ABOUT ELIN

Published by Honno
'Ailsa Craig', Heol y Cawl, Dinas Powys
South Glamorgan, Wales, CF6 4AH

The author would like to stress that
this is a work of fiction and no resemblance
to any actual individual or institution
is intended or implied.

ISBN 978 1870206 891

Published with the financial support of the Welsh Books Council

Cover image and design: Nicola Schumacher

Printed in Wales by Gomer

ABOUT ELIN

by

Jackie Davies

Honno modern fiction

ACKNOWLEDGEMENTS

I would like to thank everyone who encouraged me to finish this book:
Alex, Anne, Ruth and Clare, ex-Llanfyllin Creative Writing Course, who shared the journey;
Paul for helpful criticism; John for patience;
most of all Caroline Oakley for editorial advice and expertise, and the team at Honno who made it possible.

The extract from R S Thomas' 'The Kingdom' from *Collected Poems 1945-2000* published by Phoenix, an imprint of Weidenfeld and Nicolson, a division of the Orion Publishing group is quoted with permission.

For my mother

April 2004

Before leaving his office, Gareth Pritchard pulled open the bottom drawer of his desk and drew out a large manila envelope. Aware of a tightness in his throat and chest, he opened it and took out the contents.

He could have wept looking at them. What had he done? Had it been right? Reason said so. Then he thought of Elin. Was that when she had begun to distance herself from him? It wasn't such that others would notice but their old, easy intimacy was impaired, leaving behind a sense of loss. He felt that loss keenly. It had eaten into him as the years passed, together with a gnawing sense of responsibility, even of guilt.

He sighed. It was too late now to change things. Or was it? He took out another, smaller envelope addressed in his own hand and looked at the letter it contained. 'Time for amendment of life.' He had heard those words often enough in his job. Maybe there was still time.

Slowly, because he was tired these days, a dragging tiredness that he tried to ignore, he took a sheet of writing paper and added a PS to the letter. He would have to use a larger envelope now to hold all that he wanted sent, but no matter. He would have done what he could. He found an unused jiffy bag, addressed it, filled it and fastened it down.

Then he switched off the light, locked the office door and went home.

The Vicar

It was strange to be here without Gareth. But it was Gareth I was burying. At the back of the church I could see Elfed, his deputy in the undertaker's business. How must he feel, overseeing the funeral of his boss?

The building was packed, as expected for one so popular and well known. The village was bereft, myself included. Gareth had shepherded me through my first Welsh funerals like a kindly uncle, alerting me to local customs, warning of unexpected links between families, making sure all was in place.

As we sang the first hymn, *Mi glywaf dyner lais*, his favourite, I scanned the congregation, trying not to feel the loss of that strong bass voice carrying the tune from the back. The whole community was there. Many were standing, some squeezed into the porch, a few latecomers peered round the porch doorway.

Lily, Bryn and Megan were in the front pew, Lily smart in a new blue suit and hat.

'I'm not going to wear black, Lynne,' she told me. 'Gareth hated it. He wasn't a man to mourn.' Odd thing to say of an undertaker but true. There was always more of life about Gareth than death. What did he say to God when the heart attack catapulted him into eternity? I had no doubts about his faith. 'I'm a cheerful Christian,' he used to say, 'none of your glum faces and seriousness for me.'

I imagined him sharing a joke with the Almighty now. What had led him into this of all professions? He'd been good at it – soft-spoken, organised, reliable, always ready with the right word, respected by the whole village. Yet he could enjoy a laugh over a pint in the *Talardy* with the best of them. I would miss him sorely.

Bryn and Megan looked tense and subdued, oddly grown-up for their fourteen and sixteen years but still young and vulnerable. Bryn had removed the studs from his nose and ears, I imagine at his mother's request, but Megan's outsize earrings glinted and turned like mobiles when she moved her head. Her father used to tease her about those. Had she worn them in his honour? Both teenagers stared at the ground during the singing. I could see Bryn holding his mother's arm. 'You're the man of the family now,' someone had said during those first days of shock. But he still had years of growing up to do, years when he would have valued his father's backing.

Behind the immediate family stood Elin, Gareth's sister, a lawyer from London, on her first visit to Llanfadog for nineteen years, so Lily said. She was far the best-dressed member of the congregation in a grey suit that could be Armani, silk hat and matching gloves. I looked at her now, intrigued. Slim and erect, she stared straight ahead, her face expressionless. I wondered what she was thinking, what she was like. I'd heard conflicting reports from those in the village who remembered her but this was the first time we'd met, if you could call a handshake and a brief word of introduction meeting. At the lychgate she had appeared stiff and formal.

'Elin has standards,' Lily always said, as if standards were a disease. I gathered Elin thought herself a cut above Gareth's family. She had never married. 'She's the clever one of the family,' Gareth used to say, brotherly pride in his voice, 'she went to University College London and got a first class degree, a top job too. Travels all over the world.' There was no hint of envy, no regret that Elin had never returned to see her parents in their last years nor visited her older brother.

With her expensive clothes and assured manner she looked the essential career woman, the local girl made good, who had abandoned her rural roots to get on. Did I imagine the hardness in her face? Did her set jaw and proud bearing conceal grief or did she always look as if she thought herself better than those around? I wondered whether she would visit the family now Gareth was gone – from what I'd heard she and Lily were like chalk and cheese. Death causes so much realignment. The pattern would never be the same, not for Lily, Bryn and Megan, not for Gareth's wider family, Elfed, the whole village or myself.

I would rather have been anywhere but here in Llanfadog church, taking a friend's funeral. But I was determined to show the same professionalism that had marked Gareth's years of service to this community. My thank you to the man who had steered this greenhorn in her first living to become the accepted and acceptable minister I was now, who had encouraged my first stumbling efforts in the Welsh language and served this congregation as churchwarden and treasurer for so long.

At his request the funeral was in English – being an undertaker he knew how it helped the family to have his funeral planned years before. 'I don't want to exclude anyone,' he said. 'None of Lily's family speak Welsh. She only picked it up when she married me.' That was typical of the man. But we'd sung one hymn in his native tongue and

I'd chosen a Welsh prayer for the graveside. I announced the reading. Gareth hadn't specified the passage he wanted but I hoped Romans 8 was acceptable. It spoke with such certainty of faith and God's love.

'That was *i'r dim, cariad,*' he used to say when he thought a funeral had gone well. I hoped my efforts would be *i'r dim* – for Gareth, his family and the communities I was speaking for.

People chuckled in the address when I described my first funeral with Gareth. We got stuck in a traffic jam on the way to the crematorium and he had to do seventy on the A55 to make up time. 'Cut out what you can,' he whispered to me in the front seat of the hearse, 'and bar the way to the loos when we get there.'

They nodded when I recalled his integrity and faithfulness, his singing and his love of a good joke. They listened when I shared the faith that had been so real to him, enabling him to cope with the sad side of life without gloom or cynicism.

Then Megan stood up and began to read her father's favourite R.S. Thomas poem.

It's a long way off, but inside it
there are quite different things going on:
festivals at which the poor man
is king......

Her strong voice, clear but with a slight wobble, pierced the composure of the hushed gathering, not, I suspect, because of the words, but hearing her read so bravely reminded us afresh of our loss. Praying she would get through without breaking down, I scanned the congregation. Lily's expressive face showed maternal concern as well as sadness. Bryn stared at his hands. Elin sat stiffly upright, her eyes on Megan. She was alone in her pew. Even in this shortage of seats local custom decreed that no stranger invade the family's space. Across the aisle the Caernarfon cousins were a phalanx of solid support for Lily and the children. Behind the family stretched a sea of faces, some known, some unknown, above their sombre uniform of blacks and greys.

It was then that I saw him. He was so like Gareth that I almost dropped my service book. If he hadn't been a good deal younger, I might have imagined the young man in the crush by the font was my friend in his usual place, paying a last, ghostly visit to check all was well. It could have been Gareth's son gazing over the heads of the seated congregation – the same red hair, the same set of the head, the same build and stance. Unnerved, I lost my bookmark and had to hunt for the prayers I planned to read next.

Who was this? As far as I knew all Gareth's family were in the front three pews. But this young man looked so like him he had to be related. I glanced at my list of family members to mention in the prayers. There were no others beside those I had already met. I looked up again and saw the stranger turn his head to show a profile that was Gareth's exactly.

He must be in his twenties or early thirties, I thought, young enough to be Gareth's son. Yet Gareth was almost forty when he married. There had been no other woman for him but Lily, he said. 'Six years courting we were. And worth every minute to be together in the end.' There had been no other marriage, but had there been another woman? A son Lily didn't know about? If so, how distressing to have to creep in at the back of your father's funeral, denied public recognition of your grief. The stranger was undoubtedly grieving. It was written in his stiff posture and haunted face.

Drawing my attention away, I moved the service on. 'Let us commend our brother, Gareth, into the hands of God…' I began – mustn't dwell on this or my own grief will get in the way. And all the while my mind worried at the puzzle of the unknown mourner.

What if Lily or Elin noticed him? Would the situation Gareth dreaded, the stand-off that marred the funerals of those whose relationships were irregular or unresolved spoil his own? Maybe this was a long-lost relative who'd been overlooked. But families rarely miss a connection, especially Welsh ones.

Don't let there be any awkwardness, I prayed, as we sang the last hymn. I wanted the young man to leave, afraid his resemblance to Gareth would cause comment. Unfair of me – he had as much right as any to be there. As I led the coffin down the aisle I glanced his way, hoping he would catch my unspoken plea not to come to the grave. But he didn't see my look. He stared at the family procession as if he wanted to be part of it, his troubled eyes taking everything in. And when the congregation spilled across the churchyard he came with them.

At the graveside I focussed on the committal and the family. Lily held her children close. Megan was crying quietly. Bryn threw the first handful of soil on the lowered coffin as if in a dream. Elin stood apart, stiff and straight-backed, her confident bearing and air of detachment marking her out from the other mourners and family alike. One hand gripped the strap of her shoulder bag and she looked at no one. Perhaps she was more affected than I had imagined. I reminded myself not to judge nor be influenced by others' judgements. I'd heard gossip about her, criticism of her neglect of parents and family, even veiled complaints from Lily who was usually kind. But in this profession you learn not to listen to gossip, at least not to let it cloud your view of people. Maybe this week would give me a chance to find out what Elin was really like. Out of the corner of my eye I could see the young stranger standing some way off. He, too, looked an outsider. A city gent amongst farmers, shopkeepers and ordinary country folk. Even local professionals had a homely air.

In our part of North Wales, mourners file past the grave to pay their respects, the family first then the whole congregation. I feared there was no way the young man was going to remain unremarked with his looks. But the family didn't seem to notice him and he didn't come forward to introduce himself. He wasn't a long-lost cousin, then.

I hugged Lily – she was dabbing her eyes – and told the children, 'Well done, your Dad would be proud of you.'

Elin, cool and composed, shook my hand and thanked me in a polite, English voice. She was slighter than Gareth, I noticed, narrower about the shoulders. She turned away with a small inclination of the head and I felt dismissed. I must talk to her later, I decided. Gareth had been her only brother after all.

'I'll see you in the *Talardy* after I've tidied up,' I promised them.

The family moved off as a soft drizzle began, blotting out the nearby hills, sending people scurrying for the refreshments quicker than usual on such occasions. One or two nodded at Elin, I saw, but few went up to speak to her.

That was unusual. As a rule people flock round those who have returned from away, keen to hear their news. Even at funerals there is this eagerness to welcome the wanderer and gather them back into the community's fold. Perhaps Elin had been gone so long they didn't know what to say. She was like a stranger from another world.

I should have gone back to the church after talking with the congregation – I needed to collect my books and make sure everything had been cleared. I also wanted to tell Elfed what an excellent job he had done.

But curiosity held me back. And pastoral concern. I sensed the stranger wanted his presence recognised, his grief acknowledged. He hadn't moved when the other mourners dispersed but was standing by the grave, the last to view it, a lonely figure in a smart, wool coat that would soon be the worse for the rain. I made up my mind to speak to him, wondering, as I picked my way over the wet grass, whether there was more to Gareth than family, friends or community imagined.

'Have you come far?' I tried to look as if I was returning to check all was in order.

He turned to me, his face pale under his freckles. 'I'll never forget what he did for me.'

'Gareth did a lot for us all. Llanfadog won't be the same without him.'

'I wouldn't be where I am now without Uncle Gareth.'

Uncle Gareth? He was related then. It couldn't be a courtesy title when they were so alike. 'You look like him,' I remarked.

'Is it that obvious?' he glanced round and passed a hand over his cheek like a schoolboy caught in some mischief.

'They've gone,' I assured him.

His shoulders relaxed. 'Thank goodness. I didn't want anyone asking who I was. At first I thought I shouldn't come. Then I realised I couldn't stay away. But I can't meet the family. Gareth was clear about that.'

Was he Gareth's son, then? Born before Gareth and Lily met? Brought up knowing his father as his uncle? It shouldn't – wouldn't – make any difference to how I thought of Gareth. Yet it didn't add up. The man I'd described in church wasn't the sort to go in for furtive concealment. The Gareth I knew – thought I knew – would surely have mentioned an earlier child, told his wife about him once they were married. Or would he? Maybe he hadn't known of his existence till later.

'It was agreed I would never intrude, never try to get in touch with the family.' The stranger went on, 'Gareth had the foresight to list me as someone the business should contact if anything happened to him. That gave me the option of coming today.' He took a clean, white handkerchief from his pocket and blew his nose. 'At least I was told…' His words trailed off.

I waited while he regained his composure.

'What I would like,' he continued, 'is to tell someone how it was. The worst thing is people not knowing.'

I felt uneasy. People's emotions could drive them to offload things they later wished they hadn't. Did I want to be party to information that had to be kept from Lily and the family? I was ninety per cent certain the young man beside me was Gareth's son but I preferred not to have it spelt out. Selfish of me, I realised. In this job you have to be prepared for uncomfortable confessions. What are clergy for?

He didn't notice my hesitation. When he spoke again it

was as if he was talking to himself. 'This'll be my first and last visit to Llanfadog. I won't come back. I'll never trouble the family. But it's been good to see the place.' He turned his head to take in the grey houses and rainswept fields.

We were getting wetter by the minute but he seemed reluctant to move, standing by the grave as if glued to the spot.

'Come into church,' I suggested, 'if you need to talk. I have some clearing up to do.'

'Thanks.' He accompanied me there, squelching across the damp turf in his smart leather shoes.

Apart from a few stragglers chatting under the lychgate, the congregation had gone. The drizzle made standing outside unpleasant so there was no one to notice the stranger now. Elfed and his men had withdrawn to the pub, so had the churchwardens. Ted Evans was fetching a spade from the back of his van to fill in the grave. I let myself relax.

Inside the empty church I took off my damp surplice and waited for the young man to begin.

He stood by the font looking out at the rain. 'Gareth's been like a father to me these last twelve years.' His cultured voice betrayed no emotion but I sensed he was barely containing his grief. 'I was adopted. It was a private arrangement and Gareth had a hand in it. I believe Gareth's parents didn't know and Lily and the others were never told.' He brushed the raindrops from his coat collar with a quick, fastidious gesture and I noticed that his hands, like his clothes, were well cared for.

'When my parents – my adoptive parents – were killed in a car crash,' he went on, 'Gareth looked me up. I was eighteen, in my first year at university. When he heard what had happened he drove all the way to York to see me. He said if there was anything I needed he was there. He helped me financially till the will was sorted out, got me on my feet and gave me something to live for. I think he saved my life…' He faltered and wiped a hand over his eyes.

I looked at him sympathetically. 'Gareth was a good man.'

'Yes. That's why I had to come.' He was in control of himself now. 'We had no chance to say goodbye. His wife and children don't even know I exist. I'd have given anything to stand up today and tell everyone what he did, what he was to me. But at least I've been able to tell somebody.' He glanced at me. 'Thank you for taking the trouble to listen.'

'It's no trouble. What you've shared underlines everything I said about Gareth, his generosity, his caring.'

'I wanted someone to know how kind he was. He didn't have to look me up. It was his decision. But it made all the difference.'

'I'm sure it did. Typical of him.'

'Yes. He gave me the confidence to choose a proper career, encouraged me when I found it tough at the start. I knew he was there for me even if we only saw each other latterly about twice a year.' I could hear the warmth in his voice. 'We used to meet when he went away with the choir.'

'Ah,' I smiled, remembering Gareth's loyalty to the local male voice choir. But Lily often travelled with him. I wondered how he had kept it from her, they were so close.

'Gareth didn't like having secrets,' the young man went on, as if he had heard my unspoken question, 'but he said it was best. He wasn't the only one involved, you see. There was no point raking up the past and upsetting people.'

I nodded, presuming he meant Lily and the children or his birth mother. I picked up the service sheets Elfed had left, trying to digest this unexpected view of my dead friend. How many years had Gareth been helping this man? Ten? Twelve? And given no hint of it?

'I suppose I'd better go.' The stranger adjusted his scarf and again there was this slight tilt of the head I recognised from working with Gareth all these years. 'I'm only thankful Gareth knew where I was placed and heard what happened to my parents.'

'I expect he was thankful too.'

He stopped as if I had said something novel. 'Funny you should say that. I've been wondering about it since. I believe he *was* glad of the excuse to get in touch. I didn't think of it at the time. Too wrapped up in my own troubles. But I think – I hope – he was pleased to find me.'

'I'm sure he was.' Gareth, old friend, you fooled us all.

But maybe he had the satisfaction of seeing one son make his way in the world – if this man *was* his son, that is.

In the pause that followed, the young man took a card out of his pocket and handed it over. 'My name's Stephen Loxley, by the way. If anyone in Llanfadog ever wants to contact me, you can find me here.'

Was he hoping his existence might come to light and the family seek him out then? Despite insisting he remain unknown? I sensed a longing for recognition in his request and was moved by it, the more because it seemed impossible to fulfil.

The card was for a London firm of solicitors. That explains the smart clothes, I thought, pocketing it. I smiled.

'I could offer you coffee but it'll have to be black. There's only a kettle and a jar of instant in the vestry.'

He returned a glimmer of a smile. 'Thanks, but I ought to be going.' He took a mobile phone from his pocket. 'I'll ring for a taxi here if I may. I came by train. Saves a lot of trouble, London traffic being what it is.' His voice sounded less strained. I could imagine him as a lawyer.

While he phoned, I collected my books from the prayer desk then joined him at the back of church. I was relieved he wasn't staying longer. They would be looking for me in the pub.

'Gareth used to joke about Welsh weather.' Stephen Loxley turned up his coat collar. 'I would have brought an umbrella but I'm always leaving them on trains.' He turned to shake my hand. 'Goodbye, and thank you for what you said in the service. It helped.'

'I'm glad of that.' I watched him leave the church, pleased he seemed in an easier frame of mind.

At the porch entrance he turned suddenly. 'Was Gareth's sister there?' A casual remark but something in his voice suggested it was important for him to know.

'Yes. The woman in the grey suit in the second row. She's a lawyer in the City.'

A strange expression crossed his face, surprise, recognition, understanding perhaps. Then he smiled, a real smile this time. 'I missed her.' And was gone.

Glyn

I recognised her from her posture – upright, slender as a birch, but ramrod-straight. Unbending – like the last time I saw her. Elin Pritchard stood like that in court once in the heady days of the language campaign. What causes, if any, does she fight for now?

I knew she might be here. If I am truthful, the possibility of seeing her was one of the things that drew me to Gareth's funeral, as well as affectionate memories of an old friend. But it is still a shock. The *frisson* when I saw her in the pew behind Gareth's family was unexpected, disconcerting. It betrayed me to myself. Part of me is still attached to her. The thread that joins us may be thin as spider's silk but it is just as tenacious. I know that today may reinforce it or break it for good.

The only Welsh on the service card is the hymn we are singing. Why do I think of her as a traitor to the *hen iaith* yet accept Gareth's allowances for the English? *Duw*, but she was different. Then.

A powerful mixture, politics and passion. It consumes you, ignites the spirit till you become one, like disparate elements fused in fire. We were like that once, Elin Pritchard and I. What are we now? What is she?

I am comforted by Betsan's clear voice beside me. I have a young wife, a young Welsh wife and two Welsh children of whom I am proud. I should be content.

How long is it since Elin and I saw each other? Twenty-five years? Thirty? Time has no meaning, the memory clear as day.

Aberystwyth seafront. January, 1971. A wild south-westerly scoured the sweep of Cardigan Bay, heavy with cloud. The sea was dirty, foam-topped, dotted with showers. We were the only people on the prom. Sensible folk kept under cover. We stepped round puddles and over shingle thrown up by the tide, heading into the wind, locked in our own verbal engagement about the future. Our future – mine and hers.

I knew something had changed between us when we met beside St. Michael's. She wore the same beige trenchcoat – student uniform in those days – but differently, the collar down, a brown scarf at her throat. Her hair was up, twisted in a knot at the back of her neck, showing off her neat ears decked with unfamiliar studs. She had travelled from London for the interview and needed to look the first-class graduate seeking a research post. But there was something else. Something different inside. She kissed me as one greets a brother or bestows affection on a pet. Not with the love we once had.

I had rushed from a lecture, notes and slides in my briefcase, students' essays packed anyhow, anxious to see her again. We stopped in the shelter of a wall while I organised my things.

'Just like you, Glyn. Always in a hurry.' The old warmth was there. Perhaps all was well and I had imagined the restraint.

'What are these?' I teased, touching her ear. 'Trying to impress the prof?'

She flinched and backed away and I knew then that she had come to say goodbye.

We walked in silence till she confirmed the shattering of my world.

'Glyn, it's not easy to say this, but I think we should stop seeing each other.'

'Stop seeing each other?' My voice was raw. 'We're practically engaged. Would be, if you hadn't kept putting it off.' My hold tightened on my briefcase. 'Why?'

'Because,' she looked away from me, 'because I've made up my mind. I'm going to live in London. There's no place for me in Wales. I could go on forever waiting for things to be right. It won't happen, Glyn. I have to make a clean break.' Her voice sounded harsh.

My mind was in turmoil. 'Why? Didn't you get the research post? I thought you wanted to be in Aberystwyth so we were together. We planned it ages back…'

'It's no good. I knew it wasn't right when I walked in. Women like me don't fit in the Welsh academic world. Not yet. It's too conservative, too entrenched. I can't wait till you catch up with the rest of us.'

You? The rest of us? Her words hit me like a blow. I could almost feel her slipping away. 'We don't have to finish because of it,' I said quickly, my voice hoarse. 'We have something that will last, we always thought so.' It was an effort to get the words out. There was a weight on my chest. I gulped for air like a man about to drown.

'You're not telling me your career means more to you than us? All we had?' I added. *Had.* I took a deep breath. It was difficult to make myself heard above the roar of the wind and waves.

'No…Yes…I don't know.' She stopped speaking and stood still, hands held in front of her, fingertips touching, in that way she had when she was trying to say something important. 'It's not just my career...' she went on, 'it's my whole way of life...' She broke off again and shook her head as if she despaired of making me understand. 'And didn't we decide my career meant as much as yours? You said so yourself when I chose London instead of a Welsh university.'

'But we also decided you were coming back, remember? Or has London put all that out of your mind?' Emotion made me stop for breath. 'I went along with it because that teacher you thought so much of seemed to believe it was best. Then when you started the MA—'

'Let's not go over that again,' she cut in. 'It doesn't matter. Now's what matters.'

'So why can't we be together now?' Grief and desperation gave my voice an edge. 'We could still be married. You could spend weekends up here with me and be in London during the week. There's still no reason to break up...'

'Glyn,' she interrupted and her voice was sharp, 'please don't make it harder for me.'

'Harder for *you?* How do you think I feel?' My voice shook. 'Did you think I'd meekly accept it and wave goodbye? "Thanks, Elin. It was nice knowing you. We were everything to one another for five years but I understand you must move on to better things, fulfil yourself, do whatever you need to get on." Don't mind me. You've just torn my heart out but I'll manage.'

'Glyn, don't!'

We were facing each other. I wanted to take her by the shoulders and shake her, crush her in a desperate embrace, make her see sense, but she backed away from me. Pity, affection, sorrow in her amber eyes, but not love, not passion. And I knew there was no point fighting.

'Is that the only reason?' I had to know. 'Are you sure there isn't someone else?' Above us herring gulls screamed as they rode the wind. 'Some smooth *Sais* lecturer maybe?'

She coloured and looked away. 'It's a lot of things, like I said. But there's no future for us. Not if I stay on in London. My place is there, I'm sure of it. And you'd never move.'

'What about all we've fought for? Why leave when the struggle's almost won. We've gained equal status for the language. It's a start, surely. And a Plaid Cymru MP.'

'That sounds okay here.' She turned her back to the wind and gazed at the university buildings below the castle. 'But what about Cardiff, Wrexham and Llanidloes? Where's the support there? We're fighting each other. Like the Welsh have always done.'

I had never seen her like this. 'Why throw it all away? All that matters to us? It must be worth something.'

'What is it in the grand scheme of things? One tiny nation pitted against a powerful neighbour.' She pushed a stray wisp of hair from her eyes. 'The odds are against us, Glyn, for all your commitment and the dedication of people like you. I want to put my energy where I can make a difference.'

I was stunned to silence as she continued.

'It's no good. I've moved on. People do. They grow up, see the world differently.'

'And I've not grown up, I suppose.'

She shook her head. 'I didn't mean that. You're misunderstanding because you're hurt. You know who you are but I'm still finding out who I am. There's a whole world out there. I want to discover it, make my own way. Travel.'

We crunched across the scattered shingle not speaking.

Useless to argue, she was fixed as a standing stone. The rain began to come down more heavily, blotting out the breakwaters on the beach: Welsh rain, grief in great waves, Wales weeping for lost freedoms and lost love, for a nation bereft of itself and hearts divided.

'You'll hear no Welsh in London.'

'There are some who speak it.'

'Not many.'

She nodded, sighed. 'I'll miss that.' She looked out to sea then turned to me again. 'Please understand if you love me, Glyn.' A pleading look in her eyes – she could be so persuasive. 'I've found new aims…new ideals…the chance of a new life…'

'So you cast off the old like a worn out coat,' I broke in, my voice hard.

'Don't say that. I'll always remember you. What we had was good. What we did was right. Then.'

We parted to avoid a puddle.

Bradwr, I wanted to scream. 'After all we've been through together. Court, protests, demonstrations.' *Et tu, Brute?*

We were wet, her hair darkened by the rain. Drops of water glistened on her ginger lashes. I would have kissed them, once.

'What do you want to do? I mean now? Will you come back to my rooms for coffee?'

She shook her head. 'It's better I leave straight away. There's a train at four. I can be back this evening.'

'Not going home?'

She gave me a withering look. 'You know about that, Glyn.'

'Thought you might feel able to return now you've got

rid of me.'

'Glyn Prydderch, I could thump you, you pig-headed *twp*.'

I gave a grudging smile and it eased the tension between us. 'Let me at least see you off.'

'It'd be difficult for us both. I'd rather not.' She smiled at me, suddenly tender. 'Go on with your poetry, Glyn. Write your *cynghanedd*. You'll win the chair one day, I know it.' She pecked me on the cheek and moved away before I could hold her, before I could cling to the girl I knew and loved. Lover, romantic, passionate supporter of causes – who had become someone else.

Betsan nudges me and I sit down with the rest of the congregation but not before I have looked over their heads to the coffin in the chancel. Memories of Gareth crowd my mind and I am reminded of impermanence. Our lives can be so suddenly cut short. Yet Gareth's was a life well lived. I don't think he had a single enemy, even at school. That was where I first met Elin, though we hardly noticed each other at the time. It was only after Gareth and I had left, him apprenticed to his father's business, me studying in Bangor, that I saw her with fresh eyes.

October 1965. Tryweryn. That watershed of Welsh protests when the mayor of Liverpool came to open the new reservoir serving his city and met a response he hadn't bargained for. Elin was there, a fervent seventeen-year-old, chanting slogans in English so he would understand how much we hated the rape of our land, the uprooting of families, the subordination of everything we had and were to the needs of our greedy neighbour. Splendid she was with her long red hair and blazing eyes. She could have been one of those druid viragos, scaring Agricola's legions out of their wits. She would have hurled flaming torches in defence of her native land if they had been to hand.

I hadn't expected that she and Gareth would be there. We shared a flask together afterwards and I drove them home in my van.

'What are you studying?' she asked, squashed in the front seat between Gareth and me.

'History.'

'I'm going to read Law. Then I'll know how to bend it without getting caught.'

I was shocked. She looked so innocent. 'You'd be useful to us,' I said.

'You mean you're planning more protests?'

'Don't tempt her, Glyn. She's a proper hothead. Mam didn't want her to come today. She only allowed it because I would keep an eye on her. She's already had one detention for painting slogans on the school walls. They want her to pass her exams not end up in court.'

Elin tossed her head. 'Can't I do both?'

That was the beginning. We started to go out seriously the next year and our love grew from there, cemented by protests, risks shared. We painted road signs at night in rural Meirionydd, substituting Welsh for English names. We daubed slogans on railway bridges. We shared cider and crisps with fellow conspirators in my ramshackle van and plotted the next move. She slept in my flat, telling her parents she was staying with friends. Stirring days. Even court had its compensations as we joined the ranks of martyrs for the cause, for our language.

Elin was given a conditional discharge, allegedly the

innocent party. I received a hefty fine and we were forbidden to meet. But the enforced secrecy gave our relationship added spice. And when she was studying in London she could do as she liked, hitchhike to join me at weekends without her family knowing, go to demonstrations, stay in my Bangor flat. Even Gareth never knew.

Strange times viewed from today. Such protests seem unreal, unnecessary. Did we really have to do that? But would we have achieved what we have otherwise?

I drag my thoughts back to the funeral, anxious to give Gareth his due, glad Betsan cannot read my mind. But memories haunt me like ancient wraiths weaving in and out of the prayers. Perhaps this service will exorcise them. Thirty years is a long time to harbour ghosts, unknowing.

We stand as the coffin is carried out. The family party follows. I look at Elin as she walks past, despite my intention not to, but she is staring straight ahead and does not see me. She seems older yet not older, her face unlined but set, her hair darker than before – has she coloured it? She walks alone, part of the family yet not a part, and greets no one. What does it feel to cut yourself off from your roots? There is a cost, surely.

The sky is grey outside, threatening rain. I take Betsan's arm as we walk across the grass to the grave. She broke her ankle a year ago and it is still not strong. I am thankful she is with me, anchoring me to the present, protecting me from my ghosts.

After the interment we file past the grave and greet Lily.

'How good of you to come, Glyn. You will join us in the *Talardy* won't you?'

We murmur condolences as a gentle drizzle begins to fall. By the time we have reached the lychgate it is more insistent, dampening clothes and hair. Soft rain, Welsh rain, weeping for Gareth and the nation's lost sons.

'Come on, *cariad.*' Betsan hurries me to the pub. 'No sense getting wet. Let's have a drink before we go home.'

The function room is filling. The bar is open and the company divides between the beer-drinkers at the bar and the tea-drinkers who sit at tables. We take a corner table where neatly cut sandwiches promise sustenance, and are greeted by friends from Cefn Coch.

'Did you see Elin?' Delyth looks over her shoulder. 'This is the first time she's been back in years, I'm told. Quite the city lady, don't you think?'

'She never came to either of her parents' funerals,' Nesta Plas Gwyn adds, overhearing. 'She was abroad, they said.'

The women stare. 'Good-looking woman still,' Delyth appraises.

'She's never married. Has a high-powered job in London, so they say,' Nesta is keen to inform us. I wonder idly who are the 'they' responsible for so much information and misinformation. Material for a poem there. My mind plays with words, chasing hares.

Stan brings me back to earth, bending my ear with grumbles about foot rot and falling subsidies and the funeral tea proceeds like all funeral teas. We gossip, catch up on news – who has moved, who has died – and meet old friends. Gareth would have loved it.

'Will Elfed take over the firm now?' Delyth asks.

'Depends on Lily,' Stan says.

'What about Bryn? He might want to follow in his father's footsteps.'

'He's not old enough yet and he'll want to go to college surely. He's clever enough for Oxford, some say.'

'Like his aunt,' I said, remembering.

We looked at young Bryn, sitting next to Lily, all legs and arms, his plate piled high with sandwiches.

'He'll have to cut his hair if he wants to be in the funeral business,' Betsan adds quietly, 'poor kid. It's a rotten time to lose your father.'

'Want a drink?' Stan asks and we move to the bar leaving the women to their speculations.

She is talking to Megan at the central table. I can see the family likeness in the youngster's brow and profile. We shall have to speak before we leave. Courtesy demands it. But my stomach churns at the thought. What do I want? Revenge? Expressions of regret? Renewed acquaintance? Should I boast how well I have done since we parted – poems published, successful academic career, fine family?

People are leaving, buttoning coats against the rain. We make promises to meet before the next funeral, promises we know we won't keep.

She is standing next to Lily by the door. I can't avoid her even if I want to. As I say goodbye to Lily I sense Elin looking my way.

I turn and offer my hand. *'Elin. Ers talwm. Mae'n ddrwg gen i am eich brawd.'* The *'chi'* is deliberate, distancing us from the past we once shared, yet I feel the tug of that past as our eyes meet.

'Glyn.' She shakes my hand. She could be royalty greeting a stranger. 'How nice to see you.' She gives me a cool smile. No trace of a Welsh accent. No attempt to speak Welsh.

'You did well, then?'

'Yes. And you?'

'*Digon dda.*'

'I'm glad for you.' Her tone is formal, no warmth in her voice.

I want to disturb her poise, dent her armour, ask in an offhand way, '*Dach chi'n cofio Tryweryn?*' then smile and pretend it is a joke. But I am not that unkind. Instead I ask, 'No regrets?'

Her expression softens. I see loss in her eyes, sadness, *hiraeth,* an echo of the girl I once loved. Then she shakes her head, the mask back in place.

But I have seen beneath it. 'Will you stay awhile now you've come back?'

'I've been away too long.'

Things unsaid, questions unasked hang in the air. I sense closure but am reluctant to go. Suddenly Betsan is at my side. 'My wife.'

'I teach for my sins,' Betsan explains. She smiles at me and tugs my sleeve. 'We promised we'd be back to pick up the children.'

A strange look on Elin's face. Then she dismisses us with a polite, 'Thank you for coming,' and turns to the next departing group.

Outside the rain falls. Welsh rain, steady, relentless, a nation weeping for the children she has lost. I take Betsan's hand and hurry to the car.

Lily

When we met before the funeral it was the first time Elin and I had seen each other since 1986, when Gareth and I lunched with her in London on her leave from Hong Kong. She'd driven straight to the church and joined us at the lychgate.

It was awkward at first. Bryn and Megan had never met her.

'Your Aunt Elin.' I pushed them forward. She shook Bryn's hand, put her arm briefly round Megan, then turned to me. 'Lily. I'm so sorry,' and offered her hand.

I think she meant it. She was pale under her make-up and her knuckles showed white on the shoulder bag she was clutching.

'So am I, so are we all.' I introduced her to the vicar as the hearse drew up and we were spared further conversation. I was too numb with grief and the self-control needed to restrain it to let her presence affect me. It was only when everyone had gone and we were in the *Talardy* alone, myself standing amongst the deserted tables, Elin in the cloakroom, that I realised just how much I disliked – and feared – her. It's irrational, I know, but I blamed her for Gareth's untimely death. If she had half helped with the burden of her parents I'm convinced he wouldn't be in his grave now.

I looked round the function room, which was empty but for the staff now the mourners had gone, and blinked back the tears that threatened to overwhelm me. Gareth often arranged funeral teas here. The muted clink of glasses, the clatter of crockery being cleared in that long, low-ceilinged space recalled other times when I'd been with him at a village funeral and the knowledge of his loss hit me afresh like a shock wave. Megan and Bryn had gone home. There was nothing to protect me from his absence. Or from Elin.

I felt a sudden stab of anger against her. 'Gareth thought the world of you,' I wanted to say, 'why didn't you come and see us when he was alive? I know you didn't like me marrying him but did you have to take it out on him and the children?'

Then I remembered Gareth's love for his sister, his pride in her achievements and swallowed my resentment. *'Paid â phoeni, cariad,'* he would say when something she did upset me, when her refusal to speak to me on the phone or her failure to remember the children's birthdays brought me to tears. 'Don't take it to heart. She hasn't had things easy. You'll understand one day.'

I learnt to soldier on as if nothing had happened, bury the sense of hurt and rejection and hide it from Gareth as much as I could so as not to come between him and the sister he loved. But now he was gone it wasn't going to be easy having her to stay, not when she hadn't visited all the years of our marriage. I'd invited her to our home, for Gareth's sake. I couldn't be so uncharitable as to refuse her – and what would people think if she stayed elsewhere? But I knew I'd need all my patience and self-control to get through the coming week.

I remembered the first time Elin and I met. Summer 1984 and Gareth and I were celebrating our engagement.

'Elin, meet Lily,' Gareth said as she entered the house and the pride in his voice filled me with confidence. It's not easy to meet your future husband's family for the first time. Tad and Mam I was acquainted, if not at ease, with. I understood Gareth's difficulties with them and could recall enough of the scant Welsh I'd learnt at school to offer a sentence or two to cover the awkwardness. But I knew he and Elin were close. He talked about her a lot. Because she worked away and seldom came home, we'd never met and it mattered that I made a good impression on her. I wanted to like her and had made a special effort to look my best in a crisp, cotton dress in blue and sunshine yellow with a matching jacket. I didn't have a sister and looked forward to sharing Gareth's.

Gareth had already told her about me as we'd been going together some years, ever since Gareth handled the funeral of my elderly aunt who died in a Denbigh nursing home. But our courtship wasn't easy. I lived in Flint and worked in Chester. Gareth was tied to Llanfadog with his business and the parents. My widowed mother didn't want to lose me and worried about the age difference – he was twelve years older than me. Gareth wondered how his parents would manage if he left home. At last, with a long-awaited transfer to my bank's Denbigh branch and the possibility of a bungalow in Llanfadog, we were free to arrange the wedding. Meeting Elin seemed the last hurdle to clear on our way to fixing the date.

I smiled in welcome as we faced each other, trying not to feel awkward before her obvious elegance and polish. I noted her green, linen suit, the glowing red of her beautifully cut hair and felt that however much trouble I took I would always feel the poor relation beside her sophistication and city poise.

She looked me up and down and shook my hand. 'Congratulations, Lily. That's a name you don't hear much now. Old-fashioned.' She smiled with her mouth but not her eyes, then turned to give Gareth a hug that made me feel I was an outsider and always would be. 'Hallo, big brother. Getting hitched at last? I thought you'd end up celibate like me. Each to his taste, I suppose.' Taking his hand, she marched into the sitting room to greet her parents and I was left to follow, side-lined.

Not once during that weekend did she address me by name again. I felt she resented my presence. Whenever she could she monopolised Gareth. She took him outside to show him her car and kept him talking for an hour. When medicines were needed for Mam, she drove to Denbigh to fetch them and took Gareth along to hear how her car engine sounded. I would catch her looking at me, something like disapproval in her cold, hazel eyes. Was she envious? Surely not. She had so much to boast of compared with myself, a bank clerk with only seven GCSEs to my name. Was it my lack of Welsh? But she hardly spoke it that weekend though I heard she'd once campaigned for the language. Did she resent Gareth's commitment to me? I thought so then and still think so, though I could never see why.

Later I tackled him about it. 'I don't think Elin likes me.'

'*Paid â phoeni, cariad.* Don't take any notice. She can be preoccupied sometimes. Worried about her job, I think.'

She might have had the grace to put that aside for our celebration. Instead her brooding presence spoilt our weekend. With Tad's increasing forgetfulness – it was the beginning of Alzheimer's, though we didn't know it then – and Mam's asthma, the occasion of our engagement wasn't an unqualified success. I blamed Elin for it. Something about her flaunted intelligence – did she have to be so ostentatious about finishing the *Guardian* crossword? – her possessiveness of Gareth and her reluctance to acknowledge my presence bit deep. I was glad to see her go.

Gareth always stood up for her, I thought bitterly, praising her academic achievements, trumpeting her professional success. He defended her no matter what she did. I resisted pointing out how selfish she was, taking up his free time with long phone calls from Hong Kong or Singapore every week, not coming to her parents' funerals nor attending the children's christenings, though she was godmother. She didn't even come to our wedding, couldn't delay her overseas posting, she claimed. Though I'm sure she could have managed it if she'd wanted to. Her greetings telegram, 'Love and Best Wishes on your wedding to Gareth and my new sister-in-law' seemed patronising though he couldn't see it.

A door banged in the background and I pushed these thoughts away. What was I doing remembering Gareth like this, blaming him, resenting his love for his sister, letting bitterness sneak into my mind and spoil my memories of our precious time together? He had been a wonderful husband, lover and friend, the kindest of men. How was I going to survive without him?

Suddenly Elin was at my side. 'I'll take you home,' she said in the clipped, English voice that distanced her from the rest of us.

'I told Elfed I'd walk.' I wanted to be alone and our house is only the length of the village away.

'Don't be silly, it's bucketing down. I'll bring my car to the door.' And she was gone.

Funny how I hadn't noticed the weather. I went to the window and saw the rain sheeting across the car park, Elin hurrying through it, dodging puddles. We had nothing in common now Gareth was dead. Not that we'd had much before.

She was driving a new BMW. I brushed the raindrops from my coat and slipped into the seat beside her.

She eased the car forward. 'I suppose you still don't drive.'

I shook my head.

'You should learn. It's never too late.'

The remark aroused painful memories. I'd suggested it once but Gareth hadn't been enthusiastic. I think he liked sole charge of the car. What would he have done when the youngsters wanted to learn? Paid for lessons, I suppose. I felt suddenly irritated with him for not encouraging me. An unwelcome feeling. I squashed it at once.

The car slid smoothly up the village street.

'What had you planned for tonight?' Elin asked.

'I've got some cold ham.'

'Can it keep? I thought I'd take us out for dinner somewhere. You look as if you could do with a good meal.'

I bridled but had to admit the idea of not preparing food appealed. It let her off the hook too, of course. No need to help in the kitchen.

'Thanks. The children would appreciate it.'

They did. And eating out covered the awkwardness between Elin and myself. She had to relate to me with Gareth not there. I suspected she was finding it as difficult as I was. But she was a hit with Bryn and Megan, keeping them so entertained with tales of her travels that I wondered how deeply she had been touched by Gareth's death. Till I noticed how jumpy she was when we arrived home.

'I'll join you later.' She took a packet of cigarettes from her bag. 'I don't smoke indoors.'

I breathed a sigh of relief. A few minutes without her would be a welcome respite. I sank into an armchair while Megan put the kettle on for a *paned.*

'Have a drink and go up to bed, Mum. You look all in.'

'So do you, *cariad.*'

'I'm okay. I'll see to Aunt Elin if you like.'

'Thanks, though I'm sure she can look after herself.'

Bryn refused a drink and disappeared to his room. I imagined he would stay up listening to CDs on his headphones. It was all he had done since Gareth's death. I grieved for him. Burying your father was no way to spend half-term at fourteen. Of the three of us he seemed the most vulnerable.

Elin let herself in as I was preparing to go upstairs. 'We'd better get down to work tomorrow. As executors, I mean. Sort out the will.'

'I haven't been idle,' I snapped, 'I've been through Gareth's desk and laid things out in the dining room. But there's his desk at the office to look over.'

She glanced at me sharply. 'You haven't thrown anything away?'

'I do have some idea what needs to be done.' I stiffened.

'Okay.' She spread her hands as if placating an angry client. 'We'll go on with it tomorrow morning, if it's all right by you. You'll need my help with the business side I imagine? I can sort out what the accountant will need and take things to the solicitor.'

'Yes…that'd be helpful.'

'I'll do any running round or ferrying you want. I'm here to be of use in any way I can.' Her voice was softer, less managerial.

'Thank you.' I dragged myself upstairs to bed. It had been a hard day and it didn't look as if tomorrow would be any easier.

That night I dreamt of Elin, a haunting, unpleasant dream.

Gareth had gone away but had left his clothes and briefcase on Rhyl seafront. Elin and I were standing together, looking down at them. Suddenly, with a smirk of triumph, she swept everything up and put it in her car. I struggled to wrest the things from her grasp but she was stronger than I was. I clung to the car door, but she drove off and I fell to the ground, sobbing. She turned to look at me and her appearance changed. Her hair flamed, her eyes became slits of fire, sending sparks in my direction. I realised with a shock that she wasn't human but a creature from hell, bent on destroying my relationship with Gareth, full of envy and hate.

I awoke before daybreak shivering. I reached for comfort from Gareth's warm body to find he wasn't there.

When I'd stopped crying I got up and made myself a cup of tea, creeping past Elin's door in case I woke her. Then I sat in bed trying to read, a favourite jumper of Gareth's round my shoulders. How could I face his sister after the nightmare vision I'd just seen? I longed for the day when she would return to London and leave us in peace.

She was sitting in the kitchen when I went down at eight to refill my cup.

'Are you all right?' she asked.

'I had a bad night, that's all.'

'I didn't sleep well either. Do you want tea or coffee?'

I saw she had made herself at home and remembered she'd grown up in this house long before Gareth and I moved in when his parents were failing. The way she appropriated everything made me feel that I, and not she, was the visitor.

I gripped my cup. If Elin had been an ordinary sister-in-law, the sister I'd wanted, we could have wept together, hugged each other as Meg and I did and shared our loss. But we were wary as circling stags.

'I'll have hot chocolate.' I made myself a cup, heating milk at the stove.

'I don't eat breakfast.' She rose abruptly. 'I'm going to buy a paper. Do you want anything from the shop?'

'Milk, perhaps. They don't deliver today.' It was hard to think.

'I'll bring some then.' She went out, closing the front door with what seemed exaggerated care.

I pressed my head against a cupboard door to ease the tension. 'Oh Gareth, why did you have to go? What have you left me with?'

It was no easier when we came to go through Gareth's papers. The will was straightforward. I was the main beneficiary, apart from one or two small bequests. These included a pocket watch for Elin that had belonged to their Caernarfon grandfather. She smiled. 'It was a joke between us. I had a reputation for lateness when I was younger. Too busy daydreaming, Taid used to say. He said I'd keep better time if I had a watch as big as his. I was really disappointed when he left it to Gareth. I was eight at the time. Gareth must have remembered.' She bit her lip and looked out of the window.

In the silence that followed I was aware of our common grief. But it was a grief that divided. I thought of all the years Elin had shared with Gareth before I knew him and was reminded of my dream.

We worked on without speaking, Elin placing the papers we would need in neat piles on the dining table. Much as I disliked her, I was grateful for her methodical mind. I shrank from what seemed the closure of Gareth's life, teased by the vain hope that he would walk in one day to claim his things; even the finality of the funeral hadn't dispelled it.

Once, Megan looked in with mugs of coffee on a tray. There was no sound from Bryn's room. I hoped he was still sleeping.

Elin made a final inspection of Gareth's desk. 'This is for you.' She passed me a brown envelope. On the outside it read, 'Lily. For use in emergencies should anything happen to me'. It contained three hundred pounds in notes. I had to leave the room, overcome.

I thought afterwards as I bathed my reddened eyes, how like Gareth to think of any eventuality, always caring, always thoughtful.

Elin eyed me with what seemed genuine concern when I rejoined her. 'Have you had enough for now? I'd like to look at his work desk today if you can manage it. Elfed can see to the day-to-day running of the business but there'll be some things that need immediate attention. The quicker we can find everything, the quicker I can get to work once the will's proved.'

I wondered how she could stay so focussed, then remembered she was a professional. I might not like her but it was useful having a solicitor in the family.

'I'll cook lunch, Mum,' Megan offered as she removed our cups and we discussed plans. She was doing homework at the kitchen table. 'Will fried eggs and oven chips do?'

Elin nodded. I couldn't have cared what I ate. 'Thanks, *cariad.* Take Bryn a drink sometime, will you. He ought to be stirring by now.' I turned to Elin. 'Let's get it over with.' I felt a headache coming on.

I don't know what I'd have done without Elin at the office. Her legal and business knowledge was invaluable.

'Gareth asked me to take care of this,' she explained when we were into the task, 'he knew it'd be a lot of work if he died suddenly. I can pick out at once what needs to be dealt with.'

I was shocked by her words. They'd talked about it then. I didn't know whether to feel grateful or excluded. Gareth had only told me he had things in hand. Like most of us I imagine he expected to have more time to plan and discuss things.

'You knew he had chest pains?' She must have read my thoughts.

I shook my head, 'He never said.'

'He didn't want to trouble you.'

'I'd have made him see a doctor.'

'I tried to.' There was resignation in her voice.

My dream again. It was as if she'd stolen Gareth. Part of me wanted to scream, *Why didn't you tell me? You needn't have kept it secret.* Then I realised her loyalty was first and always to Gareth. She and I had no relationship to speak of in which that kind of thing could have been said. I stared at the document I was holding with blurred eyes.

'I tried to persuade him to tell you,' she added, 'but he didn't want you worried.'

I smiled weakly. That was Gareth all over. I couldn't blame Elin for his protectiveness. He probably felt that if he made little of it, the problem would go away. But the thought echoed round my mind. *He confided in her, not me.* And another, more troubling one. *If he had seen a doctor maybe he wouldn't have died.*

I must have looked upset for Elin laid a hand on my arm, tentatively as if she wasn't sure how I would react. 'People often don't tell those closest to them.'

'I know.' I tensed and she withdrew. Her attempt at kindness felt empty. But at least she acknowledged that Gareth and I had been close.

'I've had enough. How much more is there?' I got up from my chair and gathered the papers she had put ready to take home.

'I'll just look in here.' She pulled open the last drawer and started checking its contents, her normally deft fingers fumbling in her haste. I sensed a sudden tension in her and thought, there is something she is anxious to find.

She seized a large manila envelope and pulled it out, tucking it under her arm, then slammed the drawer shut. 'Okay, I'm ready now,' and picked up her bag.

'Aren't you going to put that with the rest?' I pointed to the envelope and offered my sheaf of papers for her to place it on top.

'No.' Her reply was curt, almost rude. 'Gareth was keeping this for me. He said he'd put it here. I thought I'd look for it before we left.' She clutched her find tightly as if to protect it from prying eyes.

Her obvious defensiveness, her claim to know what Gareth said or intended, the assumption that she could take things out of his desk for herself without consultation hit me on a raw spot and I, who rarely loses my temper, found myself going hot with rage and she saw it.

'It's only something between Gareth and me. Something confidential. Nothing to do with the will or the business.' She backed away.

'It always was, wasn't it? Between you and Gareth.' My control snapped and I spat out the words. 'Have you any idea how it's felt all these years? How it feels now? You swan in after nineteen years with never so much as a visit and act as if you own everything, as if you have carte blanche to do what you like. Telling me Gareth said this and Gareth said that. He seems to have told you so much it's a surprise he ever had the time to talk to us. You don't have the monopoly of him, sister or no. He was my husband, remember!' Shaking, hardly able to see for tears, I gathered up the heap of papers and marched out of the office with as much dignity as I could muster. 'I'll walk home,' I called as I slammed the door.

Her face was a picture. If I hadn't been so angry and upset I'd have found it funny. The self-assured, confident Elin Pritchard was white as a sheet. She looked stunned. Had no one ever stood up to her before?

After a minute or so she came after me but I am a fast walker and had a good start. I closed my ears to her calling my name and marched homewards, the pent-up rage of years boiling over. I felt ashamed yet liberated. At last the long-suffering worm had turned.

It is two hundred yards from the office to our house and by the time I reached home my fury had abated. But in its place was a cold, hard anger that frightened me. I tried to remember if Elfed had been anywhere in the building when I'd shouted at Elin in the office but assured myself he would have looked in if he had. I also realised I'd left my coat behind and wondered if Elin would bring it. Whatever she did I didn't want to see her. Not yet.

'Are you all right?' Megan looked up in surprise as I dropped the papers on the kitchen table.

'Yes,' I said. 'No. I'm a bit upset. I'm going upstairs to take a paracetamol and lie down. Call me when lunch is ready.'

'You're sure you're all right?' She watched me as I went upstairs.

'I will be.' I passed the muffled beat of rock music on the landing, guitars sounding tinny from discarded headphones. Bryn was awake then.

Now I am lying on the bed pondering what to do, how to face Elin, how to make peace with her if peace is to be made, wondering what Megan will make of it all. Elin has arrived home. I heard her come in the front door then walk upstairs. No sound from her room. Perhaps she will leave, flounce off to London in her shiny new car to continue the glittering career Gareth was so proud of. Gareth! I remember his attachment to Elin and am stricken with remorse. He wouldn't have wanted me to behave like this towards the sister he loved and admired.

Half an hour goes by and I wonder if lunch is ready. Then comes a knock at the bedroom door.

'Lily, it's Elin. I'd like a word, please, if you're not resting.'

Her voice is quiet, subdued.

Thinking of Gareth, I invite her in and am mollified to see she has been crying. She has repaired her make-up but cannot hide her red eyes.

'Sit down.' I indicate a chair and raise myself up, drawing my cardigan round me. I realise as she sinks into the cane rocker by the window that Elin is as uncertain as I am how to proceed. We are both treading new ground.

She swallows. 'I owe you an apology.' Her voice is shaky.

I incline my head, trying to feel gracious.

She stumbles on. 'What you said made me think. I've been a pretty lousy sister-in-law.'

Too true, I think. 'Yes,' I say.

'I…I don't know what to say…' She hesitates. 'I can't say I didn't mean it because I'm ashamed to say that I did. I hated having to share Gareth. For years he was – had always been – my closest friend. He got me through… well, through the most difficult time of my life. I wouldn't be here now if it hadn't been for him.'

I nod but am mystified. The cold, hard knot of anger is still there. I can't profess to comprehend, much less forgive.

'I want to say I'm sorry. It's a bit late to repair things, I know. I've made such a mess, and meant to, more's the pity. There's no excuse for that.' She looks out of the window. 'What you said just now made me realise how it's been for you. I've never thought…'

'No, you haven't.' I am hard. She will get no cheap forgiveness. 'Nor thought of what it did to Gareth.'

She nods and passes her hand over her eyes, pauses as if searching for words. 'After that difficult time I mentioned,

I told Gareth I never wanted to hear about it again. I meant to put the whole episode out of my mind. But he thought I might wish to remember one day and kept a record for me.' Her voice trembles slightly. 'I can't explain what it was – I don't want to talk about it now. Gareth said if anything happened to him I could take what he'd saved and keep or destroy it. That's what was in the envelope. That's why I took it from his desk. It was mine to take.'

She looks at her hands then back to me. 'I'm sorry I didn't explain. I could have if I hadn't been so…preoccupied. After how I've been all these years you had every reason to be suspicious – and angry. I realise that now.'

She falters and I try to sort out my response. I have no idea what she is talking about. I am not sure I need or want to know. But it dawns on me that she is in my power, asking something from me. I have the freedom to reject her as she has rejected me or I can try to start again, see if something can be rescued from the wreckage. If I choose the latter it will be for Gareth's sake, not hers. Is it worth the effort? And what of the children? Will they be the poorer if they never see Elin again?

'Was it deliberate?' I ask. 'Leaving Gareth and myself to look after Tad and Mam all these years?'

She shudders. 'I was working abroad most of that time. And I couldn't come back. Not to stay. We had a – how can I put it? – irregular childhood. You didn't know my father in the years before I left home. He and I never got on. I was always afraid that if I stayed at home any length of time we'd go back to that. I don't think he'd have liked being cared for by me any more than I'd have been able to care for him.'

I ponder this. Gareth said very little about his

childhood. All he talked of to me or the children was of what he did outside the home. Family relationships were rarely mentioned, apart from his closeness to Elin. He isn't here to explain and from what she has said I doubt if Elin will tell me. But perhaps the tensions she hints at are what bound her and Gareth so closely. My sense of being left out may not be all her fault, though her treatment of me is.

Megan calls from downstairs that lunch is ready and I realise I am hungry. I look at Elin again and see her through fresh eyes. For all her sophistication and success she seems brittle, almost fragile. I have seen through the tough exterior and am enlightened. She may be older than I am, she may have a highly paid, responsible job, but I have more wisdom than her, more compassion and more self-knowledge. I also have the children, and Gareth was mine in a way she could never know.

I remember her help with the paperwork, her generosity in taking us out to dinner, how she cheered Bryn and Megan with her traveller's tales. 'I'm sorry, too. I shouldn't have reacted as I did. Grief destroys ones defences. Shall we try to get along? For Gareth's sake?'

She nods. 'I'll try not to make things too difficult.' She looks uncertain, diffident even. 'Is it still all right for me to stay till Monday?'

'Of course. I'm not going to throw you out.'

'Thanks.'

'Let's go and eat then.'

No conciliatory embrace. It is too soon for that and we may never reach that level of trust. She is as much a mystery to me as when we first met, though not so daunting. We will probably never be friends in the sense of true friendship.

But we have reached an accommodation. We can mourn husband and brother in peace.

I can almost hear Gareth say, '*Paid â phoeni, Lily, cariad.* Leave her alone. You'll understand one day'.

Finnoula

'Finnoula Morris, you have lived too long.'

I stared at myself in the hall mirror and saw the wreck of a woman against the wreck of a home. Hairlines criss-crossed the once smooth skin, the grey curls lacked lustre, the once erect figure drooped like a bent tree. Already the house felt alien, taken over by packing cases, no longer mine. I was happy here, I thought. We were happy here. Tom and I, then Bridie and I. My husband and my sister. Now it is ended. Tom admired my beauty once, my fine bones, green Irish eyes and glossy black hair. What would he think of me now?

The innocent and the beautiful
Have no enemy but time.

I knew all about time. Hadn't I taught history once?

'Silly old fool,' I said to my mirrored image, 'get on with it now.' I limped back to the sitting room where boxes littered the floor. I would have to be careful where I put things. I didn't want to fall again. On the table, brass candlesticks, two chiming clocks and a collection of knick-knacks awaited my decision – to keep or send to *Oxfam*? Bridie would have had no trouble choosing, but she was gone. Left with only memories, I was finding it hard to relinquish the objects to which memory clung.

I had hoped it would never come to this, that I would have the good sense to die before independent living became impossible. Used to managing. I was stunned to apathy. I did not want to move.

'*Cysgodfa* is a true home from home,' the manager had said, showing me round. I was attracted by the garden, the freedom to take one's own furniture, the prospect of privacy with the option of social activities laid on.

We had entered a clean, cream bedsitting room with ensuite bathroom. 'This would be yours if you decided to come.'

I had decided. Failing health left me no choice. Thankful my savings could secure such spacious surroundings, I noted where my *escritoire* might go, my favourite Parker Knoll chair, my tallest bookcase. How many books could I bring without cluttering the place? Books were my only companions now. I could not do without them.

'You may bring your own curtains too if they will fit.'

I shook my head. My curtains, like me, had seen better days.

I need a sherry, I thought, overwhelmed by the change I faced. But instead of carrying me to the dining room where the drinks were kept, my legs gave way and I sank on to the nearest high-backed chair. What a bore old age is. I found my stick, propped against a table, and prepared to do battle with my arthritis. But first I had to be still, take deep breaths and gather strength.

It was then that I remembered Elin's letter. I had tucked it under a candlestick that morning, meaning to read it when my cleaner had gone. I reached for it, glad of an excuse to delay getting up.

Elin didn't write often, twice a year at most, but her letters always cheered me. She had been the star pupil of my teaching days, one of the few who kept in touch. We had recognised each other as kindred spirits despite the teacher-pupil divide. It was our nature to push boundaries, ask awkward questions, challenge the *status quo*. She would have made a fine historian if she had not gone in for law.

I smiled. Pupils rarely take your advice, 'specially the strong-minded ones. Elin could be frustrating beyond belief. She had a good brain but would not work. Her approach to rules was casual, her behaviour often outrageous – one speech day she arrived to collect her prize wearing a reefer jacket and her latest boyfriend's shirt. Another time she hung a Free Wales Army banner from her classroom window. She insisted on speaking Welsh whenever possible though the school taught in English. But she was quick to grasp the heart of an argument, a lover of ideas, a pleasure to teach when in the right mood.

Staff members she provoked argued with the head for tougher sanctions.

'She brings the school into disrepute...She upsets the others...You must make her toe the line.'

'That Pritchard girl! Writing letters in Science class then having the cheek to say it was to do with school because she was writing to her MP about Welsh language education.'

'Now she's appeared in court aren't you going to expel her?'

But Elin was our brightest hope of an Oxbridge place and such awards were rare for a school like ours. Despite everything she was likeable. She could talk her way out of any tight corner with her silvery Celtic tongue. She didn't go to Oxbridge though – 'Too English and too establishment,' she argued, 'I couldn't fit in.'

Couldn't or wouldn't? I asked myself. We tried to point out the long history of Welsh scholarship at Oxford and Cambridge. Wasn't Bishop Morgan, translator of the Welsh Bible a Cambridge man?

'Look beyond Wales,' I urged her, from my own experience of exile. 'You need to widen your horizons. Get the bigger picture. Learn from the best minds.'

'There are good minds in Wales.'

'I know that.' So there were in Ireland when I was young, I wanted to say. I had to get away for more than education. As you do, Elin, I thought. 'Spending your whole life in a small country can limit your perspective. You'll get locked in a narrow way of seeing before you've had chance to explore the wider options. There are other ways of looking at the world.'

Ill-chosen words. They merely fuelled her nationalist passion. I was fighting my brother over again.

'Sean, there must be other ways than violence and hate.'

'You tell me, then. Where have decades of pussyfooting got us? Ireland is still divided.'

That was why I left. I could not live with the boxes we put ourselves in, the walls around us, the insidious, suffocating myths that bind us to the past.

'Violence doesn't bring freedom. It ties you up all the more.'

'Well now, St. Finnoula, will you be telling them in the North how they get jobs and houses with all this discrimination, ask the Prods nicely will they ease up on us? See where that'll get you.'

If I had been a stronger person, a better Christian, I might have been able to stay and work for change. But the tide of events was against me. Within ten years violence had broken out in earnest and was to last for decades. I could never have taken on my whole family in that atmosphere. Not with our kind of Republicanism, which bred martyrs for the cause. They would have me killed first.

'They'll not give an inch till we hurt what they value,' Sean said. *'It's a war we are fighting.'*

I saw the same passion in Elin and her friends and was afraid for them. When you have known what nationalism can do you fear its hold on young minds. I had no wish to see her join a Welsh radical group that sanctioned violence. Many feared the growth of such then.

'There'll be time enough to return to Wales after,' I assured her. 'You can bring back what you've learnt, enrich your country, have something positive to give.'

'So why aren't you in Ireland?' She had the grace to blush then, apologise for overstepping the mark and withdraw. But her riposte left me riled – and unsettled.

That was typical of Elin. She had a way of turning things back on you, shining a searchlight on your own life. She always had the last word. Teaching her was like working a thoroughbred of great potential but wayward temperament. You had to humour, tease, cajole to get her best.

'Think about it,' I tried some weeks later, after we had discussed university entrance. She was more receptive, chastened by her brush with the police and parental censure. 'If it's Welsh independence you're fighting for, or a bigger say in your own affairs, you need to know the system. Isn't it the first rule of war to know your enemy?'

She smiled in spite of herself.

'Of course, if you think you couldn't stand the challenge of a different environment…'

She stalked away, glowering, but turned up next morning

with her UCL entrance forms filled in. She slapped them on my desk for inspection, daring me to comment. I refused to say a word.

'How did you do it?' the head asked afterwards.

'Luck. I managed to hit the right spot at the right time.'

'Well done, anyway. The sooner she's out of the nationalist orbit the better. I don't want her wasting her life in jail. She's mad enough to do anything if they put her up to it.'

'It's the boyfriend, I think, the one who was in court.'

'Let's hope she grows out of him. Separation won't do them any harm.'

Elin never came back to Wales. I am not sure why, her later letters do not say. When she finished her studies she stayed in London.

As I reached for her letter I had a mental picture of her as she was at school – long, red hair, open collar, no tie, arguing in a sixth form debate on the importance of political protest. I could envisage her then as a barrister, or politician. 'A suffragette,' Miss Phipps remarked, 'born after her time.'

'An idealist,' I corrected, 'and very much of her time.' Nationalism was the cause of the moment and Elin embraced it wholeheartedly. A few years later she would have been burning her bra.

I smiled and spread out her letter. It was satisfying to have steered Elin to university. When she got a First we were delighted and approved of her intention to do research. Then I heard nothing from her till the eighties when she wrote from Hong Kong sending a donation to a school project. I learned she was working for an international law firm, a fact that took some digesting. It was hard to imagine the Elin I knew in that world.

'Our ugly duckling has become a swan,' gloated Miss Phipps, now on the verge of retirement. 'Who would have predicted it?'

I was oddly disappointed. Elin had joined the establishment after all.

This letter was a surprise. Not the usual droll account of foreign travels, it was short and to the point. Her brother had died. She didn't elaborate but I guessed his loss had hit her hard. At school she had seemed closer to Gareth than to either of her parents. There had definitely been something amiss in her relationship with her father. It was obvious at parents' evenings when he criticised her constantly in front of others.

> *I shall be in Wales for the funeral on May 21st and will be staying for a week to help my sister-in-law put the will in hand. I thought I'd look up one or two people while I'm there. Could I call on you? Perhaps you'd let me know if it's convenient.*

She had headed it with her old address and phone number.

Looking at the calendar I realised that Gareth's funeral had already taken place. I must write a letter of condolence if nothing else. Then I wondered what to do about Elin's suggestion. The house was a mess. I was moving in a week. People from the local church would be calling to collect the things I had set aside for charity. I felt old and tired. It didn't seem at all convenient for her to come.

What the hell, I thought, suddenly invigorated. It may be the last and only chance we have to meet. I need something to take me out of myself. I'll ring to say she can come. But I'll explain the state I'm in so she knows what to expect.

Her voice surprised me. Precise, standard English, no trace of the Welsh accent she had paraded with such pride. But there was no disguising her pleasure – and her decisiveness.

'I'll take you out to lunch if that suits. Then we won't have to contemplate your packing cases. I assume you're not immobile?'

'I can get about but I'm not quick.'

'Thursday, then. I'm coming to Rhyl anyway. Shall I pick you up at twelve?'

So this was the new Elin. I felt swept along on the tide of her energy. I could do with some of that myself, I thought, and forgetting the sherry, returned to my packing.

And here we are, in the restaurant of a country pub in the Conwy valley, dining together like old friends. It is a pleasant change for me. I do not get out often and the *Derw Gwyn* has had good reports since it came under new management. I am wearing my emerald suit with the pearls Tom gave me on our twenty-fifth wedding anniversary. Elin has on a burgundy trouser suit with an orange silk scarf at her neck. I cannot take my eyes from her. For years I have lived with the memory of her as the rebellious student, careless of clothes. Despite her letters this image persisted. Now I am discovering the person she has become. Though recognisably Elin under the smart exterior, understated make-up and tinted hair, she is sophisticated and cosmopolitan. I had not imagined she would change as much as this. 'You raise your children only for them to become different people,' somebody once said. It's as true of old pupils. If only Miss Phipps could see her now.

'You're not to choose the cheapest items because I'm paying,' she warns. 'Think of this as a thank you for making me see sense all those years ago.'

'You really think we did?'

'Undoubtedly. I wouldn't be where I am now if you hadn't bullied me into applying to an English university.'

'I'm not sure 'bully's' the right word.'

'Whatever it was it did the trick.'

She scrutinises the menu for a moment then says quietly, 'I needed to get away – more than I realised at the time.'

The waiters are hovering so there is no time for comment. The way Elin handles them, even manages me without patronising, prove her the complete professional. I cannot repress a smile. She always had it in her to command people but never as graciously as this.

We chat over the meal, moving easily from topic to topic: travel, opera, modern history, the world in general. She says little about her work. I gather it concerns the regulation of companies, takeovers and financial contracts. Another world. I am sure I wouldn't understand even if she tried to explain. She says nothing about Gareth beyond acknowledging my condolences and I realise this lunch is time off for her from the business of bereavement, as it is for me from the upheaval of the move. The sun shines across the valley towards the folds of Hiraethog. This was one of Tom's favourite views.

Afterwards we take coffee in the lounge and she lights a cigarette. 'Do you mind? I ought to give it up really, 'specially as they say it contributed to Gareth's heart attack.' She blows smoke rings while I sip my coffee and feast on the view.

'So are you happy, Elin? Has your life turned out as you wanted?'

'More or less. Give or take one or two glitches I prefer to forget.'

I restrain my curiosity, though I would love to know what happened to the nationalist boyfriend.

Typically, she throws the question back at me. 'And you?'

'Apart from having to uproot now. Yes. The school did well, you know, till it was merged.'

'Do you mind very much giving up your house?'

'House? No. Independence? Yes. But it has to be done. I'd be a burden to others if I stayed there alone and now my sister's gone it's the sensible thing. The retirement home appears well run. I'll be looked after with the minimum of fuss and I can take some of my furniture with me. It's not too bad a deal.' Am I trying to convince myself?

'Don't you have relatives in Ireland?'

'Tom's family are in the States and I've lost touch with my brother's children. Besides, I've not the energy now for that sort of move.' I think of my homeland's new confidence, the changes wrought by Europe, the hopes of peace in the North. 'It seems a better place than when I left. But if I wanted to go back I should have gone when I retired. Then Bridie came to keep me company and the opportunity passed.'

'You've no regrets?'

I shake my head. 'No, I didn't really want to return. I enjoyed it here. I was happy, even after Tom died.'

'Wales has changed, with the Assembly and so on.' She looks thoughtful. 'I'm not sure full independence is possible. But a proper Welsh parliament would be good. The Assembly's neither fish nor fowl.' Her interest seems academic. No passion there.

'I always thought you'd be part of a Welsh parliament if it happened.'

'So I might if I'd stayed. But I've widened my horizons.' A wicked grin and a glimpse of the old Elin beneath the polished exterior. 'I was a pain, wasn't I? I wonder how you put up with me at times.'

'You were an idealist. An angry young woman.'

'You can say that again. Psychologists would have had a field day…' She stops speaking abruptly and leans forward to tap her cigarette on the nearest ashtray. 'That's all in the past,' she adds.

But the look in her eyes and the pause that follows tells me it isn't. Not entirely. I remember the Elin of years ago. Was it simple idealism and youthful passion that led her to behave as she did? Or was there something else? A need to be noticed, perhaps? Frustration? Boredom? Difficulties at home?

For a moment neither of us speaks. Elin stares at the distant view, frowning. Is she remembering her turbulent teenage years, or thinking of her brother? Suddenly she stubs out her cigarette, squashes the smouldering remains in the pottery ashtray, and turns to me with a half smile. 'Poking into the past doesn't get you anywhere. Best to take life as it comes, don't you think? Where would we all be if we spent our time going over things we can't change?'

Her tone is brisk, dismissive, and I get the feeling she is speaking to herself.

I raise an eyebrow. 'What are we doing now but remembering our shared past?' This feels like a return to it – we used to enjoy verbal fencing.

'I don't mean *that* past.' Her tone is sharp and I see sadness – or is it anger? – in her eyes. I sense shadows from the past drifting round us despite her resolve to ignore them and find myself teasing in response, the way I used to coax her out of her difficult moods at school.

'The past is useful, of course, if you happen to teach history.' I manage to suppress a smile. History was her best subject years ago.

She tosses her head and laughs aloud. 'I ought to have said that, Finn. You've stolen my lines.' We both laugh and our laughter chases away the shadows.

Her remark takes me back to teaching days. It is years since I was called Finn. Bridie used to call me Finnoula. Elin called me Finn to my face at school once, testing how far she could go. Outrageous child. But I proved unshockable, to her annoyance. Now, hearing the affection in her voice, I am flattered to have this personable younger woman address me by my school nickname. It was no lapse. She is grinning at me, the old sparkle in her eyes. But there is no hard edge to her teasing. Elin is not pushing boundaries but affirming our shared past.

What was it about her then that was so engaging as well as so exasperating? We let her get away with behaviour that wouldn't have been tolerated in anyone else. If she hadn't been so bright, perhaps, we might have wondered about her background, what her home was like, whether she had sufficient parental support. But her parents seemed pleasant enough on the occasions we met. Unassuming mother. Father a bit of a martinet. They didn't seem at ease together, I remember.

I return to the present and smile at my star pupil who has come so far. Had she noticed my mental absence? It's a problem with old age, I find, this tendency to wander down memory's pathways without warning. Embarrassing in the wrong company.

But Elin is not embarrassed. The silence between us is comfortable and unpressured. She turns from looking out of the window. 'I wonder if I'll come back here to live. People do, you know. Wales: the elephants' graveyard where exiles return to die.'

'If you do come back,' I say, slipping into the role of elder counsellor, 'move while you have the energy to make a new life. While you're still young.'

'Young! I'll be retiring soon. When I think of all the things I was going to do. Change the world, bring in the revolution, turn the academic scene around single-handed. What an innocent I was. Naïve and unrealistic. At least I've grown out of all that.'

'The innocent and the beautiful
Have no enemy but time.'

I can't resist quoting Yeats.

'Most of us don't die innocent or beautiful. We grow up and grow old, lose both innocence and beauty. It's what's left when they are gone that matters. And what we do with it.' I am thinking aloud, speaking to myself but Elin gives me a look, half-amused, half-serious.

'What to do with what's left? There's a question.' She

pauses to examine her hands before giving me a sudden, appreciative smile. 'You haven't changed. You always were the only teacher who could make me think.'

In the space that follows, I savour the compliment. A testimonial indeed, I tell myself. I can take this with me wherever I go. It will warm me in my wintry old age.

Bryn

'Hi, Tom.'

'Bryn. How're things?'

'Awful. Worse than last week. The house is like...' I broke off. A morgue? Death? Dad's funeral parlour? Too close. I swallowed and searched for a word.

It was hell, that's what it was. People coming and going. Being sorry. Weeping all over Mum. My blessed sister in charge. 'Aren't you lucky to have Megan, Lily? She's such a support.' What about me? I wanted to scream. I haven't got anyone now Dad's gone.

And worse. 'You'll have to look after your mother, Bryn. You're the man of the family now.' Sod them.

That's why I stayed upstairs in my room. Out of the way, where no one could get at me. My 'lair', Dad called it. 'Bryn's going up to his lair,' he'd say, with that teasing smile of his as I sloped off to avoid company or play my CDs. I sniffed.

'You still there?' Tom said.

'Yeah.'

'Pity you can't come over.'

My mangled brain switched into gear and light gleamed at the end of the tunnel. 'That's what I rang about. My aunt's coming to Rhyl Thursday. Can I call if you're home?'

'Great. How long can you stay?'

'Till the afternoon. She's taking someone out for lunch.'

'Thursday then. You'll bring your new CD?'

'Yep...And tell you something. She's got this amazing new car. A BMW, '04 reg: it must do 110 at least...'

The thought of Thursday was a lifesaver. I had to get out. I was desperate to do something ordinary with friends after all the gloom we'd lived in since Dad's death. It covered the house like toxic dust, a nuclear fall-out of sadness.

The only problem was the aunt. I wasn't sure what she'd be like once I was on my own with her. She was good fun when she took us to the *Beudy Bach* after the funeral. But she's my godmother, and godmothers lecture you when they get you on your own – at least my Conwy godmother does. It's, 'Bryn this' and 'Bryn that.' She's full of good advice. 'Shouldn't you get a paper round to help your parents out?'...'You won't be able to wear those studs if you follow your Dad into the funeral business'... 'Why don't you get a *proper* jacket?' It's a good thing she hasn't got kids of her own. She'd drive them mad.

So I got into Aunt Elin's plush BMW Thursday morning with mixed feelings, ready to be lectured but ready not to listen. I'm expert at looking like I'm listening when my mind's far away – ask Mum. But I meant to enjoy my ride in that car. It's the latest model and must have cost a fortune, top of the range, I reckon. It could do 130 miles an hour, Tom says.

She's a mystery, Aunt Elin. Megan thinks it's great she has this top job in an international law firm and (when Aunt Elin's not there) goes on and on about how much her clothes must cost. Megan would. But what kind of godmother only remembers your birthday half the time and never visits though she's your Dad's only sister?

'Take care,' Mum said as I left the house, 'and take your

mobile.' She always thinks drugs and muggings when I go to town. I could have pointed out that mobiles are an invitation to muggers but she wasn't in a state to argue. She's putting a brave face on things but anyone can see how shaken she is. It's like she's lost all colour – from her face, from her voice, from her hair even. At least she and Megan can hug each other and cry. It's all right for them. Dad was the only one who could understand how I feel. And he's not here.

Aunt Elin drives fast. I could see her reflection in the sun-visor mirror, a slight frown on her face, as she concentrated on the road. I was used to Dad's driving. Even when he touched sixty it didn't feel like it, his acceleration was so smooth. My aunt put her foot down as soon as we left the village and my stomach didn't catch up till we were at the top of the hill and looking down on the sea and across to Tremeirchion.

'Sorry.' She must have seen my face as we slowed for a bend. 'I'm not used to passengers. I do drive safely but I've forgotten how up and down some of these roads are.'

'That's all right,' I muttered. 'Thanks for the lift anyway. There aren't any buses from Llanfadog in the week.'

'Don't I know it. It used to drive me mad at your age being so cut off. I made a point of finding boyfriends with cars. Not that many could afford them in those days.'

Boyfriends? Aunt Elin? I took a sideways look at her as we swept through Trefnant traffic lights before they flicked red. She may be Dad's younger sister but she's *old*. Fifty-five, Megan says. Four years younger than Dad is.

Was. I stared at the road and forced myself to think of something else. Did Aunt Elin's car have surround sound? I turned to look at the speakers and decided it did. Could I persuade her to play one of her CDs? I'd noticed a stack of them when we drove to the *Beudy Bach* the other day. But I didn't know her well enough to ask and I couldn't imagine for a minute that she'd like my sort of music anyway. I gazed at the passing fields instead, my mind freewheeling.

'Do you go to Rhyl much?' she asked as we glided round the roundabout under the A55.

I dragged my mind out of neutral and just managed to catch her question. 'I've got friends there who go to our school.'

'I haven't been for years. Probably won't recognise the place. You'll have to tell me where to drop you and pick you up.'

'There's a car park on the front, next to the Sun Centre. I'll wait there or on the prom. That's where we always meet after shopping.'

'And where do you want to be dropped?'

'Somewhere after Sainsbury's. I can walk to Tom's from there.'

We swept past a line of vehicles all doing sixty and I was impressed. This was the sort of car I wanted if I could earn enough one day to buy one. How much *did* journalists earn? Aunt Elin's car must have cost twenty thousand at least. Not as much as that, I bet.

'See you around three then, give or take ten minutes.' My aunt braked and pulled into a lay-by. 'I'll leave the car in the car park and go for a stroll if I'm early. You'll recognise it, won't you?' She handed me a twenty-pound note as I got out. 'Treat yourself to something you want. It'll do you good to be out for the day.' And powered off as I mumbled my thanks. No lecture either. Aunt Elin went up in my estimation.

I watched the car disappear, thought what a pity none of my friends had seen me in it. Then stuffed the note in my pocket and set off.

Tom and I go back a long way. We were at the same junior school before Tom's Dad got promoted and they moved to Rhyl. Now we go to the same comp'. We're odd really. We pretend we don't care but we're gutted if we don't share out the top places in exams between us. And our interests aren't the same as the others'. When everyone else was into sport and the *Super Furry Animals* we were keen on fishing and brass bands. When homework got in the way of band practice, we gave up the local junior band and became *Catatonia* fans. Now we're into acoustic folk and the sort of sci-fi nobody else in our class reads. It must come of having fathers in unusual work, Tom says. His Dad's a pathologist and mine is – was – an undertaker. We used to joke about our families depending on death for a living. Now it's not so funny.

He was at the door when I arrived. His frown said it wasn't good news. 'We've got Sam today,' he grumbled. Sam's his seven-year-old sister. 'Mum's been called in to work and Sam's friends are all on holiday. She wants to go to the beach. I can't persuade her to sit quietly and watch a video.'

Dratia. I'd been looking forward to trying out a song on Tom's electronic keyboard. I even hoped we might use his Dad's hi-tech recording studio – he records talking books for the blind in his spare time. Now it looked like we were lumbered. What's more, though Tom has amazing patience with Sam, I'm not good with her at the best of times. It was going to be hard having her around when I felt so disconnected. I wouldn't be able to talk with Tom even if I wanted to. And our music session was off. Our sort of songs aren't a seven-year-old's cup of tea. Damn and double damn. Half of me wanted to go back home. Till I remembered what it was like.

'It's the beach or amuse her here.' Tom sighed and handed me a Coke from the fridge. We drank in silence.

'I want to play football,' called Sam from the sitting room, overhearing. 'And build a sandcastle.' Tom raised his eyes heavenward.

'Come on then.' I picked up his black and white ball from the hall floor and bounced it. 'We can always pop into McDonald's after.' I fingered Aunt Elin's note. The last thing I wanted was for Tom to be gloomy. One of us was enough.

'Bryn, you're a saint! You can't stay the afternoon, I suppose?'

I shook my head. 'Aunt Elin's picking me up at three on the front.'

'Didn't know you had an Aunt Elin.'

'She's the one whose car I told you about – Dad's long-lost sister – our long-lost aunt. She came for the funeral...' I stopped suddenly. The idea of Dad having a funeral was unreal, as if it had happened to someone else. I dragged my mind back to Aunt Elin. 'She has this top legal job in London and drives a new BMW. She's just given me twenty pounds.'

'Can't be bad.'

It was an odd day. We took Sam on the beach with the football and bucket and spade and kicked about for an hour. She surprised me by being really clever with the ball. Twice she beat me in a tackle, though with her size she could almost nip through my legs. I explained that I didn't like to play at full stretch against a kid, and a girl at that. But, 'She's tough as old boots,' Tom said. 'Don't let her get away with a thing. She's been trialled for her school team.'

The way Tom let his kid sister boss him was an eye-opener. I'd never seen him on his own with her before. She had him building a sandcastle in no time.

'Spoilt, that's what you are, young Sam,' he complained, but did nothing to stop the spoiling. 'Anything for a quiet life,' he muttered to me. I suppose it was because he had to live with her. You wouldn't catch me being that soft.

I joined in with the sandcastle but I was still missing our music session. To make matters worse, Sam looked at me as we were digging the moat and asked, 'Bryn, was your Dad buried or cremated?' I was so stunned I couldn't think what to say.

'Shut up, Sam and don't be rude,' Tom butted in, 'Bryn doesn't want to talk about it.'

'Buried,' I said, seeing her lips frame another question and wanting to forestall it.

'C'mon, Samantha Jane, let's go fetch water for the moat.' Tom dragged her away leaving me with my thoughts.

But my thoughts weren't worth having. Nothing touched this hollow feeling I've had inside since Dad's heart attack. It's physical, like toothache. Not how I imagined grief would be.

And I kept remembering things. It was being on the beach that did it.

'What are we going to build today? Conwy, Denbigh, Caernarfon?' A game of Dad's when we were little and he had time to take us on the beach after Naina and Taida had died, before he got really busy.

'No,' Meg and I would say, 'let's have a proper Welsh castle.' And Megan, who remembered the names, would add, 'You know, Deganwy, Dolwyddelan, Dinas Bran.'

Dad said once, 'That'd please your Aunt Elin if she were here.' And mum looked at him over the book she was reading and dad looked back at her. And they went quiet, as if there was something they wanted to say but couldn't because we were there.

Funny, that look. I remembered it now and wondered what there was about Aunt Elin they didn't say. Dad was proud of her, I know – he joked sometimes that I've got her brains – but she was a blank to us. A pity she never came while Dad was alive.

Sam had forgotten her curiosity by the time she and Tom returned. Maybe Tom had given her a talking to. But I couldn't be bothered with the sandcastle any more, or with anything else. I sat with my back to the sea wall trying not to think.

Far out where the Irish Sea was a blue line above the sandbanks I could see people like stick figures, walking to the sea, running in and out of the waves. Some were throwing balls for their dogs. Sunlight shone on the uprights of the new wind farm-in-the-making and an orange kite hung on the breeze. Every minute more people trickled down the steps beside me – day-trippers, groups, parents with kids, chattering, laughing, carrying towels, bags, beach balls. But I felt trapped in a sealed bubble no one could break into. It hit me that when you're sad it doesn't matter where you go or what you do: you carry the sadness inside you. Silly to think I could escape in Rhyl. I don't suppose even music would have helped.

We ate in McDonald's afterwards, which made Sam's

day. She was obviously trying to be good so we treated her to fries and a Sprite. Some people from school wandered in. They waved but didn't come over. I had a feeling it was because I was there. Silly, but that's how it felt.

It was nearly two o'clock when we finished.

'Better go back.' Tom looked at his watch.

'I'll stay in town,' I said. 'No sense walking to your place to come back here for three. I'll mooch round the shops till Aunt Elin picks me up.'

'You sure?'

'Yeah. I'll see you next week. Back in Wormwood Scrubs.'

We went our separate ways groaning at the thought of school and I was relieved to be on my own.

I bought a cut-price CD in Woolworths – a compilation of Catatonia tracks for old time's sake. Then I browsed through the videos in Smith's, had another Coke and wandered back to the sea front.

When I was nine we had a holiday in Tenby. There was a sand modelling competition the day we were due to go home and I was disappointed I couldn't enter. To make up for it, Dad spent the last afternoon with me on the beach and we built a massive sandcastle, just the two of us, while Mum and Meg went shopping. As the tide came in we made a game of trying to save it, piling up sandbanks and digging channels to stop the water washing it away, laughing because we knew we'd never succeed, but pretending we could hold the sea back. At last it surged in and our castle collapsed in ruins.

The tide was coming in but it wouldn't reach Sam's sandcastle for ages. I went to see if any of it was still there. Apart from a paw print on one of the walls it was undisturbed. For a moment I was tempted to jump on it, smash it down and kick sand over where it had been. But I didn't. Instead I stomped down to the sea.

Dad was going to take me fishing at Brenig. We were going to see Man United together, go to the *Cnapan*. None of that would happen now. I stood at the water's edge trying not to remember.

I don't know how long I was there. The children playing nearby could have been on another planet. The lapping of the waves sounded distant and dreamlike. 'Why?' I screamed silently to the sky and the sea and to God – if he existed. And, 'I never cry,' I told myself, tasting salt.

If I could, I'd have run into the sea and swum and swum till I could swim no more. Or walked along the edge of the waves to the river mouth and back. But it all seemed pointless. There was nowhere to go. Only the sea and the beach. And, eventually, home.

'Hello, Bryn. I thought it was you.' A voice behind me. Aunt Elin's. I passed my hand over my face hoping she'd think I was brushing away a fly and turned to see her standing beside me, jacket on one arm.

'Hi,' I mumbled. 'Am I late? I forgot the time.'

She shook her head. 'I went for a walk. I thought it was you and came over. Have you had a good day?'

'Not bad.'

'You met your friend?'

I nodded.

She stared out to sea. 'In heaven's name, what are those?'

'Turbines. It's going to be a wind farm. Renewable energy and all that.'

'Why on earth do they have to build it there? Spoils the

look of the beach entirely!' She turned to look at the town then west to the mountains. 'Funny, you can live without the sea for years, then when you see it again you wonder how you managed to. I love this beach. We used to come here for Sunday school trips, your Dad and I. We'd build the obligatory sandcastle then spend our money at the fair. The town's changed a lot, though.'

'Did you ever name your sandcastles?'

'Yes, so we did. Denbigh, Conwy, Dolwyddelan. Don't tell me you did too.'

'It was Dad's idea.'

'Fancy him remembering our old game.' She sounded amused.

'Megan and I always chose the names of Welsh castles, castles the Welsh built.'

'Quite right. So did we in our nationalist phase. Very patriotic we were as kids. And later. Your father was more restrained about it though. I wanted home rule and the return of Owain Glyndwr.' She sighed. 'How one changes.'

She looked up and down the beach again. 'Coming here brings it all back. We won a goldfish at the fair once and had trouble bringing it home because its jam jar had no lid. We wanted the coach driver to crawl home at ten miles an hour in case the fish slopped out. Our Sunday School teacher wasn't pleased, especially as we were the last to come aboard and made everyone late going back.'

'Dad used to say the fair was the scene of his misspent youth.'

She laughed. 'I suppose it was. That was where we let off steam when life got too serious. Did he still shoot? He and I used to compete to see who could get the most points on the shooting range when we were old enough. I don't suppose they allow such things now with the clampdown on guns.'

'He brings…brought…home a brace of pheasants every Christmas.' I could picture him, the birds hanging from his hand, recalled their limp floppiness as they hung behind the pantry door, remembered Megan touching one by accident and screaming.

'He put a dead pheasant in my bed once.'

'Really?'

'I expect it was for something I'd done – used his cricket bat to bang in tent pegs or some such. I daresay I deserved it. We were always playing practical jokes. As his kid sister I plagued the life out of him at times. Though he always gave as good as he got.'

'He played an April fool on Meg and me one year. Made scrambled eggs for breakfast and put the empty shells in egg cups to make us think they were boiled.'

We both laughed. 'Typical,' said Aunt Elin, 'he was a one-off, your Dad.'

'Yeah.'

We went quiet, but it wasn't a gloomy sort of quietness. Talking about Dad like this made me feel connected with him again. I'd lost sight of the real him, somehow, since he died.

My aunt took a cigarette from her bag, lit it with a gold lighter, took one or two puffs and said, 'I suppose we ought to get back.' But she didn't seem in a hurry to move.

I didn't want to go either. It was peaceful here with the sea and the sky and the beach all around.

'Dad never said much about when he was young,' I said.

'Perhaps he didn't want you to get ideas. We had to make our own entertainments in the country and some were pretty wacky. We ran wild a lot of the time.' Aunt Elin paused. 'I suspect it was our way of coping.'

'Coping with what?' I wanted to ask but didn't. Instead I said, 'What sort of things did you do?'

She blew a smoke ring and watched the sea breeze disperse it. 'There was the time we nearly burnt down a neighbour's shed cooking fish on a camping stove in the garden. We got too close to the shed trying to keep the stove out of the wind.'

'Then we thought we'd try bullfighting. With a real bull.' She laughed. 'My idea that was – the worst ones usually were. We were lucky it was an old one, or I wouldn't be here to tell the tale. We tested how fierce he was first by tickling his nose with long grasses. When he didn't react we thought it was safe to try proper matador stuff but the farmer saw us before we had a chance to get going. Mad.' She paused. 'Tad wouldn't allow us out of the house for a month after that. Except to school.'

That seemed hard. 'What was Taid like?' I asked, 'Meg and I never really knew him.'

She took so long to answer I thought she hadn't heard. Then she spoke slowly as if choosing her words with care. 'He was a…funny-tempered man…your taid. I think he was ill a lot of the time. We didn't realise it then, of course. People would be quicker to understand now.' She stopped abruptly and shrugged. 'Maybe if things had been different…' Her voice tailed off and she added briskly, 'That's all water under the bridge. We can't live our lives over again.'

My mind brimmed with questions I couldn't ask.

'So, how about you, Bryn?' She changed the subject. 'What do you like? Any idea what you want to do with your life? Or is it the wrong time to ask?'

Dad's death hadn't altered how I felt. But I'd never shared my ambitions with anyone, not even Tom, and specially not with the family. Aunt Elin was different though. She was family yet not family. A stranger, in spite of her closeness to Dad.

'I'd like to write – songs maybe, articles. I'm good at English – and Welsh. P'raps be a journalist if I'm good enough. I help edit the junior magazine at school.'

She gave me a shrewd look. 'Well, if I can help in any way, I'm around. I'm in London more or less permanently now.'

'Thanks.' We turned to go.

We were walking up the beach when she said suddenly, her eyes bright, 'How'd you like to go home the long way, Bryn? Via Bangor then through the mountains? I haven't been there for years – decades even. I'd love to take a look at it all before I go back.'

The chance of a longer trip in her car? You bet. I wasn't anxious to get home. 'Fine,' I said.

My aunt took her mobile from her bag. 'I'll ring your mother so she won't wonder where we are.'

As we settled in the car, she noticed me eyeing her CDs. 'Choose one if you like.' She switched on the sound system. 'Though I'm not sure they'll be to your taste.'

I flicked through them as we swung out of the car park. Monteverdi, Bach, Stravinsky, Prokofiev. Yuk. I wanted something with a bit more life.

She glanced across. 'There's a folk compilation somewhere. I bought it to remind me of student days when

I used to go pubbing in London.'

I found it and put it on. She turned up the volume and we roared down the A55 to Steeleye Span and the Albion Band. Not bad. The sound system was great. And it meant I didn't have to talk – or think.

We made it to Bangor in double-quick time. Aunt Elin may be a lawyer but she had no respect for speed limits on the A55. Her car could do over a hundred without pushing. From there we went down to Llanberis, Capel Curig, Betws-y-Coed and back over the Denbigh Moors.

We didn't speak much. My aunt made the occasional remark after the CD finished, mentioning a farm here where a friend had lived, a village there where she and Dad had known someone or a place where they'd held a rally – what sort of rally she didn't say. I think she'd forgotten I was there, she seemed to be talking to herself. I was content to sit back and feel the wind in my face and hair as we sped along with the windows open. I almost forgot the sadness – for a while at least.

As we slowed to enter Llanfadog, Aunt Elin turned to me. 'If ever you and Megan, or your mother for that matter, want to come and stay and taste the wider world, you'd be very welcome. It might help you sort out your ideas, see what's on offer.' She paused. 'I don't do advice. I was never good at taking it when I was your age. But go for it, Bryn. Aim for what you want and don't be put off – even by what's happened. Hard though it is. I found what I wanted in the end and did it. And I don't regret it. Not now. Though it wasn't always easy.'

Godmotherly advice after all. But I didn't mind. It was advice I could take.

Miss Rees

I bumped into Elin Pritchard this morning – almost literally. We nearly collided in the doorway of the Post Office as she was rushing out and I was organising myself to go in. It was a complete surprise. I hadn't seen her since she was fifteen and had no idea where she was living or whether she was still in Wales.

I didn't recognise her at first. I was too busy struggling with the door, my bag, my shopping trolley and my own slowness to look at her properly. She stood aside and held the door to let me through. 'I'm so sorry.' An English visitor, I thought, from her voice.

Then her voice changed. 'Miss Rees! It *is* Miss Rees, isn't it? Fancy meeting you. I didn't know you lived in Rhyl.' The pleasure in her voice would have been enough to light up my whole day. I looked at her face then and saw who it was.

'Why, Elin. What are you doing here?' I knew her at once even though I hadn't seen her for forty years. People age but their features don't change. I would have recognised that nose anywhere – and her distinctive hazel eyes.

'How lovely to see you,' she went on. 'You must be retired by now. You look well. May I help with the trolley?' She manoeuvred me into the building, which was crowded with pensioners like myself.

'Thank you.' I smiled at her. 'And how are you? I never heard what you did after university. Where are you living?'

'London.' She hesitated and looked at her watch. 'Look.

I've got to rush off to the bank just now. Can we meet later? I'm only in Wales for the week and I'd love to talk longer. I could meet you outside if you like – say in ten minutes or so?'

'Yes, I'd like that.' The idea that she wanted to chat pleased me. It's gratifying to think one isn't forgotten. When you've taught all your life it can be lonely once you've left the hurly-burly of the classroom. 'There are seats across the road,' I suggested. 'If I'm a long time.'

'Fine.' Her voice was suddenly brisk and businesslike. 'I'll see you afterwards then.' And she dashed off before I could take a proper look at her, though I noted her well-cut trouser suit and short hair and caught the scent of her perfume as she passed me. Fancy tomboyish Elin Pritchard turning into someone so presentable. I smiled at myself as I joined the queue.

The prospect of meeting Elin made the wait more bearable. Memories from Llanfadog came to mind as I held my trolley and followed the slow progress of the queue to the counter.

Llanfadog was my first school. It only had three classes so we knew the children well and there was a family atmosphere that made it a happy place to teach in. I started in 1951 as a full-time assistant and progressed to deputy head then head in the space of ten years. It was the start of a satisfying and rewarding career.

I'd only been there two years and had charge of the infants' class when Elin arrived. Her brother brought her on that first day. He was four years older. She was a slight little thing, as wiry as Gareth was solid. He held her hand but she pulled away from him as soon as they entered the building and fixed me with those searching hazel eyes.

'Where are the books?' she asked, looking round. 'Don't you do reading?'

For a moment I was taken aback. Then, 'We don't keep books in the corridors,' I explained. 'They're all in the classrooms. But you won't need reading books yet. You'll have to learn your letters first.'

'I know *those*,' she said scornfully as only a five-year-old can. 'I want proper reading books the same as Gareth. Not picture books that only babies have.'

I took her hand, 'Come along and we'll see what we can find.' I smiled at Gareth over his sister's neat pigtails. 'Off you go. Elin will be all right with me.'

He hovered for a moment, anxious as a mother hen, then dashed off to the boys' playground. Elin didn't give him a backward glance.

She was right, of course. As far as reading went Elin could easily have joined her brother's class. Already fluent, she soaked up learning like a sponge, forging ahead of the rest so that I had to prepare extra work to keep her occupied and often taught her one-to-one. Bright as a button, sharp as a needle, she was by far the cleverest of her year, a model pupil in her best moods. She was in my class for three of her six years at the school as I moved up to take the top juniors in her final year.

I smiled as I remembered them. Elin and her brother were often seen about the village together despite the difference in their ages. Gareth was chivalrously protective of his sister, mature and thoughtful for his age as well as something of a joker. He was a great help about the school, carrying the milk crates from the playground into the hall every day, mixing the ink and topping up the inkwells. He was liked by almost everyone.

Elin was very different. You either took to her or you didn't. She wasn't one of those quiet clever ones who get on with their work and are no trouble. She could be a handful when she was bored. If she didn't find a lesson interesting she made sure no one else had a chance to take it in. And she would exploit your weaknesses if there were capital to be made from a situation, seeing it as a challenge if she could 'make Miss mad'. We learnt to employ pre-emptive strategies on difficult days, giving her errands to run and extra work, or using her to help catalogue the library.

She could be cheeky, but I never found any malice in her backchat. She could refuse to work if she had no taste for an activity – needlework was her pet hate, I recall. But she was one of the brightest children it has been my privilege to teach, certainly the brightest Llanfadog school produced while I was there.

I followed her secondary school career with interest after she left, mostly via snippets of gossip from the dinner ladies and cleaning staff for none of the teachers lived in the village. Sometimes, driving home late from work, I would see her hanging about the village bus shelter with her contemporaries, the way teenagers will, and she would wave cheerfully at my car. Later on I read of her exam successes in the local paper. I was disappointed to hear of her involvement with a nationalist group and subsequent court appearance, though. That must have been a frightful experience for her law-abiding parents. I wouldn't like to have been in Elin's shoes then, knowing her father.

I had just learned of her university place when I accepted a headship in the South and moved away. I lost touch with Llanfadog then, but I always wondered how Elin had got on. Hadn't I used my influence once to further her education? An uncomfortable experience that had proved, right enough.

It happened over the Eleven Plus. At Llanfadog we rarely had pupils who made it to grammar school. But Gareth passed and in Elin's year we had hopes of a record score. Apart from Elin whose success was a foregone conclusion, there were two others who looked like high school material. One, Jenny Morgan, had moved to the village that year and become a firm friend of Elin's, which we thought good for them both.

We heard the results at school before any of the pupils got their letters – the village post didn't come till mid-morning. I called the fortunate three to my room to tell them the good news and they were ecstatic, as you might expect. Elin and Jenny were thrilled to be going to the same school. They danced off down the corridor till I told them they must behave like big girls now they were bound for the high school. I remember Elin's eyes that morning. They glowed like candle flames.

But by afternoon everything had changed. Elin was late returning to school, stealing into class like a shadow as I took the register. Worn out by all the excitement, I surmised, my eyes on the page; there was no cheery, 'Good afternoon, Miss Rees,' from her and no sign of that morning's bounce and elation.

I looked up as she took her place beside Jenny and saw immediately that something was wrong. There were dirty smudges on her cheeks as if she had been crying and had wiped away tears with a grubby hand.

What had happened? I walked down the room to her desk once we had started the afternoon's work and asked quietly if she was all right. 'Yes, thank you, Miss Rees,' she answered with a defiant lift of the chin. But her voice was flat and dull and she wouldn't look at me. I was concerned. A greater contrast with the morning's delighted child I couldn't imagine.

Elin's conduct that afternoon was deplorable. She wouldn't work, she kicked Ted Evans as she walked past his desk to the front to sharpen her pencil, then poked him with the point on the way back. She quarrelled with Jenny and sulked when I pulled her up about her behaviour, muttering under her breath that school was a waste of time. My patience at an end, I kept her behind when the others went out for their afternoon break.

'What's the matter, Elin?' I asked. 'You've been behaving like a bear with a sore head all afternoon. What's happened?'

At first she wouldn't say. She stared at the ground stony-faced and refused to answer. Then I realised she was trying not to cry.

'I can't go to high school,' she said at last. 'Tad says education is wasted on girls,' and she turned on me a look of such despair and anger that I could have wept. It was all I could do not to march out there and then and give her father a piece of my mind.

I tried to console her while pointing out that it wasn't acceptable to take out one's disappointment on others, however bad one felt.

'Would it help if I had a talk with your father?' I suggested, wondering if the family had financial problems.

A look of horror crossed her face. 'Please don't, Miss Rees. It'd only make things worse.' I failed to get any more out of her but was disturbed both by her response and the parental decision that had precipitated it.

Letting her go, I considered what to do. It wasn't uncommon for parents to undervalue girls' education in those days but Mr Pritchard's attitude was a surprise. I'd had no inkling of it before. It seemed most unfair that Gareth, who was bright but not exceptional, should be permitted to go to grammar school while Elin, who was well above average, possibly outstanding, was not. I cursed the blindness and insensitivity of parents, and of fathers in particular.

Talking it over with the staff after school – I was acting head at the time – we agreed that Elin's father was misguided. We didn't like to think how Elin would behave in a regime that wasn't geared to stretching her lively mind – she would either drive the staff mad or go completely off the rails. So I decided to take the initiative and call on Mr Pritchard in his workshop. I knew Elin hadn't wanted me to see him but the memory of her demeanour that afternoon, the way the light had gone out of her eyes spurred me on. She need never know I'd seen him if I met him at work, I reasoned. I had to try and do something for the poor child even if it proved in vain.

Mr Pritchard's workshop was on my way out of the village. I parked my Morris Minor at the back where no one could see.

He admitted me without question. Presumably he thought I had a commission for him. Solid, broad-shouldered and stiffly upright, he motioned me to the corner of the workshop where he had his desk, leading the way past the pieces he was working on. I followed, aware of the scent of freshly sawn pine and oak, of wood stain, sawdust and French polish.

At his desk he turned to face me and I saw the neat row of pens in the pocket of his khaki overalls, the sharpened pencil behind his ear, the folded rule in his hand. He had large hands, I noticed – craftsman's hands. It was hard to see a likeness between him and his daughter at first – Gareth was more like him physically. Then I noted his long, thin nose and the unusual colour of his eyes, pale hazel like Elin's but without her light and vitality.

He waited for me to announce my errand and I cast my eyes round the workshop, deciding how to begin. It was an old chapel with a high ceiling, an extensive ground floor and a gallery above. Dust motes danced in the sunlight that flooded in through the windows. All around were Mr Pritchard's tools and the raw materials of his trade. I glimpsed planks of seasoned wood, a dresser, a stained chest awaiting its final finish and chairs anchored in clamps for the glue to set. My grandfather had worked in wood so I knew something about the trade and I could tell the hand of a master when I saw it. How could this man be so gifted yet find it acceptable to block the development of his daughter's gifts?

He was polite and courteous till I explained why I had come. Then his manner changed and he left me in no doubt that my approach was an intrusion into private territory. I felt his impatience, saw the barely concealed hostility in his eyes and it was easy to see why he was reputed to be difficult. I realised with a shiver that there had been something of that same look in Elin's eyes when she'd hit out at Ted Evans that afternoon in class. Had someone once stamped on her father's dreams?

He heard me out while I pleaded Elin's case, even nodded as I set out the reasons why she should be allowed to take up her high school place. Then, when I was beginning to hope I might be getting somewhere, he squared his shoulders and waved his hand dismissively. 'What does she want with grammar school? Education is wasted on girls. She'll only get married in the end. Why should I keep her on an extra year or more at school when she could be earning?'

'It wasn't wasted on me,' I argued. 'And we don't all marry. Besides a good education is never wasted. It can lead to a better job. And married women have careers too. What's more an educated mother has a lot to give her children.'

He stiffened and regarded me for a moment with cold, unsympathetic eyes. I held his gaze though it was difficult to bear his hostile scrutiny. Then he picked up a square of sandpaper from a nearby bench. 'If you'll excuse me,' he said abruptly, 'I have work to do. I'm a busy man with orders to complete. No disrespect meant. But my mind's made up about the girl and I see no reason why I should change it. I suppose she's been pestering you.'

'Not at all,' I protested, 'she doesn't even know I'm here, and I'd prefer she didn't know. But, Mr Pritchard, she's the brightest child we have in the school. It would be a tragedy if she didn't make the most of her talents.'

'Tragedy, would it be? It'd be more of a tragedy if she got ideas above her station and imagined herself better than the rest of us, wouldn't it?' His tone was hard, unyielding. Slowly, he began sandpapering a length of wood that leaned against a workbench.

'Let me tell you this.' He paused to wave the sandpaper at me and it felt like a threat, though he was only making his point. 'I passed the scholarship as it was called in my day. And I couldn't go to grammar school either. It didn't do me any harm. Nor will it hurt Elin to learn she can't have all she wants in this world.' And he bent to his sandpapering once more, giving it his full attention as if the interview was over.

But I refused to go. The thought of Elin's stricken face kept me there, though I found the atmosphere intimidating. For five minutes or more, I watched as Mr Pritchard worked, sensed his growing impatience, felt the resentment in him that lapped round me like a black tide though he gave it no outward expression. I wasn't going to give up without a fight, though I quailed before his antagonism. I, too, was angry and I believed I had right on my side. I screwed up my courage for one last attempt to persuade.

'Of course,' I began – and my voice sounded puny and insubstantial in that lofty space, 'I realise you've already got Gareth to see through grammar school. Everyone will understand if you can't afford to pay for Elin too.'

I was going to explain about bursaries but his angry glance stopped me in my tracks. The fury in his eyes was almost palpable. He was outraged. If looks could kill I would never have got out of that workshop alive. I had judged he was a proud man and I was right.

He muttered something. It might have been 'how dare you,' but I couldn't catch the words. I saw a muscle twitch in his neck. His hands gripped the length of wood, tight as a vice.

'Think about it, Mr Pritchard,' I said, growing bolder. I was taking a risk but I had to for Elin's sake. He could do no worse than refuse and he had already done that once. 'There are sources that could help later on if you can't manage to keep two children at grammar school.'

Elin's father looked down at his hands. He had stopped work and stood perfectly still. Again a muscle twitched in his neck. Then he ran his hand along the surface of the wood he was finishing and swallowed. 'Thank you for calling,' he said at last, his voice hard-edged but perfectly controlled. 'Would you let yourself out, please. As you can see, I'm busy.'

'Good day, Mr Pritchard, and thank you for your time.' I forced myself to walk away slowly and calmly, though every instinct wanted to run from his barely concealed rage and the corrosive orbit of his hatred. I would not let him think he had won.

I was shaking when I got into the car. No wonder Elin has moods, I thought, as I drove home.

For two days I waited, afraid I had made things worse. The third morning Elin ran up to me in the playground before school, her eyes alive once more.

'Tad's changed his mind,' she cried, her face one big smile.

I beamed back at her. 'I hoped he might,' I said.

I never told her I'd been to see him. I didn't imagine he had either.

Elin was waiting for me outside the Post Office and I was able to take a good look at her now we were in the open. I couldn't help comparing the well-dressed woman before me with the redheaded scrap in pigtails I'd once taught. But her smile was the same, and her mannerisms, though her long hair had given way to a short style that softened her sharp features. The years had treated her kindly, I thought. She didn't look much over forty. Only a few lines showed round her mouth and eyes and her figure was slim and upright.

She smiled as I positioned my shopping trolley out of the way of passers-by.

'I'd offer to take you for a coffee but I've an appointment in a quarter of an hour. Do you mind standing here or do you want to go across the road and sit?' She eyed my full trolley.

'Here will do,' I said. It was strange to be on the receiving end of her concern. And to find that she really had lost her Welsh accent. 'So what are you doing now, Elin?' I asked, unable to contain my curiosity.

She filled me in on her career, her present job and her time in the Far East. I was thrilled to hear how well she had done. Hers was the success story teachers love to hear, especially if you've had high hopes of a pupil but are unsure if those hopes have been fulfilled. I felt myself expand with pride, pleased I had played a small part in giving her the education she deserved.

Then she told me why she was in Wales and her business errand in Rhyl – it appeared the family's solicitor was here. I was shocked by the news about Gareth. Fifty-nine is no age to die. Elin didn't dwell on details and I respected her obvious wish not to say more than she needed. I could see from her eyes how much her brother's death had affected her. I offered my condolences and we shared a few memories of Llanfadog School, laughing at some of the events we recalled. It tempered the sadness over Gareth.

'So you live in London,' I said eventually, realising where she had got her accent and her excellent dress sense. 'But I suppose you visit Llanfadog often with the family still here.'

In the pause that followed I was aware I had touched a raw nerve. Elin frowned and looked past me down the street. 'Actually, no. I'm here for Gareth's funeral. This is the first time I've come back to Wales since I went abroad in the eighties.' Did she feel guilty about that? She shifted slightly and looked at her hands.

'To be frank,' she went on, meeting my gaze once more, 'I've never been back to stay for any length of time since I graduated. I suppose I didn't fit in.'

'I'm sorry about that.' I felt a twinge of guilt. Had it been my interference that set her on the path away from home and family? I didn't like to think that it was. I know this can happen when children are educated beyond the level of their parents but it's a pity if it does.

'Don't be,' she said briskly, 'It wasn't your fault. I was always going to leave sometime. If it hadn't been education that got me away it would have been something else. We weren't exactly a happy family. I'm only thankful for what you did.'

I wasn't quite sure what she meant. 'We only guided you. You hardly needed teaching,' I said. 'Even if we did give you extra reading and tuition in organising the library.' I smiled at the memory of our various ploys to keep her occupied.

She smiled back. 'Oh yes, I remember all that. The most valuable part of my early education, that was. Stood me in good stead for later on, I can tell you. No,' and here she gave me a meaningful look followed by a grin, 'I meant persuading my father to let me take up my high school place.'

I was stunned and must have looked it for she laughed out loud.

'I know you never let on,' she continued, 'and I certainly didn't realise it at the time. I believed it was one of my father's sudden changes of direction. He could be unpredictable sometimes. In fact I'd been quiet as a mouse and as good as gold after he said I couldn't go. I hoped that if I behaved myself he would reconsider. I even wondered if it was my doing when he changed his mind.' She laughed again, 'But actually it was you. I don't know how you managed it but I'm grateful all the same.' And she gave me a beaming smile.

'How did you find out?' I recovered my voice at last.

'My father told me himself. He threw it at me in one of the rows we had later, said he regretted letting you persuade him when he saw what education had done to me, how selfish and ungrateful I'd become.' Elin was still smiling but there was an edge to her voice and she shook her head as if in repudiation of her father's words.

She grew serious. 'Like lots of young people, I'd found freedom at university, intellectual stimulation, a wider world,' she went on. 'It felt like going back to prison – the idea of coming home. But I wonder sometimes if I didn't overdo the single-mindedness. Maybe I should have considered the family more. Gareth used to come to London to see me but I never met his children till this week.' She sounded regretful.

'Let me tell you this,' I consoled. 'With your gifts you'd always have felt stifled in a place like Llanfadog. You needed a bigger stage, a wider remit. I'm sure your father was proud of you in the end. Most fathers would have been.'

'Perhaps.' She didn't sound convinced. Then she gave me a wry smile and shrugged. 'I suppose this is what happens when you get to my age. You look back and see where you've come from, ask if you could have done anything differently.'

'That's life,' I said, 'but look at where you've got, what you've achieved. You should be proud of what you've done.'

'Yes.' She hitched her bag up on her shoulder, her face thoughtful. 'It's Gareth dying, I expect. All of a sudden you realise life's half over and you wonder what you've done with it. Not that I regret taking up law, of course,' she added in a brighter tone. 'And I'm trying to look up some old friends while I'm here, to make up for all the years I've neglected them. I'm seeing Jenny tomorrow. Do you remember her? She married a farmer in Meirionydd. She's got a granddaughter now.'

'I can't believe it,' I said, 'that puts me in the great-grandmother generation.'

We laughed and I went on. 'That's what people do in middle age, of course. When the career's established or the children have grown, they go back to recover what they've left behind. Haven't you wondered why all those middle-aged men are tearing round the country on high-powered motorbikes? They're trying to rediscover their lost youth.'

'I'm not sure I want to rediscover mine.' Elin smiled. 'But I'm grateful for your part in it.' She looked at her watch. 'Goodness, I shall have to dash. I'm picking someone up at twelve.'

'I'm so glad we met,' I said as we prepared to go our separate ways.

'So am I. You're a part of my youth I don't mind rediscovering.' She was momentarily serious. 'Education was my passport to life and you helped put it into my hands.' She paused, then added, 'You should be proud of what you did.' The laughter in her eyes and the teasing smile that was not unlike the cheeky grin that had been her stock in trade at school told me she was mimicking me in the nicest possible way.

'We must meet again properly,' I suggested as we shook hands and said goodbye. 'When you're next in Wales.'

Her handshake was firm. 'I might take you up on that. If I come back that is.'

Elin sounded unsure and I guessed she was coming to terms, not just with Gareth's death but with returning home. I smiled to myself as I watched her walk briskly away. I could imagine her as a city lawyer.

What a coincidence our meeting like that, I thought, as I launched out in the direction of the flat. As if it had been meant. It had made my day, as they say.

I recalled the look in the young Elin's eyes when she was denied her high school place, the barely suppressed anger in her father's as I faced him in his workshop. Whether she was selfish or no, ungrateful or no, was between her and her own conscience – maybe you needed a degree of selfishness to succeed as a woman in her world, certainly in the days when she started out. But compared with her father, Elin was alive. There was a vitality in her, a spring in her step despite her bereavement. 'Education was my passport to life,' she'd said, not 'to a new life' but to life. Could she have been content with Llanfadog after that?

I permitted myself a quiet glow of satisfaction as I wheeled my shopping home.

Megan

It's been an awful week. Nightmarish. When Dad bought me a new navy jacket for Christmas I never dreamt I'd be wearing it at his funeral in May. Half-term, too. I should have been competing with my harp at the Urdd Eisteddfod. Dad was going to take me. Now I'm standing with Mum and Bryn at the lychgate waiting for his hearse. Dad's hearse in both senses because he owned it. He buried other people, now he's the one being buried.

But I mustn't think about this. I don't want to cry. I focus on the church instead and make myself look at it as if for the first time. I count the stone blocks that edge the familiar thick walls – the corner nearest me has sixteen from gutter to ground. Funny how you can see a place every week yet not really see it. I clutch the book from which I'm going to read during the service, a poem for Dad, and touch the earrings he used to joke about, making sure they're in place. *What are these, Megan, cariad? A geometry lesson in stainless steel? Are you sure your head can stand the weight?* His voice echoes in my ears and I struggle to blot it out along with the memory of his laughter, his teasing, his kindly smile.

A car draws up, new and black and shining. 'It's Elin.' Mum clutches my arm and I move closer as if to keep her safe.

A slim woman gets out, elegantly dressed in a grey silk hat and a grey suit that looks as if it was made for her. I try not to stare – that outfit must have cost a bomb.

So this is the sister dad was so proud of, the aunt Bryn and I have never met. I look straight at her and make no attempt to smile. She's a total stranger but she's here to share our grief. 'Why didn't you come when Dad was alive?' I want to ask. 'Don't you realise how much you meant to him?'

'Elin's the brains of the family,' Dad used to say. He and his sister were close, but she's never been close to us. Whenever Dad praised her achievements, her First Class degree, her top job, her years of work overseas, Mum would go quiet or leave the room and I grew up knowing there must have been no love between them.

Aunt Elin was abroad when Bryn and I were born and didn't come back till four years ago. Dad said she planned to visit the summer after that but couldn't because of foot-and-mouth. I remember Mum's face when he told us. Pull the other one, it said.

She's staying for a week. 'Being a solicitor she can help with the business side of things,' Mum explained as she and I made up the spare room bed. I could sense Mum's misgivings and resolved to be firmly on her side if sides had to be taken.

I nod numbly at my unknown aunt, who touches my arm and greets me but without warmth. She seems formal and distant and speaks in a very English voice. No hint of a Welsh accent, no attempt to speak Welsh. I'm convinced I'll dislike her.

The service is unreal. I can't believe Mum, Bryn and I are in church without Dad. He was churchwarden once, then treasurer. He loved this building. I keep expecting him to slip in beside us in a minute, the way he always did after handing out the books and welcoming people at the door. Tears fill my eyes and I move close to Mum, though whether for her comfort or mine, I'm not sure.

There's a hush when I go to the front to read my poem – as if the church itself is holding its breath. I'm used to performing in public but this is different. My stomach gives a lurch when I turn and see everyone sitting so still, their eyes on my face. I'm scared my voice will shake so much that no one will hear me. But I breathe deeply and begin,

'It's a long way off but inside it...'

They must hear the tremor in my voice and see my hands shaking. But after the first line all goes well, though I read much faster than I meant to.

I'm so relieved to get through without breaking down that everything seems to speed up after that, like a video on fast forward. The rest of the service passes in a blur till we're at the graveside. Here reality sinks in and as the coffin is lowered into the ground I soak tissue after tissue, though I'd promised myself I wouldn't cry in public.

Everyone hurries to the *Talardy,* then, driven inside by the rain. Aunt Elin comes and sits beside me at the central table and compliments me on my reading. 'Thank you for that, Megan. You did really well. It can't have been easy standing up in front of everyone at a time like this.' She turns and gives me a dazzling smile, 'I like your earrings, by the way.'

I feel my face going red. 'Thanks. I wore them for Dad. He always used to say they're a decorative geometry lesson.' Tears prick my eyelids and I fumble in my pocket for a tissue. 'Sorry.'

She takes a clean hanky from her bag and passes it. 'Don't be. He was worth it, wasn't he?'

I nod and as I wipe my eyes she says confidentially, 'I wore this hat for him, too. I'm not a hat person generally but I bought it for an investiture last year. Gareth teased me about going to such an establishment thing, with a past like mine, so I thought I'd wear it in his honour.' She takes it off and puts it on the seat beside her, giving it an affectionate pat. She looks more approachable without it. 'I removed the red feathers but I don't think he'd have minded if I'd left them on.'

'He'd have loved them.' Our eyes meet and we laugh. She has the most amazing eyes – yellow-brown, the colour of Mum's topaz ring – and laughter lines like Dad's. I note her subtle eye shadow, lightly applied mascara and well-shaped eyebrows and the freckles we all have that she's made no attempt to hide under make-up. When she smiles she's really attractive – not pretty but striking. I goggle at her. 'You don't mean you went to Buckingham Palace?'

She smiles back. 'It was no big deal. I went as rent-a-guest for a friend whose daughter couldn't go at the last minute.'

I wonder what it's like to move in such circles and what that past was that Dad teased her about, but I daren't ask. She goes on to question me about school and A levels and stuff like that and we chat about courses and careers. She listens to me as if I matter.

I like her sense of style and the way she presents herself. She must be fifty-five but looks younger. Her hair's darker than the usual Pritchard red, she must have it coloured. Most of all I'm bowled over by her clothes. They look classic and beautifully cut, like something out of the upmarket fashion magazines they have in the hairdresser's – *Vogue* or *Tatler*, or something. I guess she buys them in shops we can't even afford to nose in. Shows how much she must earn. It's hard not to be impressed.

To save Mum cooking, Aunt Elin drives us to the *Beudy Bach* for dinner and entertains us with tales of her travels – of elephants she saw in Thailand who paint pictures that their keepers sell and whales she watched in the seas off New Zealand. She's seen the Great Wall of China, trekked in the Himalayas and been in an earthquake in Japan. Bryn and I listen fascinated. She's a brilliant storyteller and has us both in stitches. She's like someone exotic from another world. But I can see Dad in her, bits of his humour, his liveliness, his sense of fun.

Dad's death has affected us all differently. Bryn's gone inside himself, staying in his room to play music and computer games. Mum and I prop each other up, welcoming callers and taking much needed rests between visits. I've lost count of how many pots of tea I've made this week. Mum's so strong. I'm really proud of her the way she's coping. The way she receives people and accepts their condolences with such dignity and grace. She must feel as if she's been cut in two, but she still manages to think of others. Sometimes we hug each other and cry, other times I creep off to my room and cry alone. Like yesterday when I came in and saw Dad's coat in the hall. He won't need it now.

And Aunt Elin? Hard to say how she is because I don't know what she's normally like. But she's different in the house from how she was in the *Talardy* and the *Beudy Bach*. Not so approachable. She's been brisk and efficient, helping Mum with the will, dashing about in her car, working at her laptop and going out now and then to smoke a cigarette or take a walk. A pity she smokes. Dad did and look what happened to him. But I can't take my eyes off her, what with the clothes and everything. Even her casual stuff is top-notch designer wear.

She can be charming, witty and amusing. But from the day she arrived it's plain she and Mum are finding it hard to be together. I can't put my finger on what's wrong exactly, but I can feel the tension in the air when they're in the same room, though it's not so bad now as it was the day after the funeral.

Aunt Elin's doing a lot of organising and I'm not sure Mum wants to be organised. Perhaps this is Aunt Elin's work-self coming out. I can imagine her bossing people in her job. She probably has assistants and secretaries running round after her all the time. But this is family and Mum doesn't need to be bossed. I'm sure Aunt Elin's doing it for the best but it's hard seeing them so ill-at-ease. I hover anxiously, wishing I could smooth things over but not knowing how. Sometimes they seem deliberately to misunderstand each other. They're like cats that have had their fur ruffled, but are too well mannered to spit.

Take this morning. At breakfast Aunt Elin breezed in from the garden after smoking her first cigarette. She's always up early and doesn't eat in the mornings.

'I'm going into Denbigh,' she said to Mum. 'Do you want any shopping?'

'I'll have to think about it. If you can wait half an hour, I'll come with you.' Mum looked up from buttering toast.

'Don't bother. I can take a list. I want to get some letters in the post straight away.' Aunt Elin stood at the table and flicked through a set of envelopes as she spoke, checking their addresses.

'I'd like something for supper tonight but I can't think

what,' Mum said in a vague sort of way. 'Is there anything you fancy?'

'Don't worry about me. I'm going to see Jenny Evans, an old school friend. I'll be out all day and won't be back till late. I thought I'd told you.' Aunt Elin was so brusque she sounded almost rude. Her mind was obviously on her letters. She took a stamp from her bag and put it on one of them.

Mum sighed. 'I don't remember you saying. Elfed wanted to come over sometime. I thought we might have managed today.'

'Sorry. I must have forgotten to mention it. Perhaps he could come tomorrow morning. I'll ring and arrange it, shall I?' Aunt Elin looked at her watch then at me. 'I really must be off. How about you coming, Megan? You'll know what sorts of things people like.' And she gave me her charming smile that's so hard to resist.

For a moment I was tempted to go, then I saw Mum's face as she raised her eyes to the ceiling in despair and I wanted to rush to her side and reassure her. I don't think Aunt Elin had a clue she was upset. It's like they're opposites. Mum's sadness is making her go all woolly and unable to make decisions. Aunt Elin's, I think, is making her dash about like a wound-up clockwork toy, managing everyone. And I'm in the middle, feeling for Mum yet wanting to understand Aunt Elin because she can't be all bad, not from what Dad said, how he talked about her. But when she acts as if there's no one but herself to consider I could shake her. I believe she'd organise the whole world if she could.

I don't go to Denbigh with Aunt Elin. I write a list for her and stay behind to show solidarity with Mum. To be honest I'd have liked the chance to browse in Boots for some new eyeliner and maybe talk to Aunt Elin on the way. I'd like to ask her about her career and what she actually does all day and what it's like where she lives in London. But Mum looks so low I don't want to leave her on her own.

'Elin's wearing me out,' she confesses as we sit over the breakfast things and share another pot of tea, 'I'm sure she didn't say she'd be out *all* day. Perhaps I'm losing it.'

'No you're not, Mum. She didn't say a thing when I was around. She probably forgets about other people, living on her own.'

Mum puts her head in her hands, 'And I thought things were improving.' She reaches for a tissue and sighs. 'I suppose I *am* being unreasonable. When Elin's out I think she's avoiding us and when she's in I wish she was somewhere else.'

I can't think what to say. I can see Mum's making a real effort to be hospitable, finding out what Aunt Elin likes and trying to make her feel at home. But they don't seem to speak the same language. They're locked in a pattern neither can undo. And though I'm intrigued by what I've seen of Aunt Elin, I'm beginning to look forward to the time when she goes back to London and leaves us in peace. It'd be easier if we weren't all feeling so grim and sad.

Everything's wrong, I decide later, sitting on my bed and staring at the view from my window. Even the hills don't look as green as they did a fortnight ago.

In all this unhappiness my only consolation is Huw. It's awful he's away this week in Cornwall on a field trip. Going to his girlfriend's father's funeral would have been no reason to cry off but I miss him dreadfully. He texts me and phones me when he can but his mobile doesn't work where he's staying and I have to be content with him getting to a landline when he can. I could do with him here with all this tension whirling about the house. I live for his calls but you can't hug a phone or cry on its shoulder, and it doesn't kiss you better.

'What's he like, this boyfriend?' Aunt Elin asked Wednesday night when I'd put down the phone after one of Huw's calls. She'd answered it and passed the phone to me.

'How did you know he was my boyfriend?' I've never mentioned him in her hearing. She laughs. 'The way your face lit up when I said his name. It was either that or you'd won the lottery.'

I blush. How to describe him? Huw is handsome, dark-eyed and black-haired, lover of mountains, trainer of search dogs, one-time hero of the school rugby team, and mine. '*Pishyn.*' There's a smile in my voice I can't hide. 'He's reading Geography at Aber. He does mountain rescue and he's ...well, *pishyn.*'

'That's a word I haven't heard in years. Will I get to see this paragon?'

'You might if you're here when he picks me up for the party on Saturday. I suppose it is all right to go – with Dad and everything?'

'What do you think your father would want? Would he want you to mope about or take time out to enjoy yourself?'

'That's what Mum said.'

'Sensible woman.'

It has become a joke between us. Whenever the phone

rings, Aunt Elin raises an eyebrow and grins at me, daring me to run and answer it. Once it was a business call for her from London, usually it's friends or family for Mum. Huw tries to ring every day though I can't be sure when. Yesterday I took a call and it was a man's voice, English, asking if Elin Pritchard was there. While she was coming to the phone he asked after the family as if he knew about us. He sounded kind but very public school.

'Ben. When did you get back? How lovely to hear you… No, I've had the mobile switched off…I'd better listen to your message, then.' There was a smile in Aunt Elin's voice as she spoke. I'm too well mannered to listen in but it was tempting. If I'd had the nerve I would have asked afterwards, 'Is he *pishyn?*' But I didn't.

'That was a good friend of mine,' she explained. 'He lives in Cheshire so he's suggested we meet while I'm here. I'll be out for lunch on Saturday.'

Do people her age have a love life? She's attractive still. I wonder why she's never married. Too busy with her career, I suppose. I want to marry Huw one day. Nowadays women can combine careers with family commitments, no problem. I'd like the best of both – Mum's loyalty to family and Elin's self-confidence, Mum's reliability and security and Elin's drive and career. But I'll have to work hard if that's what I want because I haven't got Aunt Elin's brains.

I can't make Aunt Elin out. Sometimes, like with the phone, she's teasing and chatty. Other times she's so busy and preoccupied she hardly seems to notice anyone else. Yesterday evening after her man friend rang I was in my room, sitting in front of my mirror with the bedroom door open, trying out a new hairstyle for Saturday.

I was getting really impatient with my hair. It wouldn't stay in place and I wanted to wear it up for the party. Aunt Elin was passing on the landing and heard me bang my brush down on the dressing table in disgust. She paused in the doorway. 'Having trouble?'

'My hair won't stay up.' I was cross by now. I pulled out all the grips and hairpins, shook my hair loose and glared at it in the mirror.

'Mine's like that,' she sympathised, 'too thick and a will of its own.' She looked me over. 'I can show you how I used to do mine when it was long, if that'll help.'

'Please.' I was close to tears. She could have chopped the whole lot off for all I cared.

She came into the room. 'May I?' and gathered my hair gently into a ponytail which she twisted in a knot on top of my head. She teased out some of the shorter strands to frame my face, twisting the curls round her finger. 'It's very thick and there's a lot of it so it's too heavy if you try to pin it all up. And this way it looks less severe. What do you think?' She busied herself with pins and grips, fixing it all in place. 'There.'

I turned my head this way and that, admiring the new style she'd created.

'Grips and hairpins aren't enough with your sort of hair,' she went on, 'you need combs. Have you got any?'

I shook my head.

'I could get you some in Denbigh if you like. That's if you like it this way. But don't let me bully you.' She stepped back. 'I know how hard it is to manage the Pritchard hair. I wore mine long for years and learnt the hard way. It didn't do to have it loose at the office. I experimented for ages till

I found something that was easy and looked right.'

It was hard to imagine Aunt Elin with long hair. 'Thanks a lot. It's much better the way you've done it. But I'm not sure I'll be able to fix it myself.' I undid my hair and experimented with it, trying to arrange it the way she had.

'I'll put it up for you on Saturday if you like. I'll be back by the time you're getting ready.'

'That's really kind. Thanks.'

'No problem. Only, do say if you'd prefer not. I've a reputation for being pushy and getting my own way.' She smiled at me in the mirror. 'You'll look stunning, sweep that *pishyn* boyfriend off his feet.'

I smiled back at her. For the first time she felt like one of the family.

She paused on her way out. 'I do like the way you've got your room, with the bed by the window. Makes it much more spacious.'

'It's my study as well,' I explained. 'Dad found the desk last summer at an auction sale. He said now I'd got my GCSEs I needed somewhere suitable to work.'

An odd expression crossed my aunt's face. Sadness? Longing? Perhaps it was because I mentioned Dad.

'This was my bedroom once,' she said slowly, looking round. She stood quietly for a moment then turned on her heel and left without another word.

I wanted to ask how she'd had it arranged, whether she loved the view from the window as much as I did, where she'd done her homework. But she was gone. And when I went downstairs after tidying my hair she was working at her laptop and didn't speak to me for the rest of the evening, which was a bit hurtful after I thought we'd got closer.

*

Aunt Elin touches base after shopping in Denbigh then dashes out again. 'See you tonight.' And drives off.

Mum and I relax. Elin's like a whirlwind in this mood. Even when she's working quietly there's this feeling of energy round her, like the force field of a magnet. Much as I like her I couldn't live with her for long. Not as she is now, at any rate. I haven't seen her cry for Dad once. Maybe she needs to go off and have a good howl.

Howl.

Today I cry my eyes out because I can't find one of the earrings Dad gave me when I did well in my GCSEs. Then I discover it under the bed, where I should have cleaned weeks ago.

For supper Mum, Bryn and I get fish and chips from the travelling chippy that calls once a week. We abandon the dining table and best china and eat off plastic plates in front of the telly. While the cat is away the mice don't have to impress.

For the first time in ages, Mum falls asleep in her chair and is zonked out all evening. Bryn and I argue over whose turn it is to empty the dishwasher and when he storms upstairs in a temper I do it, feeling martyred, then realise it's my turn anyway.

I wish I could ask Mum what went wrong between her and Elin before Bryn and I were born but I'm not sure she'd want to talk about it, 'specially if it's something Elin has done. Mum isn't the sort to complain about others. I can understand if she finds Elin difficult but I'm sad they can't get on. I wonder how Dad felt, torn between his sister and his wife. It can't have been much fun for him.

The house is so quiet without him. He was its life and

soul. I used to get cross when he laid down the law about when I had to be in at nights or twanged my harp as he came in from work. Now I wouldn't care how much he bossed or teased if only we could have him back.

That evening with Bryn upstairs and Mum asleep, I can't bear Dad's absence any longer. I need to remind myself what he looked like, what we did together, how it was. I'm afraid I'll forget his face completely. So I drag the box of family photographs out from the understairs cupboard and empty them on the dining room table. I want a picture of Dad to remember him by.

The photos, some in albums, some still in their wallets, are the story of our lives, a good part of Mum's and Dad's and the whole of Bryn's and mine. Eighteen years of family memories. It's odd but Dad feels closer as I trawl through them, as if he's laughing over my shoulder.

There's the picture of Bryn and me burying him on Tenby beach. Dad has his eyes tight shut because we're throwing sand about but there's a big grin on his face. So typical, that grin. Infectious. I remember Dad laughed so much he kept making cracks in the sand. We had to keep patting it down, telling him corpses didn't giggle.

There's one of him driving off the Friesian cow that invaded our campsite one summer at Criccieth. His arms are stretched out wide and he's waving a stick. I trace his shape and smile at his determination. I took that picture. Mum was hiding in the tent afraid to come out and Bryn was guarding our breakfast things.

Here he is, a well-padded Santa for the Church Christmas Fair two years ago - he had his picture in the paper and all the kids loved him – and as a proud fisherman with the salmon he caught at Inchnadamph last year. He looks so pleased. He showed me how to gut it and I cooked it to give Mum a break. Trouble was I left it in the oven too long and it fell to bits but Dad said that was better because we didn't have to struggle to separate flesh from bones. He could have grumbled but he didn't. I hold the photo close up and look at Dad's face, trying to print it on my mind. I want to remember how happy he was.

Birthdays, picnics, holidays, family groups – they're all here and I smile through tears as I sort through them. Dad appears open-faced and smiling, everywhere. He was so good to be with. He had the gift of making everyone feel special. If he complimented me on my clothes I felt like a star. We had fun as a family even when it was hard making ends meet before Dad's business expanded. I'm glad it was death that parted us, not divorce or separation or anything messy like that.

I pick out two photos I 'specially like, one of Dad and Bryn and me in our caravan the year we stayed at Tywyn and one of Dad in the garden here, digging over the veggie patch. He looks up, smiling, as I call his name and I've caught him just right.

The front door opens and Aunt Elin comes in. I ask her to be quiet so as not to wake Mum and she nods, inquires if I want a drink and disappears into the kitchen. We make coffee and I microwave a mug of chocolate for Bryn as a peace offering.

'Did you have a good day?' I ask.

'Yes, thanks.' She has spread her *Financial Times* on the table and is standing over it, leafing through its pink pages. But slowly. Her day out must have done her good. She looks up and smiles. 'I'll take ours into the dining room, shall I?'

When I come down from delivering Bryn's drink, Aunt Elin is going through the photographs on the table. 'This takes me back.' She has picked out some pictures of her and Dad when they were young.

I peer over her shoulder at the little black and white prints. I hadn't got as far as the earlier photos. Here are Dad and Elin on a beach – it looks like Rhyl – hand in hand, paddling. Dad must be about eight and Elin four. Another one of them in a snow-covered garden standing beside a snowman as big as Elin herself. A woman in a coat and scarf stands beside them, smiling. Yet another of them, with the same woman, in the grounds of Denbigh Castle.

'That's not Nain.' I am curious. 'Is she the woman Dad talked about who lived next door?'

'Yes. That's my godmother, Aunt Tibby, but no relation.' And I can tell from the way Aunt Elin speaks just how much Aunt Tibby meant to her. 'This was taken in their garden. Tad would never have allowed us to spoil his lawn by building snowmen on it.' She examines the photographs carefully before putting them aside.

There are more pictures of Dad and Elin, paddling in streams, climbing trees, cycling, looking out of a tent in a garden. The two seem inseparable.

'I adored him.' There's the hint of a break in Aunt Elin's voice. 'It seems no time since we were that age.' She pulls up a chair and sits to examine more of the collection. Standing beside her I'm surprised to find there are so few of Nain and Taid and Dad and her together. But there are a lot of Aunt Tibby with them.

'She and Uncle Jack took us under their wing,' Aunt Elin explains. 'They had no children of their own so they took us on. Their house was my second home.' She stacks the wallets of photographs on the table. 'They were a lovely couple. I packed my little doll's case once, when I was six, and turned up on their doorstep to ask if I could move in. Funny what children do... I thought it was quite normal at the time. I had no idea you couldn't just swap homes if you didn't like where you were.' She adds quickly, 'I'd probably been told off for something and taken offence.'

I've never wanted to live anywhere but home. I look at my aunt curiously. 'What happened to them?' I think I can remember Dad mentioning an Aunt Tibby – wasn't she the one whose funeral he saw to the other year – but I can't recall ever meeting her.

'They moved south when I was twelve. I felt it more than Gareth because Aunt Tibby always wanted a little girl and she spoilt me rotten. I was heartbroken when she left. We kept in touch though.' She pauses. 'Tibby died in a nursing home a year ago. She was eighty-six. But I was able to see her before she died. She was good to me. Not just then but later.' She changes the subject abruptly. 'I'll find you some pictures of Nain and Taid shall I?' And she riffles through some more photographs till she has discovered some family groups for me to see.

Here they are on the steps of our house, Nain and Taid, Dad and Elin. It doesn't look like it does now. There's no extension and the windows are different, but the back garden is the same with the pond and vegetable patch. Dad is grinning, holding a jar of murky water.

'His tadpoles,' Aunt Elin explains. 'We collected them religiously every year, even though Mam hated the idea of them turning into frogs and overrunning the garden. We always had to put them back where we'd found them before they got too frog-like.'

Nain, a slim woman in an apron, like Aunt Elin in build, stands behind Dad, her hands on his shoulders. Something about the way she looks makes me feel sad. Taid, very upright, like the soldier he once was, is beside her, unsmiling. Elin in front chews one of her plaits and frowns.

'I hated formal photographs,' she explains.

There's one of the family picnicking on a beach.

'One of the rare occasions we went out together.'

And another with the Caernarfon cousins. Dad and his cousin Tom glaring. 'Tom was one of the few people your Dad disliked.'

We move on to another set.

'You'll be interested in these.' Aunt Elin shows me two photographs of her and Dad amongst a crowd of angry people. Dad is holding a placard that says, 'Save Welsh Homes' and Elin looks as if she's shouting. 'Did your father tell you we were at Tryweryn?'

'So you really were. I was never sure if he was joking or not.'

'Never more serious. We calmed down eventually but I don't regret being part of the demonstration. It was a just cause.' She picks out one picture in particular. 'My first serious boyfriend was an ardent nationalist…here.' And I stare in amazement at a photograph of a young, long-haired Elin holding hands with a lean, bearded man. Her hair is loose, blowing in the wind, and she's in the scruffiest clothes – a checked shirt too big for her and faded jeans. If she hadn't told me that was her I'd never have guessed. How people change.

'See what I mean about the hair,' Aunt Elin laughs. 'And I'm wearing one of Glyn's shirts. It was the thing to do at the time.'

Her boyfriend is scruffy too but good-looking. Like a wilder version of Huw.

'He's *pishyn,*' I comment.

'*Pishyn yn wir,*' she agrees. 'We'd have married if I hadn't fallen in love with London. But it was probably for the best. We were beginning to drift apart after I got my degree.'

I hope this won't happen to Huw and me.

So Aunt Elin nearly got married. I could have had cousins. Bryn and I are the only ones of our generation in the family. I wonder if she minds now that she and her boyfriend parted. I'd like to know but of course I can't ask. I daren't. She'd back off again, I'm sure.

'Don't I look a mess?' she says, examining the photo more closely, 'I can't think what he saw in me at the time, except that we both shared a passion for Wales and the language.' She laughs. 'We had some good times, though,' she adds, then goes quiet for a moment as if remembering. 'Glyn was at the funeral. He and your Dad were friends years ago.'

I've never heard of Glyn, but Dad had a lot of friends. I wonder what it's like to be old and lose contact with people you were once close to. I'm going to make sure I keep in touch with all my friends. But then I'm never going to move away like Aunt Elin.

She puts the photographs on the table with a quick, decisive movement, 'Sorry, I've taken over,' and looks up at me. 'What were you doing before I came in?'

'It doesn't matter, just looking out pictures of Dad.'

She smiles. 'One for your room?' How does she know? 'I'd like a recent one for myself,' she says. So we sit side-by-side and sort out some pictures of Dad for her, negatives she can take prints from.

'I'll send them back,' she promises. 'Would your mother like a portrait of him from one of these, do you think? I could get it done at the same time.'

Aunt Elin is easier to talk to when she's not being managing and efficient, more comfortable to be with. I'd like to ask her why she never came to see us when she came back to England from abroad. Dad used to meet her in London sometimes, I know. But Mum never did, not that I can remember.

Perhaps things wouldn't be so difficult between them if Aunt Elin had visited. Or perhaps the problem between them was what kept her away. If Dad were here I could ask him but he isn't. The reminder that he is gone brings sudden tears to my eyes. I sniff and turn my head away. I don't want to cry in front of Aunt Elin. I know she was sympathetic in the *Talardy* but while Mum and I can share our grief and be sad together, there's this barrier with Aunt Elin, perhaps I just don't know her well enough.

She glances across and touches my arm but says nothing. For a moment I realise she understands then the moment is gone and she is her brisk, no-nonsense self again.

As I reach for a tissue she riffles through the photographs. 'Look at these,' she says brightly, 'these'll make you laugh. How not to put your hair up.'

And she shows me an enlarged portrait of herself at graduation, her hair scraped back and fastened tightly at her neck. 'Isn't it awful? The family made me have this taken but I look a fright, don't you think? I wanted to make myself look older but it worked far too well. You'd imagine I was nearer forty than twenty-one.'

She sifts through pictures of herself, Nain and Taid and

Dad taken after the ceremony. 'It wasn't a happy day. We had a running row about when I was coming home. I was determined to stay in London and follow an academic career but Tad thought that wasn't what women should do. He wanted me to come home and look after them in their old age, train as a solicitor or teach, and settle in Llanfadog. It would have killed me.'

'Weren't they pleased you got a degree?'

'Yes, give them their due… When Tad realised I was clever he let me go that far. But he thought intelligence was wasted on women. That's what his family believed. The only way I could cope was by cutting myself off entirely. I'd have been fighting for survival all the time otherwise. Your generation is luckier. You can do more or less what you like though you'll probably have your own battles to fight, same as we did.'

She doesn't sound bitter. But I've caught a glimpse of how hard it has been for her to follow her career. Dad was always so proud when I did well. He told me after GCSEs that he'd back me whatever I choose to do. I must remember that. I want to do the best I can, not just for me but for him.

'Do you mind,' I venture, 'that you left Wales and the family and everything?'

She frowns. 'There's a question. Do I mind that I left Wales? Yes, a bit. But a wise teacher once told me I needed to spread my wings and get a wider view of life. I'm glad I did that. Do I mind that I left the family? No. At the time it was a matter of survival, for lots of reasons. But I wish I'd been better at keeping in touch over the years and been less single-minded. On the other hand I probably wouldn't have got where I am now if I'd played things differently.'

She is quiet for a moment, then, 'Come on,' she says in the abrupt way she has, which, I'm learning, is just her manner. 'Let me see some photographs of you and the family. I've missed you and Bryn growing up. The downside of working abroad and being too engrossed in my own affairs.'

So I begin to show her Bryn and me from cradle till now, and all the special moments of our family life including our christenings that, as godmother, she never attended. She looks at them carefully, especially the pictures of us as babies. Is she sorry she never saw us then?

'Be thankful you had a loving father.' She picks out a picture of Dad and me on Rhyl seafront. 'Though it's a pity you couldn't have had him for longer.'

What does she mean by that? Does she mean her father wasn't as kind as Dad? I find myself thinking about Taid. I never knew him. He died when I was two. And I only remember Naina dimly, as a little woman who was ill most of the time. Dad never said much about them and suddenly I wonder why. Maybe I'll ask Mum. Or Elin. I look at her sideways and decide now isn't the right time. But I might one day, if she stays in touch.

As we go through the pictures it feels as if Aunt Elin's getting to know us properly for the first time. And I'm getting to know her better. She's still a bit of a puzzle. It's like she has two selves, her professional self, and a softer self inside. She can be kind, but she can also seem unaware of others, insensitive even. She's so different from Mum. Mum's soft on the outside but she has this steely inside self that I'm amazed at, that's getting her through this awful time and being strong for us all.

I'm trying to work out if a baby in a pram is Bryn or me

when we're joined by Mum, who's woken up and come to see what we're doing.

'I'm catching up on the family history I've missed,' Aunt Elin explains, glancing up as Mum comes in. 'We need your help.'

'The family missed you.' Mum sits down. I look at her trying to work out if she's being sarcastic. But sarcasm isn't her style. 'That's Bryn,' she decides, taking the print from Elin and examining it closely. 'He had a different pram cover. I know because I made it myself.'

I stand up. 'Do you want a drink, Mum? Coffee? Tea? Chocolate?'

'Whisky?' teases Aunt Elin.

'There's that bottle of Riesling we won in the church raffle. I rather fancy something different. How about you, Elin?'

'Yes, please.' Aunt Elin is smiling. Mum seems at ease too.

'It's in the pantry, *cariad*.' Mum looks at me.

When I return with the wine, wineglasses and corkscrew, they are poring over photographs of family outings, sitting side by side.

'I wish we'd written on the back where they were taken.' Mum sighs.

'Well, I'm sure that's the Great Orme,' says Aunt Elin. 'Isn't that a wild goat in the background?'

'I thought it was a gorse bush, though you may be right. This next one's definitely Llanddwyn.'

'Yes it is.' Aunt Elin takes the photo and scrutinises it. 'How old are Bryn and Megan here?'

'Ten and twelve, I think.'

'A favourite place of mine, Llanddwyn,' Aunt Elin says

in a reminiscing sort of voice.

'Mine, too.'

Mum opens the wine bottle and pours full glasses for them and a half glass for me and there is peace between us as we drink. I feel myself relaxing like a guard off duty.

'By the way, Lily,' Elin smiles at Mum over her glass of Riesling, 'you two have been doing all the cooking. Why don't you let me feed you tomorrow night. I can make a tolerable spaghetti or I can bring in a takeaway if you like. I passed a Chinese on the way back from Jenny's.'

It may be just a temporary truce or the beginning of something new. But as I look at the photographs spread over the table, and Mum and Elin sorting through them, I could swear Dad is smiling over my shoulder.

Jenny

'Jenny, it's Elin, Elin Pritchard.'

I nearly dropped the phone in surprise. *'Elin, ydwyt ti yn wir? Ers talwm. Be wyt ti wedi bod yn gwneud? Lle wyt ti?'*

'I'm in Wales for the week. Could I come over and see you while I'm here?' Was it really Elin? I couldn't believe her voice. It was so...English and not just the words.

I leant against the kitchen unit, thoughts racing. Elin. The best friend of my teenage years, the rebel who'd gone to London to study law and made a successful career of it. This was a turn-up. I thought we'd lost touch for good.

I switched languages following her lead while I tried to get my mind round her preference for English. What had happened to the firebrand Welsh nationalist? 'Of course, where are you?'

'At my sister-in-law's.' She paused. 'Gareth died last week. It was his funeral Tuesday.'

'Gareth! Oh no! I hadn't heard. I'm so sorry.' I'd once been in love with her gentle, fun-loving brother. And Elin had thought the world of him. He couldn't have been sixty. 'What happened?'

'He had a heart attack. Died suddenly at work.'

'Oh Elin, I'm so sorry. How are his family?' I couldn't remember the name of Gareth's wife though Tad told me years ago that he was married. Did they have any children? I'd lost contact with the family since my parents died.

'Can I tell you when I come? The mobile needs recharging.'

I reviewed my week. It would be awful to miss my old friend when we'd once been so close. Fancy Elin looking me up after all these years. She was the only friend from school I'd been sad to lose touch with. 'Can you come tomorrow? I'll be looking after my granddaughter some of the time but she's only four and no trouble.'

'Fine. It'll be lovely to see you. The family could do with a break from having me around.'

'Come for the day in that case and stay for supper. Hywel ought to have finished silaging by then. You can see him too. Do you know how to find us?' I gave instructions then put the phone down and drew breath.

Elin. After all these years. We hadn't met since my wedding, hadn't written since the late seventies, apart from the occasional Christmas card. What a lot of catching up we had to do.

I've never been one to dwell on the past. Too busy living. Farm and family are more important to me than looking up people I was at school with, 'specially those I'd been glad to leave behind. But Elin was different. The thought of seeing her made my day. I skipped through the housework, the WI minutes and the farm accounts with the lightheartedness of a child promised an unexpected treat. Even the news of Gareth's death couldn't dampen it.

Incidents from our sixties schooldays came to mind as vivid as if they'd just happened.

The day Elin took her pet mouse to school and let him out in the French lesson… Sharing the results of cookery lessons on the way home, mouthfuls of apple crumble snatched with plastic teaspoons while the school bus rattled along switchback country roads, fighting off grammar school boys who tried to grab the enamel dish from us and make us kiss them to get it back… Keeping look-out while Elin tied a Welsh flag high up a drainpipe above the school entrance because she was furious there was no official celebration of St. David's day… Shredding daisy heads in the school field as we picked over the bones of the latest romance, lamenting the fickleness of the opposite sex and swearing eternal sisterhood while plotting future conquests.

I smiled as the memories came tumbling back. Elin was a colourful character. With her Pre-Raphaelite hair, eloquent tongue and passionate loyalties she couldn't help but stand out in a crowd. I was the faithful follower who covered for her in her nationalist escapades, who hung about uncomfortably when she received the usual tellings-off, unwilling to be implicated in her crimes but loath to desert her, the foil to her idealism and daring.

'That girl will come to a bad end, or make a name for herself in politics,' my father declared when Elin and her student boyfriend had been in court for over-painting English road signs with Welsh. But the fact that she was clever and won prizes at school saved our friendship from complete parental disapproval. Even then I sensed there was something about Elin's family that bothered them. Looking back, I can see they watched out for her and gave her space in our home when things were difficult at hers. Nothing was said to me and Elin never talked about her parents. But one day my mother, returning from a nursing shift at the North Wales hospital, had found her doing homework in the village bus shelter early one morning and brought her back. 'Tad was in a mood,' was all Elin said to me after my mother had had a long talk with her. 'It was the only place I could get peace and quiet.'

From then on it was understood that Elin could have breakfast with us whenever she liked and do her homework at our house if she wanted. I wondered about it as I remembered. Sometimes I'd felt welcome in the Pritchard home, other times I knew not to cross the threshold and stayed away. Which was a pity, because for most of my teenage years, I was madly in love with Gareth, and would have died to spend more time in his orbit. But I was doomed to admire him from afar. All Elin's attempts at matchmaking, and mine, came to nothing.

I couldn't believe Gareth was dead. Elin had been so attached to him, worshipped him almost. I wondered how she was coping. I shed tears over the sink as I remembered the kind young man I had fallen for, then realised the tears were as much for my own lost youth as for Elin's brother.

'Do you remember Elin?' I asked Hywel at supper. 'My old school friend, the redhead, she was at our wedding. She's coming for the day tomorrow.'

'The talkative girl with long hair? She brought an Australian with her, didn't she? Smooth. Didn't like the chap.'

'Yes, Ian. Fancy me forgetting.' From the way they'd looked at the time I'd thought they were heading for life together. Elin had hinted as much. But Ian never figured on subsequent greetings cards. Was she married, divorced, single or what?

'I don't think she's been back to Wales for years. Had a row with her father, or something like that and…' I broke off as awkwardness rose between us.

'The weather looks good for tomorrow,' said Hywel.

He pushed his empty plate away, stood up, and, without another word, strode into the sitting room and turned on the television.

There's nothing like the prospect of meeting a long-lost friend to get you reviewing your own life. That night in bed I thought about mine. If Elin asked how I had done what would I say? That I'd taught for two years after marrying, then left to bring up a family? That I'd been a parent governor at the village school and twice president, now secretary of the local WI? That I was a member of the Community Council and helped at Clwb Ti a Fi? That I minded Ffion when Sian was at the surgery and helped with secretarial work for the farm? It didn't seem much compared with a first class degree, a successful career, a huge salary and a job overseas, which was what I'd heard about Elin from my parents when they were alive. I had misgivings about the lack of Welsh in her phone call. Perhaps she had changed so much we would have nothing in common and my hopes of friendship renewed would prove an unrealistic dream.

Next morning I peered at myself critically in the mirror. How had I changed? More grey hairs, more lines around the mouth and eyes, more weight in the wrong places. If Elin was as slim as she used to be, I would find it hard not to be eaten up with envy. Would she be so well dressed I would feel a yokel beside her? I chose my clothes with care, opting for navy cotton trousers and a Liberty print shirt. I applied some make-up though I don't usually wear it about the farm. Old friend or not, I didn't want her to think I had completely let myself go. I could give a reasonable account of myself, I thought. I was happy, wasn't I? For the most part, life was fine.

*

Elin was late. True to form, I thought, as I hovered in the kitchen finding unnecessary things to do while keeping watch on the yard. Punctuality had never been her strong point at school. But at eleven, alerted by the dogs, I looked up to see her arrive in a brand new BMW that gleamed even after its tussle with our track. For an instant my heart sank and I was glad my rusting Peugeot was out of sight in the barn. Then I forgot silly comparisons and hurried out.

I was momentarily taken aback to see her short hair. Gone were the flowing locks I remembered from our teens and early twenties. I felt a twinge of regret, then realised I could hardly expect her to look exactly the same. I certainly didn't.

We embraced in the yard.

'Elin, I'm so sorry about Gareth. It must have been a terrible shock.'

She clung to me briefly and shed a tear or two. 'Thanks. Awful isn't it? You think the people you love will go on forever.'

Again I had to make a mental adjustment to her voice. It was Elin but not Elin.

The sheepdogs danced round us, barking. I tried to stop them pawing my visitor's beautifully cut cords and suede jacket.

'Don't worry. Clothes'll clean.' She was fussing over the collies, letting them lick her hands. 'Ben has dogs. One thing I miss in town is animals. They're just the comfort you need at times like this.' I began to relax. This was the Elin I remembered.

Ben? Who was he? Friend? Partner? Son? I noticed she had no ring.

We separated to take stock.

'Jen, you haven't changed a bit.'

'Nor you.'

Lies. We were thirty years older and looked it. She was recognisably Elin, but a smarter, more sophisticated Elin, with expensive clothes and a stylish haircut. For a moment I felt upstaged even in my best casuals. Then I was pleased to note the old infectious grin, the same questioning look, the familiar teasing manner.

'What a lovely place you have.' She looked about the farmyard. 'You must show me round. I've borrowed my niece's boots in case it's muddy.'

'Later. When Ffion comes we'll go and see the lambs.'

'Ffion?'

'My granddaughter. Do you mind four-year-olds? I've got her for a couple of hours this afternoon.'

She smiled. 'I daresay I'll cope. I don't get to see many four-year-olds in my job.' She turned suddenly, 'Wait a minute,' and retrieved a bottle of wine and a bunch of flowers from the car. 'This is why I'm late. There wasn't a lot of choice in Bala today.'

'Thank you. They're lovely.' Rhodri always used to bring me flowers. It was years since I'd had any. Hywel's tokens of appreciation are less romantic.

'Let's have coffee.' I led the way to the kitchen.

It was a bit sticky at first. Elin seemed on edge and I spilled coffee and tipped biscuits off the plate in my hurry to pass them – we normally eat them straight from the packet. I needn't have bothered. She didn't eat one. No wonder she was so slim. I had three chocolate digestives. Not good for the waistline.

Then I jumped in with both feet, unable to hide my

curiosity. 'Elin, what's happened to your Welsh? You were such a campaigner for the language.'

She looked abashed, guilty even, and glanced at her hands. 'Yes. It's what I hear everyone thinking, though they're tactful enough not to say.' She looked at me, then out of the window at the sunny yard. 'It was part accident, part design, I suppose. The people I mix with don't speak it. There was hardly going to be the opportunity to speak Welsh in the Far East, and learning a bit of Japanese probably squeezed the most part of it out. The ease with it, at least. Then it became a point of principle not to bother.'

'Principle?'

'Yes. I'd decided I was never coming back. When I went to work abroad.'

'To Wales or to London?'

'Wales. Gareth was my only contact here. I didn't really know Lily, his wife. There seemed no point. Gareth got used to us speaking English.' She smiled. 'He didn't like it though.' There was a pause then she added. 'I can't explain it fully myself. I suppose it meant a break with the past. And once I've got an idea in my head I can be stubborn.'

I knew that. 'Surely not a break from Welshness, though?'

'No. From the family.'

I shuddered. Her words had stirred my own ghosts.

Elin changed the subject abruptly. 'Well, Jen. What's new? How are you after all these years?' She leaned forward, elbows on the table, chin in hands and regarded me enquiringly. She didn't seem to bear any hard feelings for the inquisition.

'Oh, fine. It's been a struggle with the farm at times but we're not doing badly. I've got a little granddaughter, as you know, and my daughter, Sian, works as a nurse at the local surgery. Her husband, Alun, runs Cefn Isa, the other farm in the business, where Hywel is today.'

'And what about foot-and-mouth? Did you escape?'

'We didn't get it, but we lost a lot of lambs in Shropshire because we couldn't move the ewes back here. They drowned in seas of mud.' I couldn't keep the anger out of my voice. The sights I had seen could still arouse a festering, impotent rage. I took a deep breath. 'We're still suffering controls on stock movements.' I crunched another biscuit. 'What makes me mad is how the Government ties farmers up in knots but doesn't give a damn about what others bring into the country.'

'Ben says the same. He lost his prize dairy herd that year. They're only just beginning to re-stock.'

'Ben?' That name again. I looked at her for an explanation.

'A friend.' Her eyes softened. 'You don't have boyfriends at our age, do you? But he's the equivalent. A widower. I've known him for years.' She smiled. 'He was once a Tory MP. How's that for sleeping with the enemy? Not literally, I hasten to add. But we enjoy each other's company and see each other when we can.'

'And you were such a revolutionary,' I teased.

A crooked grin, a glimpse of the old Elin. 'I know.'

'No wedding bells?' I was eager for romance.

She looked thoughtful. 'I don't think marriage is my thing. Too many disasters early on.' She didn't elaborate though I gave her the space.

What about Ian, the Australian? I wanted to ask, but didn't. We weren't on that level yet, still sizing each other up though we'd cleared one huge hurdle. I still couldn't get used to her voice with the Welsh accent gone. I felt like someone trying to walk familiar ground in a mist. Occasionally the mist cleared and I would catch sight of a known landmark, then it would thicken and I would lose my way again. I was searching for connections between us. Had she turned her back on everything that meant so much? I felt a *hiraeth* for the closeness we'd once had.

Turning to safer ground, I showed her my photographs of Ffion as a baby, of Sian's graduation, and of mine and Hywel's silver wedding. She examined them and made comments but I wasn't sure her mind was engaged. Family means a lot to me. From what Elin said I guessed it was low on her list of priorities.

'I saw Finn Morris yesterday,' she said suddenly, 'took her out to lunch.'

'Finn? She must be getting on.' Our history teacher had had a soft spot for Elin and Elin for her though she'd always denied it. Finn was the one who'd persuaded her to apply to UCL. 'She's moving into a retirement home,' Elin went on, 'but she's the same old Finn. Same keen mind, same personality. She'll never be old, whatever her age.'

She looked out of the window then added brightly, 'And you'll never guess who I bumped into in Rhyl Post Office just before.'

'No?'

'Miss Rees from Llanfadog School. She's retired to Rhyl apparently. I feel as if I've been meeting my past with a vengeance.'

'Miss Rees? How was she?'

'She looked well. Quite sprightly in fact. We had a chat about old times. I told her I was coming to see you.'

'Llanfadog School,' I said. 'Those were the days. Do you

remember when the classroom chimney caught fire and we all had to be evacuated?'

'And spent the afternoon watching the fire brigade put it out. That lit up our day.'

We laughed.

'And when Tony Roberts brought a lamb to school,' I put in.

We laughed again, reliving it.

'And my mouse,' Elin said. 'When I took him to French class Miss Jones wasn't a bit fazed. She let him run up and down her arms, do you remember? I'd hoped she'd run away screaming and forget to give us homework.'

'And all we got was extra sentences describing mice in French.'

Elin made a face, 'I suppose it was useful.'

'You were a real *enfant terrible*.'

She gave a wry smile. 'I suppose I was. But it was all so dull and staid – practically soporific, all those stodgy women teachers and all those petty rules. Things needed livening up.'

'You did that all right. These days they'd have you excluded.'

She grinned. 'P'raps that's what I wanted – freedom – or something like that.' She leaned back in her chair. 'And now look at me, making sure everyone else sticks to the rules. Talk about poacher turned gamekeeper.'

We both laughed. This was more like it, I thought, relaxing. This was the kind of get-together I'd hoped for.

We shared more memories of school, recalling people we'd known and trying to remember the names of others. We decamped to the sitting room and chatted eagerly about old times, what people were doing, what I'd heard of fellow pupils since leaving college, what had happened to the school since it merged and how Elin had met her old boyfriend at Gareth's funeral.

'It was strange seeing him again,' she said. 'Took me back to our sixth form days and after. He's married now. His wife's much younger by the look of her.'

'A blast from the past,' I agreed.

'Yes,' she added. 'I could have married him, you know, at one time.' She looked thoughtful. 'It wouldn't have worked out though. Not after I went to London.'

She fell quiet and stared into her empty cup. I went to fetch us more coffee.

'I'm only just getting to know Gareth's children,' Elin remarked when I came back, a trifle wistfully, I thought. 'I'm sorry I didn't see them before. They're both bright sparks. But in different ways. Megan's more outgoing but I gather Bryn's the clever one.'

'What's Lily like?' I prompted, remembering I'd once nursed dreams of becoming Gareth's wife.

Elin's hesitation spoke volumes. 'Quiet, home-loving, very family centred, and a lot younger than Gareth. Everything I'm not.' She looked at her hands. 'We don't… didn't get on. My fault I suspect. She looks unassuming but there's more to her than you think – more than I thought anyway. I'm only just getting to know her, too.' She paused as if considering what more to say and laughed suddenly. 'She speaks Welsh now. She learnt so she could speak it with the children. There's me speaking English and Lily speaking Welsh. That's ironic. The joke's on me, I think.'

We went quiet – I think we were both remembering Gareth – and I steered the conversation to my present concerns: rural services and village schools, women's place on local councils and the future of farming. 'The country would collapse without women running it,' Elin joked, 'though there aren't enough women where I work. Not at the top anyway.'

'Yes, tell me about your job. What exactly do you do?'

I don't think I was any the wiser after she'd explained. It was hard to get my mind round the responsibility she carried. But seeing her poise and self-assurance, the attention she paid to clothes, even casual ones, I could imagine her holding down a top job. Obsessively single-minded when she had her teeth into something, Elin had always had the mental capacity for such demanding work. But who would have guessed she would go so far?

'Tad thought you'd come to a bad end or be a politician,' I commented with a laugh.

'I suppose I could have done either.' She grinned. 'But believe it or not, I like the discipline of legal work, getting to grips with detail, keeping things in order. The law's a protection from business getting out of control, regulates deals and settles disputes fairly – or tries to. There's a lot of looking at the small print but I get to meet some interesting people. I train young lawyers too – I like that best – and seeing a case through, of course. I always relished a challenge.' The light in her eyes told me how much she enjoyed her job.

'No complaints?' Was I hoping for flaws in her perfect career?

She screwed up her nose. 'Not really. But the pace is faster these days. Young lawyers starting in city firms can work incredibly long hours. Hard for the women who want to start families and the pressure can be enormous.' She smiled. 'But so can the pay. I could work twenty-four seven if I cared to. But I don't. One needs a life.'

Which is where your friend comes in, I thought.

Elin frowned and went on, 'I'm not sure how long I'll stay where I am. Many city firms expect people to be out by sixty, often earlier, to make way for new people coming up. The future's not certain by any means, though I'm probably safer than most in my present position.'

I looked at her in surprise. So even the top people's jobs weren't secure. I wondered what Elin would do in retirement. I couldn't imagine her settling down to a stately old age. I was tempted to ask what she had in mind but didn't.

She changed the subject abruptly. 'It'll be interesting to see how the new law on corporate responsibility will work. It won't hurt companies to develop a social conscience. I hope I get a chance to apply it.'

'Now you are talking like a politician,' I said, and we giggled.

Joking apart, I was aware of a gulf between us. Not on a personal level. We were reviving our old friendship nicely. But Elin's mind was obviously focussed and firing on all cylinders despite her loss. Mine felt as if it had lost all elasticity and shape. Like my figure. Where does she get her energy from, I asked myself, then realised she didn't have children, a grandchild, a farm, a husband and a community to worry over. With fewer domestic commitments I might have done the same in my field...got a headship, run a school, become an educational consultant. Is that what I'd have wanted? But then I'd never had Elin's drive and energy. She would have got to the top whatever career she'd chosen.

'Do you like what you do?' she was asking, her hazel

eyes searching mine.

'Yes.' I wasn't going to envy her.

'You don't regret giving up teaching, not going back?'

'Too busy to. Anyway there were no jobs here when I wanted them.' And the country needs community builders, I could have added – people with time for people, glue in the social fabric. The trouble was our family glue had come unstuck.

We ate a salad lunch, still talking, then Elin went outside for a cigarette.

'You never used to smoke,' I accused. Hywel does and I worry about his health.

'A habit I picked up abroad. I'm trying to stop, but it does calm the nerves, 'specially when the pressure's on. Gareth dying hasn't helped.' She shook her head as if to brush the thought of bereavement away.

Sian's whirlwind appearance bringing Ffion was another sign of the gulf between our respective experiences – the career woman and the one who had given up career for family and community involvement. We inhabited such different worlds.

Elin was fired by my campaigns for better services, though, 'It's not my field, but if I can help with legal advice, I will. I know where to find things out. Are you on e-mail?'

'Thanks. I'll give you my address before you go.'

It looked as if we were going to keep in touch and I was pleased.

As is the way of four-year-olds Ffion accepted Elin as just another family member. She was in a good mood and insisted on holding my old friend's hand as we walked to the field, which made me smile. You could see from the way

Elin responded that she wasn't used to young children. She strode on absently as if her hand wasn't part of her while Ffion chattered away in Welsh. I allowed myself a tinge of smugness. This was my area of expertise. I might not be a successful city lawyer but I had brought up children and knew what they needed. Then I thought of Rhodri and the smugness vanished. Might Elin have handled him better? She couldn't have done worse.

It was a bright spring day. Our lambs, born late because of our height above sea level, looked fit and lively. Little clouds scudded across the sky, dotting the hillside with fast-moving shadows.

'Beautiful,' said Elin when we reached the top and admired the view.

'You don't regret leaving?'

She shook her head. 'Fine for holidays. I'd get bored soon, though.'

'I can't tempt you back with all these causes to fight for?'

'Not yet. Ask me in a few years. When I retire.' She was smiling, relaxed. It was good to see her loosening up.

'Do you understand her?' I nodded at Ffion who was pointing out the lamb she'd helped me bottle feed some weeks ago.

'More or less.'

'But you're not replying.'

Elin's eyes met mine. 'I don't want to confuse the child.' She grinned but the look in her eyes was stubborn.

Odd how children behave with different people. Ffion had obviously taken to Elin, insisting on sitting next to her on the sofa when we got back to the farmhouse. Perhaps she sensed Elin's sadness. She was always more affectionate with me when I was missing Rhodri.

'I can't think what I've done to deserve this.' Elin was amused.

'Push her off if she's a pain. I can always get her to help me in the kitchen.'

'I wouldn't dream of it.'

'Be warned. She'll want a story next. And it'll be Welsh. *Smot y Ci Defaid*'s her present favourite.'

'I might manage that. So long as you weren't here to notice my accent.'

A small victory, I thought.

Sure enough, Ffion fetched her favourite book and I left Elin reading aloud while I rustled up scones for tea. From the little I could catch, her Welsh sounded fine. Even if the book was meant for children.

Afterwards Elin joined me in the kitchen. 'She's asleep. I didn't know I was that mesmeric.'

'It's the fresh air. Good. She should be amenable when Sian comes to collect her.' Then we'll have an hour till Hywel returns, I thought. Time for more gossip. There was still a lot unsaid on my side. How much could one catch up in a day? We hadn't done badly so far.

Elin sat at the kitchen table while I made jam tarts and apple pie. 'You're not doing that because I've come?'

'No. The pie's for tonight. I saved making the pastry in case I needed to occupy Ffion. She enjoys having a bit to roll out. And the men like something to eat mid-morning so the tarts will come in handy for tomorrow.'

'Remember cookery at school?' said Elin, 'I threw my sausage rolls to the birds and even they wouldn't eat them. The pastry was like board. I'm not much better now.'

'Don't you cook for your friend?'

'Sometimes. But he's a better cook than I am. He likes his food.'

Trust Elin to find a man who can cook, I thought, then felt guilty for thinking it. Hywel is definitely unreconstructed. He can hardly boil an egg.

Sian turned up to collect Ffion and we chatted in the kitchen. 'Hywel usually comes in about now for a break,' I said to Elin, looking at the clock. 'But he won't be back till supper today, he's working down the hill.'

'He and Alun are scoffing my biscuits, I expect,' said Sian. 'Mam. Can you have Ffion Saturday morning? There's a meeting I have to go to.'

I looked at the calendar. 'Okay. When do you want to bring her round?'

Afterwards Elin asked, 'How do you do it?'

'What?'

'Be available all the time. Feed people. Run round after them. Don't you ever have time for yourself?'

'That's family life, I suppose. I get spaces during the day. And there are my own interests, WI and Community Council. If you think this is busy you should be here at lambing. The kitchen can be full of them in a bad year. I put the sickly ones in the bottom oven to warm up.'

'Where do you get your energy from?'

'I could say the same for you in your job.'

'Well, if you ever want a break in London, there's space in my flat. You can have it when I'm away too if you want. Go to a show or something.'

'Thanks. I'd like that.'

Elin said suddenly, 'I thought you had two children, Jen. Wasn't there a son? You haven't mentioned him.'

She was always a one for awkward questions. The subject of Rhodri had been a no-go area in the family since he left. I had sat on things too long to give a rational answer. I opened my mouth to speak and burst into tears.

Elin always said she wasn't a sympathetic person. As a teenager she could trample over people's feelings without realising it, 'specially if her mind was elsewhere. 'I must be lacking some sort of personal radar,' she lamented once, 'or too thick-skinned.' But she was round the table immediately, holding me while I cried. I needed that. I hadn't once cried for Rhodri since the day he left.

When I had finished and found some tissues to dry my eyes, she stayed my side of the table, her hand on mine. 'Come on, Jen. What happened? Would it help to talk?'

I poured out the whole sad tale. How, five years ago, Rhodri had come home from agricultural college to take his place on the farm and told us he was gay and had a lover. Hywel had gone mad. No son of his, he raged, was going to lead that sort of life. He called Rhodri dreadful names, said he was a disgrace to the family, an affront to God and goodness knows what else. I tried to reason with Hywel but he was beyond reasoning. It was partly the shock, I think, and Hywel has a temper. He doesn't lose it often but when he does it's frightening. It certainly was then. I think he frightened even himself that night. In the end he stormed out to the barn, leaving Rhodri ashen-faced and me shaking.

I tried to hug Rhodri, to reassure him that I, at least, hadn't cast him off. 'Don't listen. He's upset. He doesn't mean the half of it. Give him time and he'll calm down.' For the first time ever I felt awkward about touching my son, as if I and my sex were unacceptable and I no longer knew where I stood with him. I squashed the feeling instantly, but he'd already fended me off.

Then he rushed out too, roaring away in his old Montego, his foot so hard on the accelerator I could hear him on the main road a mile away. He came back in the early hours after I'd lain awake terrified he'd either gone for good or had had an accident. I don't think Hywel slept either. He had his back to me all night. I've never felt so cut off from him.

Next morning I pleaded with Hywel to give Rhodri a chance but he was sullen and adamant. Later I tried to persuade Rhodri to stay while I tried to talk his father round, but he had already made up his mind to leave. He waited till Hywel was at the sheep. Then brought his stuff down and packed the car. He'd cleared his room completely, even taken the model farm he had as a child. He left in a cold fury that distanced him from me even before he said goodbye.

'We haven't heard from him since,' I finished, 'though I've written many times to his old address. I can't forget what he said to Hywel that night. "If you won't accept me as I am, I'm finished with you and Cefn Ucha for good." I think we've lost him.'

I mopped up more tears and remembered how I'd tramped the fields alone the day of Rhodri's departure, sobbing out my anguish to the familiar landmarks, getting soaked and frozen in the unseasonal hail showers and not caring whether I caught a chill or not, telling myself – foolishly it seems now – that I didn't care if I never went back home. I stayed out for hours fearful of what I might say to Hywel or he to me when I returned. And when at last I braced myself to face him, he made it clear he wanted no mention of Rhodri or the row – didn't want to talk about it, for God's sake – the blasting apart of our family, the loss of our only son. Since then my grief had been locked inside, frozen like a slab of ice.

'And you've not told anyone till now?' Elin squeezed my hand.

I shook my head. 'Who could I tell? No one in the village. No one who knows us. There's gossip of course, but in the family, Rhodri's the great unmentionable. It's as though he's been edited out of our lives.'

'I've hidden all our pictures of him in my bedside drawer.' I confessed. 'I hated it when family photographs were passed round. People asked after Rhodri, naturally, but Hywel always ignored them and changed the subject. I couldn't bear it. He looked so cold and hard.' I stopped to blow my nose. 'And of course Sian and Alun follow his lead. They don't want to upset him. Hywel and Alun work together. I've no idea what Sian and Alun say when they're on their own but it feels as if I'm the only one who misses Rhodri, who still loves him. And I can't show how I feel. I can't even speak his name.'

'I don't care what he is,' I finished. 'He's my son and I love him. I'm sure Hywel cares for him too but he's too proud to admit he went over the top. Rhodri's confession hit him hard because Hywel's family sets great store by male inheritance. Rhodri won't have sons. I'm sure that's what hurts Hywel the most.'

'Poor Jen,' Elin said, 'that must have been awful. I suppose there's no chance of Hywel changing his mind?'

I blew my nose again. 'I think he's disowned Rhodri, mentally anyway, and taken Alun as substitute. I've nothing against Alun but it hurts to think our own son isn't in his rightful place. It must have taken great courage for Rhodri to say what he did. He was honest and he trusted us. It was terrible to see him so attacked as a result.'

'Families.' Elin sighed. 'I despair of them. I don't expect Hywel's thought of it from Rhodri's point of view. Rhodri must have felt terribly rejected.' She stood up. 'Shall I make another pot of tea? I can do that at least.'

'Nothing can be done to alter things,' I said, 'except hope and pray for a change of heart on both sides. That's what makes it so painful.'

As she poured the tea, Elin said, 'Don't give up hope, Jen. My rift with the family wasn't as dramatic as Rhodri's. I vowed not to return after I got my degree, but I did eventually.' She paused then said quietly as if to herself, 'Though to be honest I've not come back much in the last twenty years.' She stared at her hands.

'You don't think I'm silly, keeping on writing?'

Elin shook her head. 'If Rhodri gets your letters he'll know the door is open... To you, if not Hywel. You two might be able to meet some day even if he and his father can't. Gareth used to see me in London after I'd broken off relations with Tad.'

'But I'd hate keeping something like that secret from Hywel. I'm not sure I could cope. I'd feel I was being torn in two.'

'Not easy,' Elin agreed. She stared out at the farmyard, a distant look in her eyes, and I wondered how much Rhodri's story reminded her of her own.

I went upstairs to wash my face. I felt worn out. But I was better for having talked even if there was nothing I could do to improve things.

'Sorry to have dumped all this on you,' I said to Elin

later.

'Don't be silly. What are friends for? Even if this one only turns up once every thirty years.'

If I had feared that my revelations would affect Elin's attitude to Hywel, I needn't have worried. She had noticed his fish tanks and quizzed him about his pet interest while I served supper, always a good beginning. Then we went on to farming, the European Union and the Welsh Assembly. Hywel was in his element explaining the problems of upland farms and the effects of foot-and-mouth on rural communities. I hadn't heard him talk so freely for a long time. Elin was in good form. She'd always got on better with men than with women. She had been – and still was – a good talker, but in the years since we had last met she'd become a good listener as well. I watched, amused, as she charmed Hywel, drawing him out on subjects close to his heart.

I was taking the apple pie out of the slow oven between courses when I suddenly heard her say, 'I've met Sian. But don't you have a son? Rhodri, isn't it? What's he doing now?'

I nearly dropped the dish. What was Elin playing at? After all I'd told her? Hands shaking, I put the pie on the lid of the hot plate while I regained my composure. In the silence that followed I turned to mouth a warning over Hywel's head – he had his back to me – but Elin ignored it. Anyway the damage was done. I noted the tension in Hywel's neck, saw him clench his hands as the silence lengthened. I was about to butt in with some fatuous remark when he spoke, his tone dismissive. 'Our son left home. I've no idea what he's doing.'

'I'm sorry.' Elin's tone was conciliatory. 'I didn't mean to touch on anything painful.' She toyed with her wineglass.

'You weren't to know,' Hywel said shortly.

Liar, I thought, glaring at my friend who refused to meet my eye. She turned on Hywel a look that managed to combine contrition with sympathy. If she had fluttered her eyelashes she couldn't have been more disarming. I put the pie on the table aware we were at some sort of crossroads.

'We had a row,' Hywel explained, 'I didn't like the life he was leading and said so. He left and never came back.'

'How sad. It can't be easy being a parent. I've been spared all that.' Elin took a sip of wine. 'It must be painful when your children opt for something you wouldn't choose.'

Hywel poured cream on his apple pie and stared at his plate. 'He said he was…' he swallowed, 'homosexual. I didn't approve and still don't.'

'Difficult for you,' Elin murmured. 'And for Rhodri too, of course...' She poured cream on her pie and sampled a piece. 'This is lovely pastry, Jen. You always were a good cook.' She smiled at me across the table.

Another pause. I could feel the muscles tightening in my back. Elin, what are you doing?

Then Hywel spoke. 'Perhaps I shouldn't have been so hard on him. But a man doesn't like to see his son going down that road.' His voice was raw.

Part of me wanted to comfort Hywel in the pain he was feeling, part wanted to cheer his admission. I opened my mouth to speak but couldn't think what to say.

'I expect it was the shock,' Elin consoled.

'You can say that again,' Hywel hadn't touched his pie. He looked at me. 'Jen tried to calm things down but I wouldn't listen. It bit too deep. And the lad left before we could talk things over.'

This was the first I'd heard about talking things over. Hywel was rewriting history. But I was over the moon. Not only had he talked about Rhodri and their row, he seemed on the way to accepting that their estrangement was partly his fault! It was the first I'd heard of it. I smiled to encourage him but he wasn't looking my way.

'I don't suppose we'd have agreed even if we had talked,' he confessed to Elin, 'but I said things I regret, things that should never have been said.'

Elin was sympathetic. 'I shudder when I think of some of the things I've said in my time. But I've realised life's too short to lose touch with one's family.' She looked at Hywel. 'At least Rhodri trusted you to say what he did. There are many families where a young man wouldn't dare.'

'Is that so?'

'At least,' said Elin, finishing her drink, 'he hasn't robbed a bank or set up a chain of brothels. Then I *would* be worried.' She grinned at Hywel, her hazel eyes flashing amusement. 'Which reminds me, have I told you how one of our staff sniffed out a money-laundering operation? Right under our noses.' She embarked on one of her stories. Hywel and I looked at each other and smiled the ghost of a smile.

As I stood up to make the coffee I touched Hywel's shoulder and he reached for my hand. Relief flooded through me. He wasn't going to pretend this conversation hadn't happened. I might be on the way to regaining the husband I'd lost when Rhodri went away. Hywel would still have problems coming to terms with Rhodri's lifestyle. We might never find our lost son. But at least we might be able to talk about him again. The long silence had been broken.

Afterwards I saw Elin to her car. 'I couldn't believe what you were doing back there,' I told her as we walked across the yard.

'You should have seen your face.' She laughed.

'How could you lie with such conviction?'

'Sorry about that.' She grew serious. 'It seemed the only way to introduce the subject. I didn't like to think of you not being able to talk about Rhodri when you're missing him so much. Bad enough losing a son without him being – what did you say? – edited out of your life.'

'How did you know it'd work?'

'I hoped Hywel would take it from me. I gambled on the fact that he wouldn't want to quarrel with a guest, 'specially one he hardly knows.'

'Thanks anyway.' I gave her a heartfelt hug.

'I hope it's helped. At least you're talking about Rhodri. Now it's up to you two.' She looked round the yard. 'Thanks for a lovely day, Jen. It's been good to get together after so long.'

'You must come again. And bring your friend, Ben wasn't it…' I added as she got into her car.

She put the key in the ignition and wound down the window. 'I may take you up on that, you never know.' She paused. 'Don't give up on Rhodri. And if you do need to talk, I'm at the end of a phone. Though I'm not brilliant at this sort of thing.'

You underestimate yourself, I thought.

She was about to start the engine when she stopped and looked at her hands. 'I had a son, too, you know. He was adopted. I've no idea where he went or where he is.' Her words were matter-of-fact but her normally clear voice was thick with emotion. She shrugged, disclaiming it.

I stared at her in surprise. 'Elin, I never knew.'

'Nobody did except my godmother and Gareth. We kept it secret in case Tad got to know. It'd have been another stick for him to beat Mam with if he'd found out. And then it became easier not to say.' She fiddled with her fingernails. 'I'd hoped to combine motherhood with an academic career but it didn't work out. I think of him sometimes and wonder what happened to him.'

I could feel her sadness. 'You can always trace them, you know. With the new law.'

She shook her head. 'Better not to, I think. He's probably best left undisturbed. He went to a good family, I was told.' She stared out of the windscreen for a moment before starting the car then she turned to me and smiled. 'Anyway I'd have made a lousy mother.' And her voice was bright once more. 'The kid would have suffered indigestion all his life.'

'You can be honorary *nain* to Ffion any time you like,' I promised.

'Thanks. I'd like that. *Diolch am bopeth, Jenny. Tan tro nesa. Pob hwyl y ti.*' The old wicked grin.

'*Pob hwyl.*'

It was only when I was back in the farmhouse that I realised she had been speaking Welsh.

Ted Evans

So Gareth Pritchard's sister came to his funeral after all. I had a bet on with Elfed that she wouldn't but he said I'd lose. She was bound to be there, the two being so close. I wasn't sure. The village hadn't seen sight or sound of Elin Pritchard since before Gareth married. If she hadn't visited while he was alive why should she come when he was dead? She hadn't come to her parents' funerals.

Odd, never coming to see your family... Elin used to phone Gareth from Singapore – Gwen heard Lily talk of it in the shop once. But she's not in Singapore now. She's been back in London four years. She's never seen the children, Gwen says. You'd think she'd want to meet them.

I was curious to see what she was like after all this time. We were at school together, Elin *bengoch* and I. In the same class. We had a love-hate relationship you might say. It started when I cornered her behind the bike shed in a game of 'kiss chase'. She struggled like a wild thing, bit me on the arm and nearly drew blood.

We were both shocked at what she'd done. She drew back and stared at the teeth marks, her face white, fists clenched. 'Sorry,' she said, and backed away.

She turned and raced to the shed corner then stopped to look at me. *'Mochyn, pen swejen,'* she called. 'I'll set my brother on you if you do that again.'

'Gast, diawles,' I yelled back. But she'd already run off. The last I saw was her red plaits as she turned the corner.

Good for a laugh, those plaits. Elin hated having them pulled. When she had one of them undone by the nit nurse and undid the other to go with it, I couldn't keep my eyes off her hair. It was like a red waterfall, shiny and glowing. Some of the girls liked to comb it for her when it was undone to practise plaiting. I wanted to grab it, hold it, cut some off to take home.

I never told Miss Rees about the biting. I'd have been in for it as well. But Elin plagued the life out of me after that, making fun of me for not being so quick at my lessons as she was. She would pinch me when I walked past her desk. Two could play at that game. I used to put my foot out when she went by to see if I could trip her up. Till she stamped on it. That bloody hurt. But you had to admire her spirit.

When there was a new skipping rhyme the girls used in the playground:

Silly old Ted
Should be sent to bed,
He acts like a monkey with a hole in the head.
If he tries to kiss you, run for your life
Cut off his fingers with the carving knife...

I knew where it came from. Elin was there, leading the chanting, shouting it louder and smirking in triumph when she saw I was listening. It wasn't *fingers* she said either. Miss Rees wasn't in earshot that day, more's the pity. I bet she had no idea her precious teacher's pet knew words like that. I didn't care. At least the girls knew I was there, took notice of me.

Elin dared me to rise to her teasing, dared me to notice

her. But she was already noticeable with her red hair, freckles and tiger eyes – as well as for being top of the class. 'T E loves E P,' I saw chalked in the playground once but I doubt if it was Elin who put it there. We played at being enemies the way boys and girls do at that age. No real harm in it.

She was a bit of a flirt later. We were at different schools then. She went with the clever clogs to High School. I fancied my chances with her for a while when a gang of us used to hang round the bus shelter of an evening. But she soon showed me I had no hope. None of us village lads did. She was good for a laugh and a mock fight but inside she was as cold as ice. Freeze you with those yellow eyes, she would, if she thought you were trying it on. And cut you with her sharp tongue. I never had the wit to answer back fast enough but others tried and always lost. Too clever by half she was and made sure you knew it. She wasn't pretty but she was the life and soul of a group. When Elin laughed, we all laughed. When Elin sulked, the sun went in.

I wasn't surprised when I heard what she did later. A top degree and a top job were always on the cards if she stayed out of trouble. She was one of those who got away and got on. The village would have forgiven her that if she'd cared for her parents. And if she'd bothered about Gareth's family after.

Gareth had her photo in his workshop. Two, it turned out, though I only recognised the one at first. I noticed it when I called for my grave-digging money one day. It was on the wall above his father's old desk, next to pictures of Lily and the children.

He saw me looking. 'My sister,' he said. 'But of course you remember her from school. Wasn't she in your class?'

'Yes.' I leaned forward to see. There was Elin in a light coat, Tower Bridge in the background. She looked much the same as when I'd last seen her – thin face, long hair, cheeky grin.

'That was taken the day she got her MA,' Gareth said proudly, touching it. '1972. Seems a long time ago now.' He drew on his cigarette and breathed out the smoke. 'The next one's her, too.'

It could have been a travel advert – like you see in holiday brochures – a woman at an outdoor table, sunshade above, palm trees in the background, bright blue sky – a drink on the table in front of her, a cigarette in her hand. She was wearing a low-cut blouse and her hair was short, curled round her face. I had to get close to be sure it was Elin, I didn't recognise her till I saw the nose. She looked different. Not older but more serious for all she wore the same grin.

'All right for some,' I said, nodding at the palm trees.

'That was taken in Thailand,' Gareth said. 'On one of her holidays. She gets about a bit, my sister. Works hard and plays hard. She went to the base camp of Everest last year.' He sighed. 'She ought to be coming back soon – in a year or two. We might see more of her then.'

A pity about the hair, I thought, comparing the photos. The London one was the Elin I remembered.

'She's a high-powered lady now,' Gareth said, 'earns much more than you and I put together, moves in another world.' He sounded sorry as well as proud.

'Is she married?' I asked. I'd presumed not from the gossip, but I was curious to know.

'No time in her life for that sort of thing. Too busy, she says.'

He showed me the postcards Elin had sent. He'd stuck them to the side of his old filing cabinet. It was covered in them. 'I've kept every one,' he said, 'travelled the world second-hand so to speak. She's been almost everywhere she can now.'

Not Wales, I thought, but I didn't say it.

We looked back at the photos in silence. 'I miss her,' he said at last. 'You wonder where the years have gone when you look at these. Sometimes I wish I could go back, have the time over again. Don't you?' He laughed though he hadn't said anything funny. Then he turned to get on with our business.

When I left he was gazing at Elin's picture, frowning as he smoked his cigarette.

'You lost your bet,' Elfed said over a pint in the *Talardy* the evening after Gareth's funeral.

'I know.' I'd seen Elin Pritchard arrive in her flashy car when I was sitting in my van, noted her city looks, heard her voice through the open window as she spoke to Lily and the children.

I'd kept clear of her. It wasn't just that I didn't want to be seen in my work clothes. I was angry because of what she'd done to Gareth, for the way she'd let him down after he hoped to see more of her. It was none of my business, I know, but why did she wait till he died before she came back? What's the point of university degrees and top jobs if you can't make time for family?

'A pity she didn't come back before.' I stared at my drink.

Elfed was diplomatic. 'Well, she'll be a help to Lily now. She's already said she wants to see me in the week. She and

Gareth had it worked out, seemingly.'

He sighed and ran a hand through his hair. 'It doesn't seem right without him, does it? I kept turning to speak to him this afternoon, forgetting he'd gone.' He sipped his beer. 'He wasn't just the boss, he was a good friend.' His voice cracked and he stopped speaking, then he squared his shoulders. 'Better get on with the job. It's all I can do. There's another burial next week. Can you open a grave for me?'

I nodded. It's a good remedy for sadness, hard work.

I saw Elin Pritchard several times that week, dashing here and there in her expensive car. She was always in a hurry.

'She's like a human dynamo,' Gwen said, reporting what Lily had said in the shop. 'And talks like a duchess.'

Elin didn't mix much. Went to the shop for cigarettes but drove to Denbigh to get her paper and do her posting. Maybe she was keeping out of people's way. I was walking the dog Thursday morning when she shot past in her car with young Bryn in the front seat. I caught a glimpse of her face as she stared at the road. She drove like a rally driver. You have to admire her, the way she handles that car.

Half of me wanted to meet her, to see if she remembered who I was, half wanted to give her a piece of my mind about Gareth. In the end I thought, why should I bother, too late for poor Gareth, leave well alone, keep out of her way.

And I would have done if it'd been up to me. But when I parked my van by the churchyard early Saturday morning to take a look at the grave Elfed wanted opened for Tuesday, to see where it was and whether there was a kerb to be lifted, she was there. At the lychgate, looking into the churchyard. She had her back to me but I knew it was her from the way she stood – straight and upright – and from her hair. No one in Llanfadog has hair that colour except the Pritchards, though hers was a darker red than it used to be. Red-rinsed to cover the grey, Gwen says, 'Gareth was starting to go grey wasn't he?'

It was half past six, not the time you expect people to be about. I sat in my van for a minute willing her to move. But there was no avoiding her, not unless I wanted to stay in the van till she went away. And she didn't look like doing that. Still as a statue she was.

'Don't be soft,' I told myself, 'you're not afraid of Elin Pritchard just because she's got degrees and talks posh. She's not going to bite, now, is she?'

Remembering how she was at school made me feel better. I got out of the van, slammed the door to tell her I was there and walked up to the lychgate. 'Excuse me, please,' I said, 'I'm on a job. I've got to look at a grave.' I didn't want her to think I was some mugger about to knock her on the head for her money.

She swung round. 'Heavens, you gave me a fright.' Then she laughed. 'Of course. I'm in the way. Sorry.' She moved to one side and opened the gate to let me through. I couldn't believe her voice now I heard it properly. Posh wasn't in it.

I was aware of her looking at my face but I didn't return the look. I wanted to get away as quick as I could.

'Don't I know you?' Her question stopped me in my tracks.

'I turned to look at her then. 'Ted Evans,' I said. 'We were at school together, weren't we? You're Gareth Pritchard's sister.'

'Of course.' She laughed and her laugh was like Gareth's. 'Ted. I didn't recognise you after all these years. How are you?'

'*Ddim yn ddrwg.*' I'd heard she didn't speak Welsh now. 'Not bad. I hear you've done well.'

'*Ddim yn ddrwg.*' She grinned.

We stood staring at each other. She was behind the gate, holding it back. I was a yard or two beyond it, on the churchyard path.

I could take a proper look at her now. Same eyes, same freckles, same nose, same chin. But she was different and it wasn't just the hair, though it was longer than in Gareth's picture and curled over her ears to touch the yellow scarf at her neck, nor that she was older. It was her expression that had changed. Sharper, you might say, more focussed, laughter lines and worry lines mixed together. She looked as if she could drive a hard bargain. But she was an attractive woman even without the long hair.

'I'm sorry about your brother,' I said at last.

'Thanks.' She fiddled with her scarf.

There was an awkward silence. I knew I ought to move on but now I didn't want to. 'How long are you staying?' I asked. I already had the answer – the whole village knew – but I was curious to see if the Elin Pritchard I remembered was still there.

'Till Monday.' She looked past me to the church then back again.

'It's been a good long while since you were in Llanfadog.' The words slipped out. I hadn't planned to say them. I could have bitten my tongue off after. But I watched for her response, thinking of Gareth.

She frowned and looked down at her hands holding the

gate. 'Yes. Nearly twenty years. I've been working abroad.'

Not for the last four, I thought. I could feel my anger rising as I remembered Gareth's hopes.

'Gareth was looking forward to you coming to see them after you got back.' I had to say it now. I wanted her to know how disappointed he was.

'I know.'

When I saw her face I was sorry. She didn't need telling. Perhaps that was why she was there, haunting the churchyard, looking over the gate when most people were in bed.

'Better be going. I've got work to do.' I made as if to go but she stopped me. 'Ted.' Her voice was sharp, commanding. 'You worked for Gareth, didn't you?'

I nodded, aware of her eyes on my face. I saw the sadness in them.

'Did you see much of him? What was he like when you saw him last? How was he – in the weeks before he died?'

I hadn't expected her to ask anything like that. I thought for a moment. 'All right,' I said. 'Cheerful. His usual self. He was always all right, wasn't he?'

'No particular worries?'

'Not so far as I know.'

I wanted to undo what I'd said. If I hadn't been so upset myself I mightn't have said it. No point twisting a knife in a wound when it's already there. I mightn't be as clever as she was but I could tell regret when it was real.

'I should have come back earlier.' She shook her head. 'First it was foot-and-mouth, then it was the 'flu, then it was work, and…other things…' She was talking to herself.

I wasn't sure whether to stay or to go. It seemed our conversation wasn't finished. I wanted to put things right somehow. All my anger at her for not seeing Gareth and the family had vanished. I stared at my boots.

'He thought a lot of you,' I said at last. 'He kept all the postcards you sent; had your picture in his workshop.'

She nodded. 'I know. I've seen them.'

I'd never seen her cry. I'd seen her angry, teasing, arguing, flirting but never with tears in her eyes like now. She didn't even cry when she fell off the shed roof at school and hit her head on the playground. Tough, she was.

But she wasn't giving in. She shook her head and gazed into the distance, fiddled with her fingers, twisting and untwisting them.

'I dare say people are talking.' She frowned.

I didn't answer.

She turned towards me and her face was angry all of a sudden. 'Well, they can say what they like. I don't care a damn what people say or what they think.' Her voice was fierce and she tossed her head like the Elin Pritchard of years gone by. 'But I do – I did – care about Gareth,' her voice shook slightly. 'I care that I didn't get to see him before…this happened. God knows why I didn't. Too busy, I suppose.' She looked at her hands. 'But that's my problem. I can't do anything about it now. I'll have to live with it, get on with life.' She lifted her chin and looked me in the eye. 'Do you understand?'

I nodded. It didn't seem safe to speak.

'Sorry.' She waved her hand. 'Don't take any notice. I'm sounding off that's all. I didn't sleep last night. I came for a walk to clear my head.' She felt in her jacket pocket, took out a packet of cigarettes and lit one. 'It's just that it hits you, the result of your choices. You wish you could go back, do things differently, have your time over again.'

Elin smiled and her smile was like the old cheeky grin. 'At least I don't bite now. Not with my teeth anyway.' She laughed and I laughed with her, relieved she seemed less upset.

'This is a bit different from before, isn't it?' she went on, 'from when we used to annoy each other in the school yard and you were always pulling my plaits. Talking in a graveyard. Shows our age, I suppose. Do you remember the teenage gatherings at the bus shelter years ago? I saw a gang of kids there last night. Some things don't change, though I expect they've all got mobiles and i-Pods now.' She puffed at her cigarette and nodded towards the churchyard. 'Don't let me keep you. It's time I was going. Lily'll wonder where I am.'

She hadn't changed. Not completely. Pity about the short hair, though.

Stephen

'How're you doing?' asked Sarah when she rang at nine from her coaching course in the Midlands.

'Nothing so far. But I've eliminated a lot. I suppose that's progress of a sort.' I shifted in my seat at the computer, aware of stiffness in my back and shoulders.

'You still think she's the one?'

'Yes. She's the most likely. Gareth had cousins in Caernarfon, he said once. I suppose it could be one of them. But I've no idea who they are nor whether they're male or female.'

'Good luck then. Don't stay up too late. We're out tomorrow evening, remember?'

I smiled as we said goodbye. With Sarah away there was no one to mind if I went to bed late. And tomorrow was Saturday, anyway. I could stay up all night if need be. I got up to make more coffee.

That was five hours ago and I'm still at the computer. My eyes ache from staring at the screen and my hand feels as if it's stuck to the mouse. I promise myself I'll turn in soon but it's hard to stop because I'm trying to find out who I am – or rather, who my mother is.

'You're obsessed,' I tell myself. I'm sure Sarah thinks so, though she's doing her best to be supportive. Much as I love her I'm not sorry she's away this week. I can indulge what she calls my 'mother-quest' alone. I'm wary of going on about it too much in case she gets fed up with me. I don't want to drive her away.

I sip black coffee and decide to try one more line of enquiry before going to bed. I've been at the computer three nights in a row, now. Every spare evening since I came back from Gareth's funeral. But I can't stop till I've trawled the website of every city law firm I can think of. Because she might be there. Gareth's sister. The woman I'm convinced is my mother.

I've been sure of it for years, though it was Gareth I suspected of being my father at first. Why should he be so concerned about me after my parents died? Yes, he'd been a friend of theirs but I hardly knew him. Kind of him to take an interest, but there must be something more.

And then there was the likeness. How come we looked so similar that people in York thought he was my father when he came for my graduation? I teased him about it once I got to know him better, asked obliquely, in what I hoped were subtle, jokey ways till one day I tackled him outright: 'Gareth, please would you tell me, honestly, whether or not you're my father.' We were having a pub lunch in a village outside York on one of his visits.

He looked at me straight this time, no teasing smile, no amused twinkle in his kind blue eyes. 'No, Stephen,' he said seriously, 'I'm not your father. But I wouldn't mind if I were. You're the sort of son any man'd like to have.'

I saw truth in his eyes then and trusted him. But there was still a mystery. Why didn't he introduce me to his family? Why did we have to meet on my ground all the time, not his, as if he were keeping me at arm's length for some reason? But I didn't inquire any more. Not directly anyway. I felt more probing would spoil the relationship we had.

Then I found out about his sister. Call it instinct, call it a hunch, but the moment Gareth mentioned her, a shiver ran through me. That's her, I thought, I'm her son.

It's been strange having this inner knowledge I couldn't prove. Difficult. Gareth didn't want to talk about her – he only mentioned her the once. And then I wasn't fishing for information but bemoaning the lack of family to share my grief over the loss of my parents.

'There are distant cousins in Canada, but Mum never kept in touch with them. And Uncle Edward, Dad's brother, died without marrying,' I grumbled. 'If I had brothers or sisters it wouldn't be so bad.'

'One of the problems of being an only child,' Gareth sympathised.

I looked across at him – we were standing on the Ouse Bridge in York two years after the accident. Below us the river, brown and swollen after recent rains, rushed past on its way to meet the Trent. 'Are you an only one, then?' I asked.

He didn't answer at once, as if he was thinking hard what to say. 'I've got a younger sister,' he replied, after what seemed an age. 'She works abroad so I don't see much of her now.' His curt tone, so different from his usual way of speaking, put me off asking more and he wouldn't look me in the eye. Perhaps that's what gave it away. I didn't mention his sister after that. I never even found out her name.

But she lived in my imagination. Hardly a day went past when I didn't think of her. The urge to seek her out grew the more I became aware of being alone and rootless now Mum and Dad were gone. Gareth was the only person I could remotely call 'family' though I hardly knew him before the accident. 'We met when your Dad worked on Deeside,' he explained, 'and I had a hand in your adoption.'

I knew the story. My parents had had three sons before me and all died as infants. They'd given up hope of having their own children by the time they met Gareth. And the various agencies judged them too old to adopt. 'Then Gareth told us about you,' Mum said, 'and you were an answer to our prayers. God chose you for us.'

I liked the idea of being chosen. It made the thought of being given away easier to take. I've met adopted children who have grown up with a disabling sense of rejection, of not being good enough, of being thrown out like so much rubbish. I never had that, though I do remember waking up feeling sad sometimes, overwhelmed by a longing for something lost I couldn't name.

Bereavement reactivated this longing. And the longing crystallised round the image of Gareth's sister. The knowledge that she was Welsh and Welsh-speaking added romance to my notions but, even before that, I'd felt an inexplicable affinity with the Welsh language. I was keen on folk songs as a teenager and collected tapes of songs from around the UK. One day I bought a tape of Welsh folk songs in a Chester charity shop for fifty pence. Playing it in my room afterwards I was overwhelmed with a sense of belonging, the language felt so familiar. One song in particular had me in tears, a jolly little piece about a miller trying to woo his lady-love by listing all his possessions. I was so overcome whenever I played it that I hardly dared put it on unless I was alone. The only word for what it aroused in me, I learned later, is *hiraeth*, Welsh for a sense of homesickness, a nostalgia for something lost.

With Gareth's stonewall reticence there was no way I

could find out more about my mother even when adopted children were granted rights to details about their birth. It would have been disloyal to push it. I valued his affection and the last thing I wanted to do was upset him. My instincts told me he'd be grieved if I tried to trace my origins. He often talked about how things were now and how lucky I was to have had a good home and loving parents.

Once I looked up Pritchard in the North Wales telephone directory, wondering if any of those listed could be her. Then I remembered she was abroad. Besides there were too many of them – Welsh surnames are singularly unvaried – and she could be married anyway. So I was left to my own speculations. What had made her give me away? Inconvenience? Inability to cope? Had she been a teenager when I was born? Or a career woman for whom a baby would have been a handicap? And what about my father? Who was he? A lover? A passing fancy? A rapist even?

My mind teemed with questions that had no answer. I pondered all sorts of scenarios, romantic and hopeful, dark and depressing or just mundane. Girl meets boy, girl and boy have affair, boy deserts leaving girl pregnant, result – me. There were times when my imaginings led me to hate my own sex because of the selfish and careless way we can behave with women, times when I found myself beginning to hate the mother who'd got rid of me like an unwanted toy. Then I remembered the date of the abortion act and was grateful I'd been allowed to live at all. 'I could have been one of those foetuses that never saw the light of day,' I consoled myself in my worst moments.

I kept all these conjectures within bounds. They never interfered with my daily life or my legal career, though they grew more morbid during a time of depression when

I found I was unsuited to work at the bar and switched, with Gareth's encouragement, to train as a solicitor. All in all, by the age of thirty, I was coping pretty well with being an orphan and uncertain of my origins. I felt I was putting the effects of bereavement behind me. Then, suddenly, Gareth died.

In the midst of the shock and the devastating sorrow, a thought struck me. 'I can look for my mother now. There is no one to mind.' Immediately I was overcome with guilt. Was that how I saw Gareth? Just an obstacle to finding my mother? I was appalled at myself. All the more reason to go to his funeral, I decided, even if he *had* been emphatic about keeping myself and his family separate. Aware of the physical resemblance between us, I knew I couldn't make myself conspicuous, express my condolences directly to his grieving wife and children, but surely it wouldn't hurt if I sat anonymously at the back, I thought. I had to say goodbye. Naturally I wondered if his sister might be there, but my main reason for going really was to give thanks for a wonderful man who'd been more than an uncle to me over the last twelve years.

In the event I missed Gareth's sister. That was justice, I thought. The church was so crowded I couldn't get a clear sight of the family and though I watched the procession down the aisle I saw no one that could be her – I'd always pictured her as a female version of Gareth – and in the front pew, where any sister would surely have been, were just his wife and children. In the churchyard I stationed myself at a distance to get a long view of the mourners at the graveside but again I saw no one who fitted the bill. The only lead I got was from the vicar, who told me afterwards she is a lawyer in the City. I came home planning to search for her, even if it meant looking up all the law firms in London.

I stifle a yawn and click on the last name on my list for tonight. Uttley Stannaway is an old-established firm that has gone global in the last twenty years. Rumour has it they are picky about who they employ, only applicants with first class degrees need apply. But I decide to try anyway. I click on 'Lawyers' and 'London office' and scan the list of names. A Pritchard at last. And a woman. Heart racing, I click on the name and stare at the emerging image of Elin Pritchard, Senior Partner, specialist in Mergers and Acquisitions, responsible for training. Could this be her?

My heart is thumping and my mouth is dry. Now the picture is complete, I stare at it critically.

At first I am disappointed. This woman is nothing like Gareth. Her short, wavy hair is red, but not the same colour as Gareth's or mine and she has a thin face and pointed chin whereas Gareth's features were broad and square. There could be a similarity about the nose – Gareth had a long nose, too, I remember – but that's all. Then I realise she can't look like Gareth because I missed her at the funeral, that siblings aren't necessarily alike and that Elin is a Welsh name.

I gaze at the photograph testing what I feel. There is no shiver, no *frisson* such as I experienced when Gareth first mentioned his sister. Does that mean this isn't the woman I'm looking for? But would you recognise the mother who had you adopted thirty years before?

I search her face for clues but find none. She isn't unattractive but she doesn't look motherly. She gazes straight at the photographer over half-moon glasses and wears the uniform dark suit, the typical professional lawyer of a certain age, Sarah would say. The only sign of personality is in her half smile and slightly inquiring expression as if she has just been asked to look up from her desk and is amused. Does she appear approachable? And how would I feel if I were told this is my mother? I don't know how to answer but I can't suppress a rising excitement. I could be on to something at last. A pity it's too late to ring Sarah.

Elin Pritchard's CV is below her picture…

> Ist class honours University College London, 1970. MA 1972, articled 1976, Partner 1986, Senior Partner 1996. Hong Kong office 1985-90, Singapore 1990-2000. Specialist M. & A. Training 1996-2000 (Singapore), 2000 London.

Worrying… I only got a II:1. What would this woman think if she found she had a hack criminal lawyer for a son?

I dismiss instant reactions and check the detail. Elin Pritchard was in Singapore when Gareth said his sister was abroad. And my birth in May 1973 would fit in the gap between her second degree and the beginning of her legal career. Though I'm disappointed to have no flash of recognition, no intuitive 'yes' or 'no', I realise the evidence doesn't rule this woman out. Then I remember the words of a friend who researches family history – 'Don't assume a connection till it's proved.' – and try to keep Elin Pritchard, Senior Partner with Uttley Stannaway, in the pending tray. But I allow myself a small flicker of hope. My late nights may be paying off.

I print her profile even though it feels as if I'm intruding into this woman's life without permission. This must be what stalkers do, I realise, and shudder. Then I put the printout by my bed. 'Don't pin too much on this,' I warn myself, 'Elin Pritchard may not be Gareth's sister and Gareth's sister may not be your mother. You've no proof despite your secret hunches.'

I am too excited to sleep. I toss and turn, my brain working overtime. If this woman *is* my mother, would I like her? Would she like me? She isn't what I've imagined. I've always dreamed of a warm, solid, earth mother-type with welcoming arms – a red-haired, Welsh version of Mum, I suppose. Elin Pritchard doesn't look like this. But I can't wait to find out more about her. Is there anyone in the City I can ask?

By four a.m. my thoughts are less optimistic. If my mother has rejected me once might she do so again? And if she is Gareth's sister, did he avoid mentioning her because he knew she wanted no part in my life?

At half past seven, feeling distinctly the worse for wear, I text Sarah then stagger downstairs for my first fix of caffeine to discover the post has come. There's a packet for me bearing a North Wales postmark. I revive myself with a mug of strong, black Arabica, freshly ground, then open it.

Inside is a jiffy bag addressed to me in Gareth's handwriting, and a letter:

Dear Mr Loxley,

I regret to inform you that my brother, Gareth Pritchard, died suddenly on May 14th. The enclosed was found amongst his effects to be sent to you in the event of his death.

If there is anything arising from it, or any matter you wish to discuss in relation to his estate, please feel free to contact me at the above address.

Yours faithfully,

Elin Pritchard, Executor.

The business address on the letterhead confirms my suspicion that Uttley Stannaway's Elin Pritchard is Gareth's sister. My stomach plunges. Coming on top of last night's discovery, this feels a massive coincidence. The answer to a prayer I haven't dared pray.

I seize the jiffy bag, tear off the parcel tape and remove the staples underneath. Out falls something small wrapped in tissue paper.

The something small is cufflinks. The letter is Gareth's goodbye. Full of affection and fond memories, it brings tears to my eyes. When was it written, I wonder. It has no date. Did Gareth suspect he was going to have a heart attack? The letter can't bring him back but it softens the impact of his death. It's consoling to think I mattered enough for him to leave me something personal. I blow my nose and read on.

The cufflinks were his, Gareth explains, handed down from his grandfather. *'I never wore them but when I saw you in your Jermyn Street shirts I knew they'd be just the thing for you. Wear them when you become "something in the City" and remember your old Uncle Gareth as you pass the port.'*

I smile. Gareth always teased me about my clothes. *'You'd better stick to high-class crime the way you dress,'* he said once. I pick up the cufflinks reverently, enjoying the feel of the smooth, old gold on my palm, fingering their embossed pattern. I will treasure them always, even if I never get to wear them.

But it's the extended PS that sets my pulse racing.

Dear Stephen,

I've thought long and hard about adding this but I believe you have a right to know it. I am sorry if I haven't been straight with you before about your past. That was my fault. I wasn't sure what to say because it involved others than myself and I allowed family loyalties to override my duty to you.

I want you to know that my sister, Elin, was your natural mother. Your father was an Australian academic to whom she was once engaged to be married. I have never told her I've been in touch with you, and I am not sure how she would respond to any approach on your part. But I am certain she would want you to know that she let you go for adoption believing it was best and was pleased you went to a loving and stable home.

The enclosed photographs are enlargements of snapshots taken in your first few weeks. I thought you would like to have them.

What photographs? Hastily I feel in the jiffy bag and find them, fingers clumsy in my excitement. My heart misses a beat. There are four enlargements almost the same size as the bag, three of myself with my mother and one of me with Gareth. I fall on them like a starving man on food, greedy for information, ready to devour all they have to tell.

They are windows into another world, another time.

My throat tightens as I see pictures of my mother and myself, and Gareth as proud uncle. They give no sign that I will be given away for adoption, no hint of anything wrong.

I spread them on the table and examine each in turn, my eyes misting. This is me, I think. My past, before I came to be with Mum and Dad. And here is Gareth's sister. My mother. At last.

At first glance she is nothing like the successful lawyer whose profile I took from the internet. Pretty, smiling, full of life, she looks young enough to be a teenager with that long red hair, though she must have been in her early twenties when she had me.

And I am so small. Tiny. A few weeks old, if that. I gaze at the self I have no memory of and bite back tears.

The photographs are poignant in view of what came after. I am breathing as hard as if I've just run a hundred yards. My life is being turned upside down, my sense of identity undone. Tectonic plates of personal history shift to disclose new patterns, new truths, and I feel as if I've been shot through the middle, blasted by some inner earthquake.

The first shows my mother cradling me in one arm and offering a finger for me to touch. My tiny fingers curl round hers and she looks down, smiling. I see tenderness, a playful love in that smile. Her hair is loose and she wears a patterned summer dress. Closer examination reveals her thin face, angular chin and long nose. *She does resemble the woman on the website after all.*

In the second I am very new, possibly newborn. My mother sits in bed, holding me. She smiles at the camera, pride in her face, ecstatic as the cat that got the cream.

'Look at my baby,' she seems to say, as if I am the first baby ever to be born. Cards and flowers flank the bed. *So there was delight at my birth. After years not knowing, I feel I have been welcomed, given permission to be. Not just the me my parents took on, but the whole of me, the person I was before.*

The third shows us in a garden, forest trees in the background. My mother holds my face towards the camera. She is grinning, a wide, mischievous, Cheshire cat grin, lifting one of my tiny arms for the person taking the photograph. Her hair is tied back but she still looks very young. The fun in the picture is infectious. I find myself responding to it, humming aloud a tune that seems to go with the party mood, though I can't remember its name.

The images of myself and my mother look so full of joy that my heart aches. What happened to make her let me go when she seems so elated at my coming? Something must have. But there is no inkling of it here, no shadows, only warmth and love. Something inside me unknots and I realise I have been haunted by a buried sense of rejection all my life and not known it. 'You weren't cast off at birth,' these pictures tell me, 'you were wanted. You were loved.' And I wipe my eyes on my sleeve.

But I don't dissolve in tears. I sit immobile, as if encased in glass. The hum of the fridge seems unnaturally loud. The tick of the kitchen clock echoes in the quiet room. I can hear my heartbeat and sense the accelerated rhythm of my breathing. I stare at the hand that holds the photographs as if it belongs to someone else. It's the shock of Gareth's death, my parents' deaths all over again. But this isn't death, I tell myself, it's a beginning. *My* beginning. It could even be the start of something new.

Then emotion kicks in again. Excitement, elation, relief,

sadness and uncertainty hit me in a jumbled mix. I am euphoric at finding my mother, discovering who she is, knowing I can contact her, learning her name. I am also haunted by grief, by *hiraeth* for the love I never knew. Part of me wants to open a bottle of wine, get in touch with my mother at once, tell her who I am, reclaim our lost relationship. Part holds back, unsure what her response might be.

I am assailed by questions. Why did the bond between myself and my mother, so plain in these pictures, have to be broken? Why did she give me away? Did her fiancé desert her? Did my father desert us both? The answer to my life's one big question has spawned a hundred others. 'What happened?' I want to demand, 'What went wrong? How could she let me go after all this?' But there's no answer that I can see.

I glance at the clock and reach for the phone. It's not too early to ring Sarah. They have breakfast at eight. I dial her mobile but can't get her. She's probably in the shower knowing her, or luxuriating in a bath full of bubbles. I leave a voicemail. 'Sal, I've found her. I was right. She *is* Gareth's sister. Tell you all about it when you get back. Love you lots. Stephen.'

Time passes and I continue to gaze at the photographs. I compare the successful company lawyer my mother is now with the vivacious young woman whose smile lights up these pictures and draws a smile from me in response. Her joy doesn't look forced, but people put on their best faces for the camera. What was going on behind these scenes? What do they hide?

I pick up my mother's letter, the letter she wrote to her son, though she had no idea who I was when she wrote it. I trace her signature with my finger, examine her handwriting. What is she like, this efficient-looking woman with the top job and dazzling CV? Would she want to meet me? I know I won't rest till I've found out. But the uncertainty Gareth expressed in his PS warns me off precipitate action.

Don't do anything yet, I tell myself. Take time to think. Get advice, put out feelers. Talk it over with Sarah. You've waited years for this. It won't hurt to wait a little longer.

But I can't help singing as I shower and dress to face the day. It's only as I'm shaving that I recognise the tune that's been playing in my mind since I looked at Gareth's pictures. It's the miller's song from my old Welsh tape.

Benedict

'How did it go?'

'All right. There were a lot of people. The church was overflowing.'

'And how are you?'

'Fine. Busy. Surviving.'

'And how are you really?'

A long pause. 'Tell you Saturday.'

Walking the dogs after breakfast on Saturday morning, I went over Wednesday's phone conversation with Elin. We'd gone on to chat about her week so far, the people she'd met, the family, but she wasn't giving much away. Busy? Yes, she'd certainly be busy with all the running round you have to do after a death in the family. Surviving? Of course. Elin was a survivor par excellence. But fine? Hardly. Which was why I'd arranged to meet for lunch. I needed to see how she really was.

I was worried about her, had been worried all through the charity conference in Paris that prevented me going with her to the funeral. With her mobile switched off and myself occupied with meetings all hours, there was no way we'd been able to speak.

'I'm fine.' That was what she'd said the day she heard about Gareth's fatal heart attack. Arriving at her flat that evening I'd found her rushing round, organising everything that conceivably needed organising, unable to stay still. I'd almost had to force her to sit down and eat. And then I think she only gave in because I'd gone to the trouble of cooking the meal myself and wouldn't take no for an answer. Outwardly she was coping, but fine? My foot.

I smiled to myself. Funny, exasperating, argumentative, adorable woman. She could drive me mad at times with her pigheadedness and stubborn independence but I couldn't live without her. Did she love me as much as I loved her? I thought so, hoped so, but only time would tell.

'Why don't you and Elin get hitched, Dad?' Lara had said after we'd spent Christmas together as a family, Elin included. 'Get her to make an honest man of you.'

I wasn't sure about being 'made' an honest man. I was being as honest and honourable as I could, I thought, trying not to push Elin into a more definite commitment than she could manage or might want, keeping my desire for her within bounds. But I wanted to make her my wife one day. No doubt of it. The question was when.

We came to the lake and I called the dogs to heel. Tess, Brandy and Thistle aren't to be trusted when there are waterfowl in range and the moorhens weren't doing well this year. Too many mink about. I needed to talk to Jem about the best way to deal with them before we were overrun.

I stopped to look at a flotilla of Mallard ducklings feeding with their mother, swimming busily in circles – 'like giant fluffy gnats, buzzing about,' Elin says. She loves to watch them. Could I see her settling here eventually? I hoped so. If there was enough to occupy her active mind and plenty of trips to London to stave off boredom, I thought we could be happy. I smiled again. We're an odd mix, both of us. Country-loving but cosmopolitan. Lovers of the natural world but needing the buzz of the city.

Taking the path by the lake, one of her favourite walks,

I reviewed our shared history...

We met in October 1977, at a party given by old friends of mine in Bromley. It was the year after my father died and I was running the estate by then. Karin and the girls were already settled here, but I had a case to complete for my old firm which meant staying in London during the week till it was finished. Tony and Zelda had asked me, I suspect out of pity for my enforced solitary state.

I arrived early and Elin was already there. I found her on her own in the large sitting room, examining the bottles on the drinks table one by one, picking them up to read their labels. From the back she looked like a teenager. The straight black dress emphasised her slimness. The red-gold hair that tumbled to her shoulders made her look younger than she was. One of Alice's schoolfriends, I assumed, Tony and Zelda's eldest was sixteen at the time.

But when she turned round, I found myself facing a woman with a thin, freckled face that was attractive rather than beautiful. Her pale hazel eyes met mine in a look that was both quizzical and amused. 'Are we the only guests, do you suppose? And should we help ourselves?' She picked up a corkscrew from the table and turned it over in her hands.

'Tony ought to be doing the honours. He loves to play barman. Where's he got to?' I looked round for other signs of life. Nine-year-old Debra had let me in then vanished upstairs to where I could hear a television game show playing.

'He was here five minutes ago then disappeared. Something domestic I imagine, from the screams.'

'That'll be the twins. They probably want to stay up and

see everyone arrive.'

'My fault. My coming upset things. I used to have a reputation for being late at home, now I'm disgustingly early. Must be the effects of city life and solitary living.'

Did I imagine the lilt in her voice?

'So, you're not a Londoner?' I took the corkscrew from her hand and opened the bottle of Chardonnay she'd been scrutinising. 'This do? I'm sure Tony won't mind.' I poured us both a glass.

When we were settled on the window seat she asked. 'Is it obvious? That I'm not from the city?'

'Only the hint of an accent. You're from North Wales, I assume.'

'And I've been trying to sound so metropolitan.' She wrinkled her nose.

'But I'm from Cheshire, so I have an ear for a *Gog.*'

Her face lit up. 'You speak Welsh?'

'*Tipyn bach yn unig,* I'm afraid. My mother was from Holywell.'

'*Byd bach.* Did she give you a good Welsh name?'

I shook my head. 'A good Catholic name – Benedict. But I was baptised in water from St. Winefred's shrine.'

'Well, well.' She stopped speaking and blushed. 'Sorry about the pun.' But her accompanying grin was impish. 'A bad habit. I'm Elin Pritchard.' She kept her hands firmly round her wineglass.

'A good Welsh name. So what are you doing in London?'

'Training as a solicitor. I'm a late starter. I spent time working for a PhD'

'Dr. Pritchard, then.'

She shook her head. 'Sadly, no. I messed up along the

way. Had time out and couldn't get back into it. This is my second attempt at a career.' The defiant lift of her chin dared me to commiserate. I found her honesty appealing.

'And are you enjoying it?'

'It's not bad. Maybe it'll get more interesting as it goes along.' She looked round the room. There was still no sign of other guests. 'I suppose this is the right night?'

'It is. I know what a muddle this room would be if it weren't.'

'You must be old friends, then.'

'Yes. Tony and I were at Downside together. Then Oxford.'

'He's my immediate boss. So, what do you do?' I was aware of her searching gaze.

'I have land on the Cheshire-Staffordshire border so that makes me a farmer. But I was a solicitor before that and still keep my hand in. I'm also a political animal and like to be where the action is.'

'True blue? Or am I misjudging you?' Seeing my nod, she added, 'Ten years ago I'd have been demonstrating against your lot. Against any English, actually.'

'We're not all bad. You're a nationalist, then. I've always wanted to meet one of those.'

'You make me sound like something out of a zoo. I'm not sure where I stand these days, though I think Wales has had a poor deal.' She looked into her glass. 'I'm not a Tory as I expect you can guess.'

'I'm not a high and dry Conservative.' I needed to justify myself. 'Being part Welsh I can understand a little how you feel. And I don't hunt if that makes me more acceptable.'

'So long as you don't shoot the peasants.' She grinned at me, finished her drink with a flourish and gazed at her glass. 'I shouldn't have another, should I? We must leave something for the rest. I haven't had much today.'

I found a bowl of peanuts and passed them. 'I presume you mean food not alcohol.'

'Thanks. I forget to eat sometimes.' She helped herself. 'Too busy. You know.' She waved a hand.

I didn't as it happened. Even away from Karin's excellent cooking, I made sure I ate well. I suddenly felt much older than my fellow guest, though, as I discovered later, there were only five years between us. Talking to her was like meeting my undergraduate self.

She said between mouthfuls. 'So what do you think about the nuclear deterrent? And equal pay for equal work?'

'You're not a feminist, are you? If so do you want an argument or a pleasant evening?'

Her eyes flashed. 'Can't we have both? What's wrong with a lively discussion between civilised adults? You might be persuaded to see things in a fresh light.'

'Much as I'd like to be illuminated, we don't want to end up at each others' throats. Or spoil the party.'

'Sorry. I like to spark off a good debate.' Her voice softened. 'Not everybody does. I realise that now. Maybe I'm growing up.'

The switch from political idealist to apologetic schoolgirl was endearing.

'I can see you in politics.' I removed the peanuts before she finished them and poured her a glass of soda water and fruit juice. 'Have this. It'll fill the gap without addling the brain. You can argue better if you're sober.' She laughed and I caught her eye. It was then that I came under her spell.

'I see you've introduced yourselves.' Tony appeared holding a plate of warm vol-au-vents. 'Elin's our brightest recruit, Ben. She'll give you a mental run for your money any day.'

'So I've noticed.' The impression of a sharp intelligence was well founded, then.

'I've told her she'll go far,' Tony put the plate down and winked at me, 'if she can learn tact.'

Elin made a face and we laughed.

We circulated separately for a time when the other guests arrived but spent most of the evening together, making outrageous puns and putting the world to rights. I found her company refreshing after the unrelieved intensity of work. She helped me forget the miles between myself and my family and the loneliness of living apart from them. I was uncomfortably aware that what I felt for her was more than a married man should feel for a girl at a drinks party.

Afraid she might feel the same, I told her I had a wife and children in Cheshire. I didn't want there to be any misunderstanding. But she seemed pleased for me. I was ashamed to find that I minded.

I interrupted my musings to watch a heron plunge his beak in the water and come up with one of my trout. I couldn't begrudge him his breakfast, but was glad when the dogs disturbed him and stopped him taking more. He flapped slowly away to plunder someone else's lake.

'They're so beautiful,' Elin said in defence after she'd seen a heron swallow three trout in succession and I'd scared it off.

'So they are but if you run a sporting estate they're a problem. I don't want all my young fish to disappear.'

'You'd never kill one, though.'

'Of course not. They're protected. But I'm not putting up a sign to say "eat all you like".'

'It's striking a balance,' I explained. 'I don't mind herons taking one or two trout a day. But I want them to leave something for the anglers who pay to come and fish.'

Did I get the balance right between my friendship with Elin and my love for my wife? A tricky question. I pondered it as I walked the familiar path. Was my feeling for Elin all those years ago more than friendship? Can you be in love with two women at once?

I struggled with it at the time. How could I be in love with Elin? I was happily married with two lovely daughters. Karin, Lara and Ismene meant the world to me. My commitment to Christian marriage meant I could never think of Elin except as a friend. Yet I did think of her. More than was comfortable.

I never told anyone about this. I was shocked, I suppose, to find myself as prone to temptation as the next man. I clung to biblical promises of strength in time of need and proverbs that told me 'you can't stop birds flying round your head but you don't have to let them nest in your hair'. Difficult when thoughts of Elin came at me in unexpected moments, like hibernating butterflies beating against a window when they should be asleep.

I called Tess off from chasing a pheasant. Why agonise over this now? I asked myself. Thank God that you stayed faithful to Karin and never broke your marriage vows. She was your childhood sweetheart, a wonderful mother to your children. She gave you peace and rest when you came home worn out after political infighting and party battles. She was warm, compassionate and kind and you loved her to the end.

I'd been humbled by Karin's courage in her illness. And by her faith, which was stronger than mine, though I was the churchgoer when we married. Across the lake I could just make out the young Dawyck beech I'd planted in her memory, next to her favourite ride. By the time Karin developed breast cancer Elin was half the world away and thoughts of her had receded. But I'd still been haunted by guilt. Had I sacrificed too much for my parliamentary career, given too much time to London friends, Elin included, and neglected my wife and family at home in the country?

'Do something for others,' advised a priest when I poured out all the guilt and self-recrimination. Wise man. I needed to be taken out of myself. Grief can make you turn inwards.

How was it affecting Elin? I wondered. She'd rung her brother every week, been close to him though they didn't meet much. She was going to miss him badly. She might put on a brave front but I knew she'd need me. Spirited, irrepressible, stubborn she might be, but I didn't think she could cope with this on her own.

It was her fighting spirit and independence that had drawn me to her at first. And her energy, idealism and sense of fun. With her quick mind and skill in repartee she swept into my life like a breath of fresh air. Her no holds barred approach to debate forced me to re-examine old certainties and look beyond accepted beliefs. I never for a moment ditched the loyalty to country and family that formed the bedrock of my life, but Elin made me question it. And she challenged my intellect. At Oxford I'd wanted to be an academic, but family duty and my father's ill health ruled it out. It was Elin who revived that side of me, breathing new life into my thinking, sharpening my mind against hers.

Could she have become my 'bit on the side'? I frowned at the question but I needed to be honest with myself. Perhaps, with today's morality. But only if we'd been different people. True, there were enough affairs going on in politics when I started my career to make everyone look to their marriages. Too much separation from family was always a risk. But I was sure Elin hadn't wanted a love affair any more than I had at the time. We were good friends and stayed that way. Didn't someone – Jack Dominian or C S Lewis – say friends stand side by side and look at the world while lovers look at each other? That definition made us friends, though ours was a close friendship.

What did trouble me was that I shared more of my inner self, my ideals, doubts and political questionings, with Elin than with Karin. But Karin wasn't interested in these things. She didn't want what I shared with Elin and couldn't give me what Elin gave back. They only met once, at a dinner party at Tony's, on one of the rare occasions I managed to persuade Karin to leave her beloved horses and dogs and come to London. Then Karin was bored with the talk at table. 'I can't cope with your City friends,' she told me afterwards. 'They're too high-powered for me.' So Elin remained my friend not ours.

Did our friendship develop because I was married and Elin felt safe? That was always a possibility, knowing her as I do now. Did she want to avoid commitments and concentrate on her career? Very likely. Promotion would have been impossible at that time and in that firm if she'd been married with a family. But I worried then that our friendship distracted her from meeting other men, men she might have married. Now, of course, I'm not sorry it did.

I had news of Elin off and on after that first meeting. Tony kept me up to date with her. She was a challenge to him too. 'I can't find enough work to stretch her.' He said, 'She's as keen as mustard. Certainly keeps me up to scratch.'

'And breaking hearts,' added Zelda. We were having supper one Wednesday night. 'Men are fooled by that innocent look. They find they've bitten off more than they can chew when they get to know her.'

'If she allows them long enough,' Tony said. 'Our Ms Pritchard doesn't suffer fools gladly. It'll be a brave man or a very intelligent one that snaps her up.'

Zelda snorted and went to fetch the cheese. 'Snapping her up indeed! You ought to read Germaine Greer. Women are more than ornaments to please the opposite sex.'

'See what Elin's done,' Tony said, 'corrupted the wife as well.'

Elin and I ran into each other several times while I was finishing my London job: at a dinner party to which we'd both been invited, a business reception, a book launch, a symposium on pensions law, a conference on unemployment. In large gatherings we'd gravitate towards one another and end up arguing in a corner. She didn't seem to have many close friends, though I knew she and Gareth meant a lot to each other. And she had few women as friends, though she made a great deal of her feminism. Knowing her, she saw sisterhood as a principle, a grand ideal, nothing to do with real-life people. But she sparkled in male company. She'd had a series of escorts, Tony said, though none lasted long.

'I'm afraid she'll end up an office dragon,' he admitted, 'which would be a waste. She's too attractive for that.'

'Or a politician,' I suggested, thinking of my own leanings in that direction.

We began meeting in 1983. I gave a talk on the Morality of Capitalism at a lunchtime Lent series in one of the city churches and Elin was there. When I'd finished, she pushed against the flow of departing people to question something I'd said. She was on her academic high horse, the would-be constitutional historian quoting parliamentary acts at me and we could hardly hear ourselves over the buzz of chatter. Since I had only a hazy idea of what she was saying and our discussion was becoming heated, I suggested we adjourn to the nearest pub to continue in peace.

'Let me buy you a drink and we can talk about this in comfort. I don't need to be anywhere till two.'

'I've only got half an hour.' She looked at her watch. 'But if you can spare the time, I'll be happy to put you right.' Her half smile told me she was joking but I knew she wouldn't let me off lightly. If anyone could spot a hole in an argument, she could.

She'd cut her hair, I noticed. A pity. She'd looked like an ancient warrior queen with those long, flowing locks. But I supposed that sort of style was hardly appropriate for an up-and-coming lawyer in a City firm, especially a firm as long-established and conservative as hers.

When we got down to discussion I had to admit she had a point. Annoying that, why was she always right? But I didn't agree that it demolished my whole argument. With both of us more or less satisfied – 'One all,' Elin said, with her usual ironic smile – we fell to debating the possible confrontation between the Government and the miners. It looked to be on the cards should the Tories win the election.

'Are you really going to stand?' Elin was shocked when I told her I was a candidate. 'How can you support that woman? I find it shaming that the country's first female PM should come from the Right.' She tossed her unfamiliar thick bob.

'She had to come from somewhere,' I pointed out, 'and I suspect socialists are a lot less open to women's leadership than the Tories. The working classes are very conservative – small c.'

'Benedict Palmer, you're an unregenerate snob.'

'And you're a hopeless idealist. Is it time you went, or may I buy you another drink?'

Elin said she'd never speak to me again if I was elected. Instead we found ourselves meeting fortnightly for lunch in our favourite City pub, debating the issues of the moment.

I smiled remembering those days. I could see Elin now, waving her fork at me, eyes alight, as she pointed out some flaw in a loved theory of mine. We were opposites politically. She was a natural left-winger, City lawyer or not, and railed against what she called the lunacy of letting the country's industrial base decline. She disliked tax concessions for the rich and the plan to sell off council houses. I believed in a free market, encouraging thrift, and giving people choice in matters like education and health. We rarely agreed. She challenged everything I stood for but was so witty about it that we laughed more than we argued. And half the time she'd be so engrossed in discussion that she'd forget to eat. 'Don't worry,' she said once. 'I'm dining with a client tonight. That'll make up for it. Anyway ideas are more interesting than steak pie.'

We've mellowed since, I thought, keeping a close eye out for rabbits. Years ago Elin took great pleasure in debunking any notions I had about mine or my party's right to rule and I enjoyed pointing out inconsistencies in her brand of socialism. Now I'd given up all illusions about Tory superiority and she fumed about the proliferation of laws under the present Government. I smiled. We were obviously older and wiser.

But I loved our verbal battles. I used to leave those lunches with a spring in my step, better able to face opponents within and outside the party. If I could survive one of Elin's grillings, I reasoned, I could cope with anything. And she kept my feet on the ground. 'Cheer up,' she said one day after a bruising debate in the House. 'If you don't get re-elected, you can always go home and keep fish.'

'I could have become a party political bore or a right-wing fanatic, if it hadn't been for you,' I told Elin recently.

'No you wouldn't. You're too nice. Anyway, you weren't ruthless enough to be an out-and-out Thatcherite. You cared too much about people.' I was flattered by her observation but I wouldn't have been years ago. I saw myself then as a man of principle, strong minded, astute and committed to maintaining the right course no matter what. Perhaps I needed Elin to show me other ways of seeing the world.

I smiled and took one last look at the lake before retracing my steps to the farm. The heron was back and I didn't have the heart to disturb him. Elin would have been pleased.

She always said she enjoyed our lunchtime discussions.

I suspect there weren't many who could cope with her sort of verbal combat.

'I expect it's my way of letting off steam,' she admitted in a moment of rare self-disclosure as we parted one day. 'The antidote to being polite to clients.'

'You went into the wrong branch of law,' I told her. 'You should have been a barrister.'

'I started too late,' she said, 'and it's harder for a woman there than in my line of country.' True then. But her career was progressing well, fulfilling all Tony's predictions.

In May '85 she rang me unexpectedly from work. 'I've got a new job. They're setting up an office in Hong Kong and want me there. I'm clearing my flat to let it. Could you store some boxes for me?'

I considered my Holland Park apartment. 'Yes, I can manage that. And congratulations. You deserve it after all your hard work.' I tried not to think how much I would miss having her in the same city.

'I'll feed you as a reward,' she promised, 'I can order a takeaway.' Cooking was never her strong point.

'When do you leave?'

'As soon as possible. Next week if everything can be sorted out in time. I'd like to see Gareth first, of course.'

We moved her things that Friday evening then ate a Balti in her Dulwich flat with a bottle of wine I'd bought to celebrate.

'I'll send you a postcard from time to time and give you the low-down on Far Eastern politics,' she promised, as we relaxed in her first floor sitting room.

I was determined to be pleased for her and squashed my mixed feelings. We started discussing women's ordination, a hot topic then.

'I've joined The Movement for the Ordination of Women,' she announced. 'Being agnostic doesn't bar me, apparently.'

'Most Anglicans don't know what they believe anyway,' I said loftily, 'I'm not against ordaining women myself.'

'Your Pope is.'

'He isn't "my Pope". And English Catholics have a flexible approach to authority. I know many nuns who'd make excellent priests.'

'Ah, but what about married women?'

'I'm not so sure about that.'

'See! Sexual stereotyping raises it ugly head. The Virgin Mary's okay, nuns are okay, but what about ordinary women who do regular jobs and raise children and—'

'Motherhood's a full-time job, or should be.'

'What about your beloved leader then. Margaret Thatcher has children and look what she does. Or doesn't she count?'

I shifted uncomfortably. Trust Elin to find my weak spot. 'She's an exception. And anyway she has help and a supportive husband. And she's excellent at time management.'

'So it's all right for the rich, but not for the poor.'

'I'm not saying that. I'm saying, as a general rule, that it's the mother who should give up work to care for the children. After all it's the most important job in the world.'

'God, Ben, I hate it when you're pious...and pompous.'

'Pompous or not, it's true.' I ploughed on aware I'd been sliding over shaky ground but trying to recover the moral ascendancy. 'We wouldn't be in the mess we are now if working mothers weren't leaving their children prey to God knows what.'

'You talk like a bloody Tory politician. I should expect rubbish from a traditionalist. And a country landowner too.' She threw a cushion at me.

'I *am* a Tory politician in case you hadn't noticed. And you can't flout biology, my good woman. Females, *on the whole*, are meant to look after their offspring. Not dump them in nurseries and prance off to feather their own careers.'

'Don't you mean further? And don't you "good woman" me! Where would the country be if half the clever women, half the population, sat on their backsides and did damn-all – to say nothing of giving their daughters inappropriate role models?'

'They're a quarter of the population, probably less. And bringing up children isn't damn-all. Ask Karin, ask Zelda, ask any mother.'

An uncomfortable silence ensued. I picked up the cushion she'd thrown and put it on the sofa with elaborate care. 'Not a bad shot.' And settled back in my seat. 'Anyway, what do you know of motherhood as a career woman?'

I expected a witty riposte. Instead Elin went white, said she would make the coffee and stalked out, tight-lipped.

'Fool,' I told myself, 'you've upset her now.' This wasn't supposed to happen when we were on the verge of years apart. But I couldn't think what I had said to offend. It was no holds barred when we argued. Elin always gave as good as she got, better usually.

I followed her into the kitchen. 'Sorry.'

'Go away.' She was leaning over the work surface and refused to look at me. I realised from the shaking of her shoulders that she was crying. That feisty Elin Pritchard should be in tears was unnerving.

I put my arm round her. 'I'm sorry, Elin. I was patronising and arrogant. I had no right...' But she pushed me off.

'You can say what you think. That's what we've always agreed. It's my fault. I shouldn't have pressed the point.' She splashed milk into mugs of coffee, spilling it on the work surface, scraped a spoon in the empty sugar bowl and searched in the cupboard for sugar without success.

I looked over her shoulder and found it. 'Here.'

'Bother you.' She turned to face me, defiant. 'If you really want to know, I had a kid when I was a student and had it adopted. So all this talk of motherhood's a sick joke. I even failed at that.'

What could I say? That I'm sure it was for the best? That at least she didn't have it aborted? That it was better for a child not to grow up in a single-parent family? As I absorbed this bombshell my pious rhetoric crashed about my ears. I saw the depth of her feeling and was powerless to touch it.

'And now I can't find the bloody tray.' She glared at me, torn between laughter and tears, then gave way to both. For a moment she sobbed on my shoulder.

'Sorry,' her voice was muffled. I caught only snatches of what she was saying as I held her and struggled to find a clean handkerchief.

'I didn't want to give him up...Gareth said it was best...'

It came home to me then how significant Elin's brother was in her life.

She detached herself abruptly, took my handkerchief and blew her nose.

'Thanks. Sorry about that. It must be the move stirring up the past.'

I hovered uncertainly. I wanted to ask what had happened but didn't like to pry. Instead I found the tray she had mislaid and put it on the work surface.

'Thanks.' She managed a smile. Setting our mugs on the tray with a box of After Eights, she said with forced brightness, 'let's consider the subject closed, shall we?' and led the way to the sitting room as if nothing had happened.

Neither of us felt like resuming the argument. We sat on the sofa while I tried to get my mind round Elin's surprising revelation. I wondered how to reassure her that I thought none the less of her for giving up her child. But the subject was closed, she said. With Elin that was final.

Time ticked by as the evening drew in. The last rays of sunset faded from the mirror opposite the bay window.

'Thanks, Ben.' Elin broke the silence. She had kicked off her shoes and was curled up beside me, her head on my shoulder. It was unusual for her to be so quiet. 'You're a good friend. I'm going to miss our spats.' She smiled up at me. 'We're like a pair of old shoes. We pinch occasionally but we're comfortable most of the time.'

'I'm not sure I find that flattering,' I said, stroking her hair. 'What am I going to do without you around to sharpen my wits?'

'You'll cope. Maybe it'll be good not to see each other for a while. I might give away too much after tonight. God knows what else I might say.'

I wondered what she meant by that. I'd always realised there was much about Elin I didn't know, about her past or what she felt. Ideas were our main currency.

We were relaxed, edging towards a physical intimacy we had never entertained before. Part of me thought, this is the last time we'll see each other for five years at least. Make the most of it while you can. But my conscience signalled danger. I thought of Karin and of Elin. What if Elin and I crossed the well-defined boundaries of our friendship? Where might it end? Could she, could we, cope with that level of closeness? I had glimpsed a side of her I'd never seen before. For all her fighting spirit, she was more vulnerable than I'd imagined. I didn't want to destroy the friendship we had.

She must have caught my thought for she sat up suddenly and looked at the clock. 'Half past eleven. You'd better be going. Haven't you got a train to catch in the morning?' She felt for her shoes. 'And I must think about packing. There's so much to do.' She gave me an affectionate glance. 'A pity one can't crate up one's friends and take them as well.'

'Thanks for the meal, even if you didn't cook it.' I stretched stiff limbs.

'Be grateful for small mercies. You'd need a box of Rennies if I had.' She stood up and smiled at me. 'Thanks for helping out, Ben. It'll be strange working so far away, but I'm looking forward to it. I like a challenge.'

'You'll do fine,' I assured her as we went downstairs.

She paused before opening the front door and laid her hand on my arm. 'Am I forgiven?'

'What for?'

'For being a hard-nosed career woman rather than a good Conservative mother?'

'I'll have to mind what I say in future speeches.'

'Maybe I've done you some good after all.'

'You'll write?' I asked on the doorstep.

'Try to.' She hugged me and I kissed her on the cheek. Then she pushed me into the night.

We didn't see each other much in the next fifteen years. We met sometimes on Elin's annual visits to the UK if I happened to be in London at the time, but our paths and the tenor of our lives diverged.

In 1990 we managed a lunch in our old sparring place. Elin arrived bright-eyed and excited. 'I'm moving to Singapore,' she said, barely able to contain her pleasure. The firm's setting up an office there and want me to be in at the start.'

'That's a feather in your cap.' I was pleased for her. 'And how is life in the capitalist Far East?'

She gave a rueful smile. 'You're right about the capitalist bit. My socialist principles are under attack. But I try to give good service and keep my nose clean.' She paused and shrugged. 'I try not to delve too closely into the records of some of the clients I deal with – human rights and so on. But it's not too bad. And I get to meet lots of interesting people. How about you?' She gave me one of her searching looks.

I fingered my glass of bitter. I didn't want to cast a shadow over our reunion.

'I suppose I've lost my edge, or mislaid my vision somewhere along the line.' It was the first time I'd honestly faced my feelings of discontent.

'Your party's been in power too long.'

'Maybe that's it.' I gave a sigh and finished my drink. 'I might be cynical in my old age...' I paused, searching for words.

'But?' she prompted, looking me in the eye.

Yes, there had to be a 'but'. 'I suppose I'm fed up with all this squabbling and back-stabbing,' I began. 'The poll tax was a disaster. Anyone could have seen that it was going to be. And no one seems to care about the long-term jobless – you know, those families where unemployment runs down the generations. Or the young people in our cities...' I stopped and looked at her. 'I could go on.' Somehow it didn't feel disloyal to be talking this way with Elin for all her instinctive criticism of my party. She was abroad now, an outsider.

'They'll make a socialist of you yet,' she exulted. Then seeing my face she added sympathetically. 'I'm sorry it's like this for you. Politics is a funny game.'

'You can say that again.' I managed a smile.

'And how are the cows? I hope you're not going to tell me you've had BSE on the farm?'

'No. At least that's one area that's going all right.'

'Let's drink to that, then,' she said brightly. 'Good health to the Palmer herd. And to their owner.' And she gave me her old teasing smile.

Two years later I was wishing she'd said the same for my wife. It was still hard to look back on that period. So many events came together that left painful memories. First I found myself moving to the left of my party, joining the so-called 'wets' who were much derided in the Tory press at the time. Then the government ran out of steam and passed a number of hasty measures I'm sure we'll come to regret, to say nothing of getting mired in 'sleaze'. Worst of all Karin, lost her battle with breast cancer in April 1996. It was the darkest time of my life.

By contrast, that same year, Elin received the just reward for all her hard work. 'She's got a Senior Partnership,' Tony told me at Christmas. 'About time too. If she wasn't a woman she'd have got it years ago. She's far and away the best person for setting up new projects and looking after trainees.'

I wrote to congratulate her. It was the first time we'd corresponded since Karin's death. We began to write regularly after that. I needed someone to pour out my thoughts to, especially after the 1997 election debacle.

'I can't say I'm surprised at the Labour landslide,' she wrote back – and I was eternally grateful to her for not crowing. 'It's been coming a long time. But I'm sorry you're out of a job. What do you plan to do now? Are you going to farm quietly or will you get involved with some of your good causes?'

I did both though it was hard concentrating on anything for a time.

'You're depressed, Dad,' Lara said when they came to the farm that Christmas. 'Why don't you take a holiday?'

'Yes. How about going to stay with Auntie Val in New Zealand,' Ismene put in. I could smell a conspiracy but thought, why not? It'll be summer there in January. And the family could do with a break from me in this state.

Odd, how things work out, I thought, joining the access road that leads to the farm and starting on the last half mile. Would Elin and I have got together if I hadn't made that visit to Valentine's stud farm? Of course there's no knowing. But it certainly made it easier.

I had to break my journey in Singapore so I rang Elin to see if I could call on her.

'How long can you stay?' she asked, 'I could take time

out and show you around if you like. I'm due some leave.' So I spent two nights in her apartment on the fifth floor of a modern condominium.

It was good to meet again. Elin greeted me warmly and seemed as pleased to see me as I was her. Maybe she was making allowances for my bereaved state, but she seemed gentler and less combative than usual. She listened sympathetically while I brought her up to date with my doings and fed me an excellent curry. It was a relief to be in the company of an old friend with no need for pretence.

'Your cooking's improved,' I told her as we relaxed over coffee in her ultra-modern armchairs. Elin's living room was all glass and chrome and contemporary lighting. I thought of the Dulwich flat's softness with regret.

'I'm not sure you ever tried it.' She smiled. 'I was too kind to force it on you, remember? Didn't we always eat out?'

'I've missed our sessions, putting the world to rights.'

'We can resume them in a year or two if you want. I'm coming back to London in 2000.' She paused as I put my cup on the glass-topped table between us, 'More coffee?' and came over with the jug to refill it. I caught a hint of her expensive perfume and realised how starved I was of feminine company. Daughters were all very well but Lara and Izzie had been bullying me. I was glad to be away from them for a while.

Elin sat down, crossing her legs gracefully. 'Having trained a team of local lawyers,' she continued, 'I've worked myself out of a job.'

'Is that good or bad?' I asked. 'For you, I mean?'

She looked serious. 'I'm not sure. I wonder if I've hit the proverbial glass ceiling. The firm's very male-dominated.

Younger women on the way up will have a better chance than I have of making it to the top. After fifty you're on your way out in this line of business.'

'Come on, Elin. That doesn't sound like you. Where's your feminist fighting spirit?'

She smiled. 'Oh, that's not gone. But maybe I should look for other battles to fight. I could go into politics, for example. After last year's election disaster and its traumas over Europe your party needs to rediscover its soul – I could help them find it.' She raised an eyebrow and grinned at me. 'Or I could write a scurrilous novel,' she went on, 'about mega-deals and mergers, call it *The Lawyers* and make a mint selling the film rights to TV companies. Or,' she paused, 'I could go back to my first love and finish my PhD.' She ticked these off on her fingers, a mischievous light in her hazel eyes.

'You're teasing,' I accused her.

'Not about the last, though I'd choose a different subject now. "A Comparison between English Medieval Law Codes and the Laws of Hywel Dda" doesn't have the appeal it once had.'

'Was that it?' I stared in amazement.

She laughed. 'Maybe it was a good thing I gave up. Or,' she added with a wicked grin, 'I might find a nice Japanese millionaire to marry and save myself the hassle of deciding.'

'Elin Pritchard, you're incorrigible,' I told her. 'You haven't changed a bit.'

But she had. She was more attractive, more sophisticated, better dressed and less abrasive than she once was. It occurred to me then that if she didn't find a Japanese millionaire, a Cheshire landowner might be an acceptable substitute.

I squashed the idea. A typical bereaved person's hunger for affection, I rationalised. But after that our letters became more frequent. We shared more of ourselves. And we discovered the immediacy of e-mail.

We were nearly back at the farmhouse now, facing the slight rise up to the farmyard. I paused at a gate to look over our new Holsteins, who were grazing or sitting quietly in the early sunshine. The ravages of foot-and-mouth were still a bad memory, 'specially as ours was a contiguous cull, none of our cows had caught the disease. But things were looking up. We'd gone ahead with re-stocking and our new calves were a sign of hope. Life with Elin had taken on a new and more hopeful turn as well.

When she returned to England I arranged for Elin to stay in my apartment till she found somewhere of her own. I'd been renting it out since the election defeat and it happened to be empty.

I met her at Gatwick on a dull February morning. She greeted me, smiling, the old buoyant Elin. At her insistence we stopped at a service station before the M25. 'I must boost my caffeine levels or I'll wilt.'

As we drank cappuccino and caught up on news I realised the old attraction was still there – we could spark off one another, teasing, punning, laughing. But there was something else on my side. I am in love with her, I thought. Did she feel the same for me? It was hard to tell. Elin was her usual animated self despite jet lag; we were friends with a long history. Then, in the midst of swapping stories, we glanced at each other and something like an electric charge passed between us. For a moment we stopped talking, then struggled to pick up the conversation again. But everything had changed. Leaving the café I reached for her hand and we shared a smile of recognition.

'I've missed you, Ben,' she said. 'I hadn't realised how much till now.'

It took time to come to terms with the realisation that we were more than friends. We had to adjust to the changes in each other. Elin had become more thoughtful – 'Tony was right. I needed to learn tact. I hope I'm beginning to.' The total loss of her Welsh accent was disconcerting – it had always been part of her. Somehow I'd not noticed that in Singapore. And Karin's death hadn't just given me grey hairs; that and the election defeat had turned my life upside down. I hoped I was a wiser, more tolerant person as a result.

I took her out to dinner that night.

'Does every tenant get this treatment?' she asked, teasing.

'No.' I smiled across at her. 'Special attention limited to Welsh redheads back from Singapore who must be partners in a law firm and have a first class degree.'

'Very limited.' She laughed.

Afterwards we talked late into the night despite the fact that she'd been awake for hours. 'Where do we go from here?' we asked ourselves.

'A nice, romantic friendship? No strings?' Elin suggested.

'Fine. See where it takes us,' I agreed, hoping it would take us to marriage in time.

'And slowly,' she added, 'no need to rush.'

By then I had more time to socialise, with Jem, Izzie's husband, managing the farm. But Elin was now her firm's

Senior Training Partner and busier than ever. We met as often as we could. We spent a weekend in Dublin, a holiday in my sister's villa on the Algarve, a week in Edinburgh and had various outings in London. But Elin spent just one weekend with me in Cheshire before foot-and-mouth forced us apart for months. She kept me sane then with her phone calls and witty e-mails, pulling me out of the depression caused by the loss of our sheep flock and pedigree dairy herd.

Soon friends and family were seeing us as a couple. We could go weeks without meeting but phoned or e-mailed most days and often knew each other's thoughts without needing to voice them. 'Years of practice arguing,' Elin joked.

We spent Christmas 2002 with the family at the farm. Elin had hoped to visit her people in North Wales while she was with us but the whole household came down with 'flu and she couldn't go. Instead we spent a relaxed convalescence by the fire with the dogs at our feet. We listened to CDs and Radio 4 and worked through a pile of detective fiction and crosswords while the younger generation recovered to loud music and TV soaps at the other end of the house. Despite our coughs and colds it was one of the most pleasant Christmases I could remember, certainly the best since Karin died. I began to think that if we could cope with one another when we were scratchy and convalescent we could surely consider being together on a permanent basis. But Elin's work was based in London. How might our lives fit?

We didn't discuss marriage. I wasn't sure how Elin would respond. We'd shared a hotel room once when late bookings left us no choice, but having made clear my disapproval of Jem and Izzie sleeping together before their wedding, I wasn't about to break my own rules. We set our own boundaries and kept within them out of respect for each other, though it wasn't always easy.

After Christmas Elin hit a busy stretch when the pressure of work seemed relentless. Her only trip North in three months was to share a balloon flight she'd bought for my birthday. We drifted over Dovedale and the Roaches one glorious May evening and came down in a quiet field just before sunset.

'We must have more time together,' we promised ourselves and agreed to make it a priority.

But it didn't work out. We'd arrange a weekend and Elin would phone at the last minute to cancel. I'd stay with her and she'd be so busy we'd hardly have time to talk. She altered arrangements on the flimsiest excuses yet rang at once if I didn't keep in touch. I didn't want to pressure her. I knew the stresses of her job, how she was anxious to hold on to her position with younger lawyers below her pressing for promotion. But I began to wonder if there was more to her elusiveness than a heavy case load. Was she trying to tell me she'd had enough?

The next time she was at the farm, I tackled her about it. We were walking the fields, the day she was due to leave.

'Is everything all right?' I asked. 'Work and so on?'

'Mmm. Busy but it always is.' She was watching rabbits by the hedge, her eyes narrowed against the afternoon sun.

I was wishing I'd brought my shotgun. 'You seem run into the ground. Isn't there anything you can do to cut down?'

'I'm fine.' She kicked a clod of earth.

'Not changed your mind about making more time for each other?'

We walked the next hundred yards in silence, Elin frowning. Then she said, 'I'm feeling pushed, that's all. There's a lot to do.' But she didn't sound convinced or convincing.

I was confused. She was warm and demonstrative one moment, elusive and distant the next. Elin was becoming impossible to pin down. I wondered where we were heading. We seemed stuck in some kind of trough.

'Come and see how the calves have grown,' I suggested on the way back.

She laughed and took my hand. 'Is this pet therapy or something?'

'No, but animals keep their own counsel.' Living close by, Jem or Ismene could walk into the farmhouse any time.

Scratching the head of the youngest heifer, Elin admitted, 'I can't hide, can I? You know what I'm thinking before I know it myself.' She looked at me then away. 'Work *is* busy but I realise I've let it become the excuse for not meeting. I don't know why. It's not what I want, deep down. I wish I could explain.'

'Try,' I prompted.

She squeezed my hand. 'I think it's because I've not been close to anyone for so long. I'm finding it hard to adjust. It's not your fault, Ben, it's me.'

'Would you like me to back off? Ease the pressure?'

'Definitely not.' She glared at me. 'But something changed at Christmas didn't it?' Her voice softened. 'We're closer. I'm not used to it. If we go on like this…' She shook her head. 'Please stick with me, Ben. I'm trying to work it out. The last thing I want is to lose you.'

'I'll stick as long as you like. If that's what you really want.'

It came to me that Elin was afraid. Of commitment? Of close relationships? Of love? It was unexpected in someone so confident and strong. What lay behind it, I wondered.

Packing her car to return to London, she paused. 'Ben, promise you'll pull me up if I start being elusive.'

'So long as you promise not to explode.'

She grinned. 'I'll try not to. Though I can be combustible at times, as you know.'

'I'll dig myself a bunker.'

Afterwards I mulled over what she'd said. I knew from the odd remark that she'd never been close to her parents. I knew about her broken engagement years before and the baby she'd had adopted. What was the matter and how could I help?

Thinking it over on one of my morning walks I remembered an incident from childhood. Before I went away to school, a stray cat came to the farm, dragging a paw. Eager to make it better, I chased it round the yard till it climbed on top of the straw bales in the barn and sat spitting and glaring.

'That's not the way,' my mother said when I ran indoors, upset. 'You have to be patient. Watch.'

She left a saucer of sardines and a saucer of milk in the barn. Next day both were clean. We put food out every day and the cat took it. Gradually we moved the saucers nearer the house and in a fortnight we could get close enough to tend the cat's paw and take it to the vet. He became a loved pet – Barney, the barn cat.

I didn't think Elin would be flattered to know I

compared her with a limping stray cat, but similar patience might help the situation, I reasoned. I tried not to crowd her but made sure she knew I wasn't going to give up in a hurry. I didn't budge when she played 'go away, closer' and challenged her when it was clear she was avoiding me. She could spit and glare like Barney. I could withdraw, confused. But our love, friendship and sense of humour held us together when we got it wrong. In spite of the difficulties – perhaps because of them – we were gradually moving towards a more settled relationship.

We saw each other regularly as far as our commitments allowed, spending weekends in London but mostly at the farm since Elin found it restful here after what she called the 'hectivity' of the office. 'You really are like an old married couple,' Izzie said once, finding us asleep on the sofa one Sunday afternoon with various bits of *The Sunday Times* and *Observer* around us on the floor and the dogs snoring gently by the fire. I couldn't imagine life without Elin. I knew one day I'd ask her to marry me. At the right time.

But what had made her so insecure?

'My father told me I was rubbish,' she said once, 'a misfit. I spoilt everything.'

'*That* was rubbish,' I said at once. 'You're a very attractive woman, intelligent, lively and fun. And you have the most beautiful eyes.' Then the meaning of her words sank in. 'Surely he wasn't serious? What on earth was he thinking of?'

'It's not worth discussing.' She shrugged it off, clamming up as she always does when her parents are mentioned. 'And flattery will get you everywhere, Ben Palmer.' She smiled and kissed me then changed the subject. But there was sadness in her eyes.

Was her father the problem? If so I wished I could have wrung his neck. I thought of Lara and Ismene. I'd done my best to assure them that they were special and loved, to make them feel good about themselves. When they'd got above themselves as teenagers, I was tempted to think I'd overdone it, but that was far better than what Elin's father seemed to have done to her.

I decided to find out more. I'd spoken to Gareth once on the phone. When we eventually met, I thought, I'd ask about their father and what their home life had been like. But before I could talk to him, Gareth died.

I was sorry to have missed my chance of seeing him. I'd always felt I'd understand Elin better if I met her brother and I'd wanted to meet him for himself. Elin was always singing his praises. I hoped I'd see his family one day, though that was up to Elin.

I met Ismene in the yard, going to saddle her horse. 'You're seeing Elin today aren't you?' she said.

'Yes. We're meeting at Delamere.'

'Give her my love, I'm really sorry about her brother.'

'I will.' I looked at my watch, put the dogs in their run and went into the house. Two hours and Elin and I would be together. I decided to spend an hour form-filling in the study to make the time pass more quickly.

She was waiting for me at the car park entrance, standing, arms folded, her eyes on the road. Her face lit up as she saw me arrive and she came over to where I parked the Volvo.

'Ben, it's good to see you.' Her voice was even but she looked tired about the eyes.

I hugged her and she shed a tear before pulling away. 'Don't, love, I can't let go. Not yet.' But she held my hand as we walked to the garden.

'I thought we'd eat outside. Enjoy the view. And it'll be quieter out here.'

We chose a table where we could sit side by side and look across fields to the forest.

'So how was it really?' I asked when we'd finished ordering.

'Okay. You don't think about death do you? Not till it happens to someone close.'

'I know.'

'Of course you do. I don't want to re-open old wounds.'

'If it helps, there is healing. In time.'

She nodded, searched in her bag for cigarettes and lit one. I hadn't the heart to remind her she'd promised to give them up. 'Two days ago I was painting a rosy picture of my job to one of my old teachers. It wasn't untrue but when something like this happens it feels so unimportant. I feel my foundations have been rocked.' She spread out her hands.

'And the family?'

'Stunned of course. And I'm not sure I haven't made things worse by being there. It's hard to stay in that house, 'specially without Gareth.' She wavered then went on. 'I'm like a cat on hot coals there. If I'd got to know them before it wouldn't be so bad. But we're complete strangers trying to cope with each other plus a bereavement. Lily, Gareth's widow, is an exceptional person. I realise that now. I've not been fair to her over the years.' She looked out across the forest and gave a small sigh. 'Whether that can be repaired or not…' Her words tailed off.

'You've never said much about your family.'

'No. I've spent most of my life running away from them, except Gareth. We went through a lot together when we were young...' She stopped speaking suddenly and I put my arm round her. 'You are allowed to cry, you know. It's not forbidden. You don't have to be the tough guy all the time.'

'I know.' She shook her head and smiled apologetically. 'But I'm not good at it. Years of training I suppose.' And wiped away a tear.

She tried her best to eat but wasn't succeeding. 'Would you like my meat?' she asked, pushing her plate towards me.

'Are you sure you don't want it? I'll get fat.' But I took her lamb shank onto my plate. I hate to see good meat going to waste, especially when some farmer's gone to all the trouble of raising it.

'I've been good all week.' She watched me. 'I'm even cooking for the family tonight. How's that for dedication?'

'Yours or theirs?' I teased.

'Theirs of course.' But she sounded tired.

I wanted to kidnap her and take her home. 'Stop over on the way back. Have a rest, recharge your batteries.'

Her eyes brightened. 'I'd love to. But I'm meeting a client on Thursday and the paperwork's in the office. Besides, I haven't got much leave in hand. I've overstayed as it is.'

She changed tack abruptly. 'There is one thing I haven't mentioned. I'd almost forgotten. The day Gareth died, before I heard, a friend of Tony's rang. He wants to start a small firm offering to run in-house courses. There's a good market for them with all this new legislation coming out.

He's asked if I'd like to go in with them. I can't get my head round it at the moment. It's flattering to be approached and I've been unsettled as you know. But is it too great a risk? Do I want to play safe or is this the challenge I've been waiting for?'

'That depends on you,' I said. 'Of course, if we were married the risk might be lessened. I could support you if things went pear-shaped. And you could put all your millions and jewels in my name. Then if you went bankrupt they'd be safe.'

'Ben!' She sounded shocked. 'I wouldn't dream of expecting you to underwrite my risks.' She laughed suddenly. 'Idiot. What jewels? What millions?'

Then the full meaning of what I'd said hit her. 'You can't be serious.' She turned to me, amusement in her eyes.

'Can't I? What do you think?' I reached for her hand. 'Elin, don't you think we ought to consider it seriously – being together for good? Marriage even?'

'Ben, you silly old romantic.' But her fingers grasped mine.

'I am serious,' I went on, 'though I didn't mean to mention it now nor quite like that. I should have waited till you'd had time to recover from Gareth.'

Elin looked from me to the distant view, then back again. 'I'm not sure I see myself as marriage material, Ben. I don't know if I'm up to that sort of commitment.'

She grinned. 'What would you want me to do? Leave London and become a farmer's wife? Make jam for the WI? Dispense broth to the tenants?'

'Don't be silly. It's not a job I'm offering.'

Her face grew thoughtful. 'I know.'

'Don't answer yet, love,' I said quickly. 'Bereavement's

not the time for decisions. As I said I shouldn't have asked now. But it's been in my mind for some while.'

'I can't say I hadn't suspected this would happen some day. But do we know what it might mean? For either of us? Do you really want an insomniac workaholic for a wife?'

'We could always have separate bedrooms if you felt the need for nocturnal prowling.'

'We could keep separate houses.' She laughed then stopped suddenly and said with a hint of the old asperity, 'This isn't a rescue package by any chance? Because if it is, I refuse point blank.'

'Rescue? From what?'

'Work. The firm. Difficult decisions.'

'Good God no. You're not a washed up has-been. You've got so much to offer. But maybe you need to change direction, try something new.'

'And this could be it?' The usual teasing grin. 'Company lawyer meets country landowner and lives happily ever after.'

'Ex-Welsh Nationalist and ex-Tory MP. A marriage of opposites.'

'A loose partnership, perhaps.'

'A lawful union.'

'A professional association.'

'We could run our own consultancy. Pritchard and Palmer. Anything legal considered.'

We looked at each other and laughed. Whatever happened we would always belong together. Somehow.

Meryl

'Do you mean she never came to her parents' funerals?' Linda Travers leaned over the counter of the village shop and stared at Nesta Plas Gwyn in amazement.

'No, she didn't.' Nesta frowned her disapproval as she bent to take a pack of assorted crisps from a bottom shelf.

'What's more she only saw them once or twice in the last ten years they were alive.' Eirlys Jones looked up from the pet food she was collecting.

I moved away from the two friends, unwilling to get caught up in gossip. Nesta and Eirlys had a gift for shredding reputations. Hadn't I been their target once upon a time?

It was Saturday teatime and the three of us were stocking up for Sunday. Linda, who runs the shop but isn't a native of Llanfadog had asked, innocently, 'What's all this about Elin Pritchard? What's she like? She seems pleasant enough when she calls in but I get the feeling people don't like her.' And her question stirred a shower of disapproval from the other two, like muck from a muckspreader.

I tried to put a word in – I don't like to hear people being criticised when they can't answer back and I knew how it felt to be subjected to such treatment. But Nesta and Eirlys are unstoppable once the knives are out.

'She's the prodigal returned,' Nesta snorted, 'but unfortunately she's come back too late. Too late to make it up with her parents, too late to see her brother. I hope her conscience is troubling her at last.'

'Not likely,' Eirlys had said. 'Hard as nails that one.'

'She was a tearaway when she was young,' Nesta went on to explain. 'Out of control. She ended up in court for defacing road signs. I was so sorry for her parents. They were quiet and respectable, always kept themselves to themselves. It must have been dreadful for them having it all over the papers.' She put down her basket on the floor and squared her back as if preparing to make a speech, 'But people could forgive her that if she'd shown a bit more respect, if she hadn't dropped her family once she went to London.'

I ventured an opinion then. 'She's not exactly a prodigal. She's one of Llanfadog's successes. You must have heard Gareth talking about her sometimes. He was so proud of her successful legal career it wasn't true. But…'

There was always a 'but' with Elin. Three years her senior and a fellow pupil at the high school, I had watched her progress through adolescence as my own children grew. I would wait with Llinos in the pram when the school bus returned, whether to show off how grown-up I was, or to keep in touch with friends I'm not sure. You couldn't miss Elin with her red hair and voluble chatter. She was always the centre of whatever was going on.

She was one of the ablest girls at the school but one of the most wilful. You don't get to know many in the classes below you but Elin was one who came to everyone's notice. She gave us prefects a hard time. I could picture her now, arguing with the head girl while her friend begged her to come away.

She campaigned for the Welsh language but never knew where to draw the line. The village had never forgotten how mortified her parents were when she was up before the magistrate. That was in a different league from my own less original misdemeanours.

She would stand up for any cause she thought right but was insensitive to people's feelings. I remember her sticking up for a kid who was being bullied, chasing two older girls to get the girl's bag back, then ignoring the victim afterwards.

She was fearless and outspoken but did things behind her parents' backs that would have given them heart failure if they'd known. She spent a weekend with her student boyfriend once when she was supposed to be sleeping over with a friend from school. My brother saw them in a Bangor pub and was shocked at some of the political stuff Elin was spouting. 'The girl's a bloody revolutionary,' he said, 'God knows what she'll get up to when she leaves home. Blow up the Houses of Parliament, I shouldn't wonder.' But Elin thought it a hoot when he recognised her. She made him promise not to tell her family in return for buying him a drink – or rather the boyfriend buying him a drink for she was only seventeen at the time. I was cheered by this. I wasn't the only one breaking the rules, it seemed, prepared to defy the conventions of Llanfadog's moral mafia. And breaking the law was much more serious than getting oneself pregnant at sixteen. I could allow myself a degree of smugness. There's always someone worse than yourself.

'Elin's done well, that's true,' Nesta admitted, 'but there's many in the village that don't like the way she treated her family. However successful you are, it isn't right not to come and see your parents. 'Specially when they're old. It's callous and ungrateful.'

'Gareth said she was too busy,' Eirlys put in, her tone implying that she didn't believe a word of it.

'Too self-centred more like,' judged Nesta.

I was silent. There was no defence for Elin's conduct. A pity because I had admired her spirit when she was young. Trapped in an early marriage, with two children before I was twenty, I had followed her career with interest and some envy. Not many from our village got as far as university in those days, particularly young women. I saw Elin's success as a beacon for ordinary people, an encouragement for girls who would never have considered higher education before. She had taken full advantage of the opportunities I had thrown away but I felt let down by her subsequent behaviour. Her disregard of family and community was a poor advert for education. It showed disrespect and a lack of generosity. I was disappointed with her. But that didn't give me an excuse to join the mud-slinging.

'Elin came home just two or three times in thirty years,' Nesta said, 'and they were only flying visits. She turned her back on Wales and the family. People were upset for her mother's sake. What kind of daughter is that?'

'Not much of one, I'd say.' Eirlys put her basket on the floor the better to join in the disembowelling. 'Poor Mrs Pritchard. She had a hard life. She could have done with a daughter at home. Elin should have come back after her training and got work as a solicitor here. There was no need for her to stay in London and cut herself off. Mr Pritchard was a difficult man. Elin might have made things easier for her mother if she'd been here.'

'She might at least have helped pay for their care.' Nesta was scathing. 'All that money she was supposed to be earning and none of it sent home as far as I know. Mean, I call it. Gareth and Lily did a lot but it's the unmarried daughter's place to look after the parents, or always used to be.'

'Too wrapped up in her own career to think of anyone else, that was the trouble.'

I had to butt in. My own experience, being on the receiving end of distortion and rumour when my divorce was going through, has made me a bit of a stickler for truth. 'I'm not sure it would have helped for Elin to be at home. I got to know old Mrs Pritchard in her last years – after her husband died she used to come to lunch club in the village hall. From one or two comments she let slip it sounded as if Elin and her father didn't get on. Her father was over strict with her, she said.'

There was a short pause. Nesta and Eirlys didn't look convinced.

'Of course Annie would defend her own daughter,' Nesta was dismissive. 'What would you expect? A pity Elin didn't show the same loyalty.'

Eirlys sniffed. 'Father and daughter were cut to the same pattern, that's the top and bottom of it. Tom Pritchard was an odd-tempered man. You never knew if he'd speak to you or not. Walk right past you some days, he would, as if you weren't there.'

'And Elin took after him,' Nesta said tartly. 'The last time she was here she didn't acknowledge me in the street, didn't even see me. Gareth was far the nicer of the two.'

Mention of Gareth stemmed the flow of criticism for a space.

'It's such a shame. He was so well liked. We're going to miss him dreadfully.'

'Yes, he was kind and generous. And he did well by the family.'

'He had a kind word for everyone. He was so good with

Ruth when poor Herbert died.'

'And his children are a credit to him.'

We went quiet remembering the village's loss.

'Poor Annie Pritchard always wore that shell brooch Elin sent from New Zealand,' resumed Nesta after a decent interval. 'Do you remember? She liked to show it off and tell everyone where it came from.'

'As if it was the only thing Elin ever gave her, poor soul.' Eirlys pursed her lips. She turned to Linda. 'Annie was so proud when Elin got her degree, telling everyone she'd been awarded a First and they were going to London to see her get it – she never said much as a rule. Gareth drove his parents down and they made a weekend of it. For Elin not to come home after that must have been heartbreaking, like a slap in the face.' She paused to take a packet of soap powder and put it in her basket. 'Did you see her at the funeral, by the way? She hardly spoke. It's a wonder she deigned to come.'

'She and Gareth were close,' I defended, 'they were always together as children. I expect his death hit Elin hard.'

I had a fleeting memory of the pair dipping in a stream, grubby as street urchins, Elin's red plaits splashed with mud. I had watched enviously, unable to join in because I was wearing my best skirt. I also sensed that their friendship excluded others though Gareth was in the same class as me.

And another memory – of a tinier pre-school Elin running up the village street to look for her brother because he was home late for school and she had forgotten it was football practice. We were dawdling home after buying sweets and Elin shot past us like a little bullet, quite distraught, calling Gareth's name. One of the older girls who lived near the Pritchards ran after her and took her back, I remember, though Elin fought hard not to go.

'Why didn't she come and see him, then?' Eirlys demanded. 'She's had time enough. Been back four years from Singapore or wherever it was.'

I shook my head. No one knew the answer to that.

Eirlys looked at Linda. 'Most people in the village think Elin hard and uncaring, you'll find. She's got on and she hasn't bothered about anyone else in the process. That's why we don't like her.'

She turned to Nesta. 'Do you remember how Tom Pritchard was in the end? Wandering about the village in his pyjamas all hours. Lily and Gareth were wonderful then. They cared for Annie too when she was so ill. Elin didn't lift a finger to help. Even if she and her father didn't get on, you'd have thought she'd come and see her mother before she died and her so ill for six months.' She sighed. 'I shouldn't wonder if all the strain had a bearing on Gareth's heart attack even if it was some years ago. These things take their toll.'

There was murmured assent from Nesta and a pause while we resumed our scrutiny of the shelves. Eirlys rummaged in the freezer. Nesta started picking out cereals. I thought that was the end but then Eirlys said, loudly so that Linda could hear her at the till. 'You should hear our precious Miss Pritchard talk. Not a trace of a Welsh accent. She doesn't speak Welsh at all now, people say. Left it behind the way she did the rest of us.'

'And flaunting that new car just to show how well off she is. Have you seen her in it?'

I was unhappy with the way the conversation was going

but I didn't like to challenge the other two. Eirlys and Nesta are Llanfadog veterans of long standing, pillars of the chapel establishment, with impeccable reputations and undeniable influence.

'I can't think why she should think herself above the rest of us. She was no better than she should be when she was at school.' Eirlys lowered her voice. 'Do you remember that bearded boyfriend of hers? Goodness knows what they got up to between them, breaking the law and such. And she a lawyer herself now, of all things.'

'It takes a thief to catch one,' Linda observed mildly.

'I daresay she's changed since then,' I said, stung, 'I expect we all did things as teenagers we wouldn't approve of now.'

The others smiled indulgently and I realised, too late, that it was the wrong thing to have said. No doubt they, unlike me, had never done anything to be ashamed of. The pair continued, unabashed, to pick over their victim's past.

I gave up trying to inject any charity into the discussion and moved away. I imagined I was still 'no better than I should be' for all my years of respectable living. I meant to close my ears to the rest of the conversation, intent on finishing my shopping. But it's hard not to overhear in such a confined space.

For Linda's benefit, Eirlys described in detail Elin's brush with the law at eighteen, her doubtful morals ('out till all hours, she was, even at fifteen') and her undesirable reputation at school ('We thought they were going to expel her after the court case.') She would have demolished what was left of Elin's character if Linda hadn't given a sudden, loud cough and shot us a warning look.

The village shop is L-shaped with an entrance at one end

and the counter where the two wings meet. Being in the aisle furthest from the door, we three couldn't see anyone come in but took Linda's hint and stopped speaking. The silence that followed was like the quiet after a gun has gone off. You could have heard a pin drop.

Eirlys, Nesta and I looked at one another.

Linda said, 'Good afternoon,' and smiled in the direction of the door. Then we heard Elin Pritchard's crisp, English tones in reply. 'Good afternoon. Not too late am I? I'm not sure when you close on Saturdays.'

'We're open till ten lottery nights,' Linda answered.

The things that had been said seemed to hang in the air, accusing us. I felt myself go hot, even though I'd contributed very little and tried to distance myself from any unkindness. Nesta looked at her feet, Eirlys counted the tins in her basket. The shop door was open so Elin could have caught snatches of conversation before she came in. What, if anything, had she heard?

I racked my brain for something to say, anxious to defuse the tension.

'There's always another side,' I said at last, 'we don't know everything that goes on in people's lives, what makes them do what they do.'

And with that I walked to the counter with my basket and set it down for Linda to ring up my purchases. I was in sight of Elin now. I glanced over my shoulder to see her pause in front of the wine and spirits.

She looked up. 'Oh, hallo. It's Meryl, isn't it? Meryl Williams. I wondered who was there.' Was that a challenge? But her tone sounded friendly enough.

'Not Williams now, Hardy.' I said, 'I've re-married. Arwyn and I split up years ago.'

She obviously hadn't heard about the divorce. 'Sorry. I'm out of touch. It's a long time since I heard any village news.'

I could see Eirlys and Nesta exchange glances. 'Whose fault is that?' their eyes said.

'Gareth never said much about what was going on,' Elin added. 'Men aren't good at that kind of thing, are they?' She paused, perhaps because she had mentioned Gareth and remembered he was no longer with us. Then she asked, 'How are the children?'

I didn't know if she was really interested or just being polite, but I was pleased she had remembered them. 'Llinos is married and lives in Rhyl – she's got two children and works in a bank, David's teaching in Birmingham – he's not married – and Bethan's a vet in Liverpool.'

'That makes me feel old,' Elin said. 'They sound a credit to you, anyway. They must have inherited your brains.'

I smiled. Yes, I had been heading for training college or university when I came unstuck. But shotgun weddings aren't the best. Arwyn and I had been madly in love for four years then it fizzled out. He hadn't liked being tied to a wife and children so early and I had resented giving up my education when the future seemed so promising. Thank goodness modern youngsters didn't have to suffer the same social pressures we had.

Had Elin remembered this? She had admired Llinos in her pram, I recalled. 'I'm going to wait years till I have children,' she said with the certainty of a fourteen-year-old, 'but when I do I want lots, all girls. And I'll bring them up to think they can do anything boys can.'

I had smiled to myself from my superior knowledge of life. At seventeen with a husband and the experience of childbirth behind me I had felt older than my years – and wiser. 'You can't order what you want just like that. And you'll have to find a husband first,' I joked. Elin frowned then, fiddled with the strap of her satchel and walked off quickly with her friend, as if the reality I hinted at was too much for her. She hadn't produced her hordes of children, then. I wondered if she minded.

She was picking wine bottles from shelves and reading their labels, a Mona Lisa smile on her face as if recalling some private joke. I had expected her to look sad but I suppose you can't go round being mournful all the time. Yet she was more cheerful than I had expected. She hummed softly to herself while she inspected what was on offer.

'Do you have any cheaper red?' she called to Linda at last. 'I'd like some for cooking.'

Linda hurried to help and Elin explained, 'I'm making a meal for the family. I'm not a brilliant cook but I wanted to serve something special. Lily's been seeing to most of the catering. I feel guilty for not doing my share.'

I could sense grudging approval from the other two – difficult when you've just been taking someone apart behind their back.

'I'm sorry about your brother, Miss Pritchard,' said Linda who had missed the funeral.

'Thanks. I still can't believe it. How Lily must feel I don't like to imagine.' Elin's tone implied she didn't want to talk about it further and we waited while she and Linda picked out a suitable wine. Nesta and Eirlys caught my eye.

'Do you think she heard?' mouthed Nesta, raising her eyebrows.

Eirlys shook her head and shrugged. 'It won't hurt if she did. Make her think.' But she seemed less sure of herself, her whisper barely audible against the murmur of Linda and Elin discussing prices. Our earlier conversation was beginning to appear cheap and mean-spirited.

'Is that all you'll be needing?' Linda asked as Elin took a bottle from the shelf.

'Yes, thanks. I bought most of what I wanted earlier.' Then she hesitated. 'No, there is something else,' and glanced round the shop, 'I've just come back from Chester. I meant to stop off in Denbigh but forgot. You don't have combs for holding hair in place, do you?'

Ours is an excellent village store. I could sense Linda's pride as she found what Elin wanted.

'Thank goodness,' Elin said, 'I promised to get them for Megan. I'd have had to go all the way back if you hadn't produced these.'

She added the combs to her basket and joined me at the counter. I noticed she was wearing a delicate scent and amber earrings that matched her eyes. The hands that clasped her basket and soft leather shoulder bag were well manicured and she wore only the lightest make-up. This was a far cry from the scruffy student I remembered from school. She was still attractive, I thought. And there was a light in her eyes that seemed out of keeping with her bereaved state. In fact she looked as if she was suppressing a smile. Was she laughing at us?

'It's good to see some things haven't changed,' she said, looking round. 'Hallo Mrs Evans, Mrs Jones,' she nodded at the other two and put her basket down. 'This takes me back. I spent many happy hours here as a child, waiting to get my mother's shopping while the women gossiped. It was quite entertaining in a way. What people say about others says a lot about them, don't you think?' And she gave us all a charming smile. 'If the cap fits, wear it,' her eyes said.

I busied myself packing groceries in plastic bags while the others looked at the floor, the shelves, anywhere but at Elin. I could almost hear the air crackling with their embarrassment. But Elin Pritchard, perfectly at ease, handed over the money for her wine and combs and smiled at Linda. 'Thanks for finding these. You've done a lot to the shop.' And she put the combs in her jacket pocket.

Nesta cleared her throat, fumbled with her basket and said, 'It's good to see you back, Elin. *Ers Talwm.*' I left them exchanging pleasantries and hurried outside.

I didn't go straight home. I waited on the pavement to have a quick word with Elin when she appeared. I needed to assure her of my goodwill, I suppose. I didn't know how much she had heard but I didn't want her to go away thinking I agreed with all that Nesta and Eirlys had said.

In a few minutes she joined me, her bottle of wine on one arm. 'So what are you doing now, Meryl?' She smiled. 'You said years ago that you wanted to continue your education sometime.'

'Fancy you remembering.' I was flattered.

'Oh, you made quite an impression on me.' She grinned. 'You were a dark horse, a real surprise to the rest of us. We saw you as a heroine in a way, leaving school suddenly like that to have Llinos and get married, not caring what people thought or said. I admired the way you braved the gossips and shamed them all.' She paused. 'You gave me the courage to do my own thing and not give a damn about other people's opinions.'

'I gave *you* courage?' I was surprised. If she had known

the half of what I had been through at the time, the parental recriminations – 'Throwing all that education away. We wanted you to get a decent job with prospects and now you've let us down. What will the neighbours say?' The village talk – 'I could have told you where it would end. Too serious too young, they were and left alone too much.' And, worst of all, the patronising pity – 'Poor thing. It's always the decent girls that get caught. Too innocent she was.'

There had been nothing for it but to stick two fingers up at the world and get on with it. Blowed if I was going to be cowed by their hypocritical hand-wringing. They'd all enjoyed a good gossip at my expense but I had brazened it out, refused to wear the regulation sack cloth and ashes and flaunted my expectant state round the village even before Arwyn and I had our registry office wedding.

I remembered Elin's question. 'Yes. I did go back. Years later. Arwyn left me, you know, with three young children to look after. It was tough but Mam minded the kids while I worked in a care home. Then I did a night course and an Open University degree and trained as a teacher. It's been a long haul but it was worth it, though I only work two days a week now.'

'You said you married again,' Elin prompted.

'Yes, eight years ago. Andy's a wonderful man, teaches disturbed children in Wrexham. The children think the world of him. I'm so lucky.' I smiled my happiness. 'That's why I gave up work full-time. Two of us in school every day was too much. We needed quality time together and my job was going nowhere.' I shrugged. 'So I do a lot of things in the community. Hear children read at school, help with the old people's club.' Did it sound too idyllic?

But it was true, even with our present financial pressures I was happy, had never been happier in fact.

'Wasn't it difficult adjusting?' Elin asked, 'after so long on your own?'

I thought about this carefully. 'I suppose it could have been but we're very good friends. We've both been married before, had our corners knocked off, so to speak.' I smiled to myself. 'There's something to be said for getting together at this age. You're more accepting, and more content. You don't have any illusions about human nature, don't expect too much of each other.'

'And what do the children think? Did they mind you marrying someone else after all this time?'

'They all like Andy,' I explained. 'He's a much better father to them than Arwyn is now. It's only Llinos who still keeps in touch with her Tad. And anyway, we've all got our own lives to lead. They've turned out surprisingly stable, everything considered.'

Wondering why Elin was quizzing me in such detail, I went on, 'I never expected to marry again but it's been good – like being given a second chance after all the mistakes and struggles of the past.'

'I'm glad for you,' Elin said, 'you deserve it.' She hitched her bag up on her shoulder and looked back at the shop. 'You've lived down your past, I haven't. Not in Llanfadog. It hangs round my neck here like an albatross.' Her light laugh suggested she wasn't overly concerned though I couldn't be sure.

'That's because you never came back,' I observed, without thinking. I could have bitten my tongue off when I realised what I'd said. I put my hand to my mouth, appalled.

She only laughed again. 'Don't worry. You don't last

long in my job if you haven't developed a thick skin. And mine's as thick as elephant hide. Too thick, perhaps...' She frowned, serious all of a sudden. 'I couldn't come back, you know,' she said. 'It wasn't possible. Not then. And afterwards, well…' she looked down at the hand that supported her wine bottle, 'I was working abroad.' She hesitated and I thought she was going to say more but she didn't.

I nodded, not understanding but wanting to.

For a moment I saw something different in her face. Sadness? Regret? Self-reproach perhaps? Then she shrugged. 'You were right, there's always another side.'

So she *had* heard something in the shop, but how much? I wondered briefly if she was teasing. She was hard to read under that polite, brisk, superficially good-humoured manner. What was she thinking? What did she mean?

She smiled suddenly and waved a dismissive hand. '*S'dim ots.* Don't worry. Actually I'm glad I ran into you, Meryl. You've encouraged me, and made me think. You were an example years ago, when I saw how you handled things – a challenge if you like.'

Me a challenge? 'More an "Awful Warning",' I corrected with a smile.

'Weren't we both?' Elin smiled as she unlocked her parked car. 'What's more,' she nodded towards the shop, 'I think I still am. Wouldn't you agree?'

Huw

'I like your aunt,' I said to Meg as we got out of the Land Rover the afternoon after my brother's eighteenth birthday party. 'There's more to her than you think. She was really interested in search dog training when we talked yesterday. You didn't mind me saying she could come and watch, did you?'

'Not so long as we have time to ourselves after.' Meg brushed the hair from her eyes and scanned the moorland that stretched as far as the eye could see. 'She's a puzzle, Aunt Elin. Some days I think I'm getting to know her then the next day it's as though the day before never happened. We had a really good time looking at family photographs the other evening and she was brilliant, showing me how to do my hair. But between times she's been rushing around, going out visiting, acting like we're a hotel. I can't make her out.'

'Perhaps that's how she copes with missing your Dad,' I suggested.

'Maybe,' Meg said with a frown, 'but she's going home tomorrow and the way things are she might not visit again. I don't want that. She's like the last link with Dad when he was young and...' she trailed off and I put my arm round her while she wept a tear or two into my anorak.

Meg returned my hug. 'I wish you didn't have to go back tonight, Huw. I've missed you awfully with Dad's funeral and everything. It's not going to be easy at home. Even with the tension around Aunt Elin we've had to keep our spirits up because we hardly know her. We're going to feel the loss of him horribly once we're back in our ordinary routine.'

'You can ring or text any time,' I promised. 'You know my timetable.' She nodded and I kissed the tears from her cheeks. I loved her even more now she was sad. Her need made me feel protective. Her father's death had been a terrible shock, coming out of the blue just as she was about to sit her AS exams. And our summer plans were in the melting pot too. Not that this seemed important after what had happened. But we'd planned to have a month in Ireland together. Would Megan want to leave her mother so soon?

She raised her head from my chest and looked down the road. 'Here she is. I'd recognise my old green jacket anywhere. At least she was tactful enough not to accept your offer of a lift.'

'As I said, there's more to your aunt than you think.'

Megan detached herself. 'We'd better behave while she's with us.'

'She's not the thought police,' I replied. 'She seemed quite open-minded when we were talking last night.'

'You two got on so well, I should be jealous.' But Megan grinned.

'She's too old for me.' I grinned back. 'And who wants a middle-aged maiden aunt when I can have you. Even if she is a legal high-flier earning pots of money.'

'Aunt Elin a maiden aunt?' Meg giggled. 'That doesn't fit her at all. Anyway she's got a boyfriend or whatever you have at her age.'

'There was this Ben she mentioned.'

'That's him.' Megan looked thoughtful. 'She had lunch

with him yesterday. She's been in an odd mood ever since.'

'A lovers' tiff?' I teased.

She frowned. 'I don't think it's like that, though I don't know. She must stay with him a lot. When she borrowed my coat and boots she said all her unsmart stuff was at his place. Perhaps he's a secret partner and they haven't got married for tax reasons.'

'They don't have to be married,' I said. 'But if he's a proper farmer he'll want to stay where he is. It makes sense for her to visit him rather than the other way round – *and* leave her scruffy clothes there.' I was amused at the amount of energy Meg can put into speculating. I take people as I find them.

Meg looked annoyed. 'A farmer? How come you get to know these things and I don't?'

'My natural charm. Women confide in me.' I dodged the expected playful punch but Meg only frowned. 'I suppose it's that we hardly know her, except for what Dad told us. And he never said much except about her degree and job and stuff. It's like there's a whole area of her life – and our family history – that we don't know. They phoned each other often enough but he never told us what they said.' Her eyes widened, 'Anyway, what *did* you talk about while you were waiting for me last night?'

'Oh, this and that…' I grinned. I'd roused her at last. She came for me and tried to push me into a drainage ditch – a mistake because I'm too strong for her and we ended up wrestling on the edge. 'Aunt Elin'll think we're having a row,' Megan said. So we leant on the Land Rover bonnet and watched Aunt Elin walk towards us. Inside Teg whined and pawed the windows, eager to be let out.

'So what *did* you talk about?' Meg persisted.

'Oh, how clever you are, how pretty you looked with your hair up and what a stunning outfit you were wearing,' I said airily. 'Things like that.'

Meg tossed her head and sniffed and I was struck by the similarity between her and her long-lost London aunt. They weren't alike at first glance but they had the same mannerisms. Strange considering they'd never met till last week. And they were both equally persuasive. How *had* Aunt Elin managed to wangle the invitation to come dog training this afternoon? They must both possess the same 'get my own way' gene.

I stared at the figure in the green waterproof jacket striding up the road and remembered our meeting the day before.

'You must be Huw.' The woman at the door had looked familiar though we'd never met. Then I realised her smile was like Megan's father's though she wasn't like him, apart from the freckles.

'Come in.' She waved a wooden spoon she was holding to indicate the hall. 'Megan's getting ready, Lily's having a rest, God knows where Bryn is.' And she wiped her hand on her apron before offering it for me to shake. 'I'm Elin Pritchard, Megan's aunt. Pleased to meet you.'

I was taken aback at first. I'd been psyching myself up to meet the family after their bereavement and had my condolence speech all prepared. Then here was this chatty woman in trousers and apron with floury hands welcoming me in a posh English accent and the family nowhere to be seen. It seemed surreal.

But it made things easier. I'd been apprehensive about

going to the Pritchards' for the first time after what happened, wondering what to say, wanting to get it right. You don't expect people like Megan's Dad to drop dead suddenly. And he'd been a friend, someone I'd been growing to like and respect. I didn't dare think how they all felt. It was less awkward with a stranger, especially as she did all the talking.

'Sorry we had to meet at such a sad time,' she said. 'It'll do Megan good to have an evening out. It's been a beastly week for them all.'

I'm not usually sensitive to atmosphere but I could feel the sadness in the house. 'Yes. I'm very sorry. I can't believe it. He was joking last time I saw him. I never dreamt...' My voice tailed off. Looking at her face I realised that under her cheerful talk Megan's aunt was feeling it too but didn't want to discuss it. I was glad of that – it removed the awkwardness.

She offered me coffee. 'You can have it in the sitting room or keep me company in the kitchen. Either way I won't mind. There's a *Daily Post* somewhere. Megan's deciding what to wear.' This remark was accompanied by a raised eyebrow and an amused smile.

'I'll need the coffee then,' I said and we laughed. I decided I liked this aunt.

I sat at the kitchen table while Megan's Aunt Elin made supper. 'At least Meg's escaped my Bolognese. Saved herself untold miseries, I expect,' she said, stirring something at the stove.

Her throwaway humour helped me relax. I scanned the sports pages while she watched the pan and sipped red wine from a glass on the work surface by the cooker. Seeing my look, she said, 'I'd offer you some but you're driving,' and twirled the glass by its stem appraising the contents with a critical eye. 'It's only cooking quality but I need something to keep me going. I don't drink much generally, but I've a lot on my mind.'

Was she making excuses? She didn't look like an alcoholic but you can't tell. She poked at her cooking then sat opposite, her chair at right-angles to the table so she could watch what was happening on the stove. Suddenly she looked at me and asked, 'What's this I hear about training search dogs? You must tell me how you do it.'

I was floored at first. I'd been reading the obituary for Welsh rugby and was engrossed in dismal predictions about the team's future. Then I connected with her question. 'Yes. I've got a young dog who's at the second stage of grading. Megan's my dogsbody.'

I waited for the usual reaction but didn't get it. Instead she grinned, 'I bet you enjoy telling people that,' and laughed aloud. 'I presume that means she plays the part of missing person.'

'Spot on, but it makes a good conversation starter,' I replied and we both laughed. Then I told her how search dogs are trained, how we start with puppies and bring them on, how you have to be a fully qualified member of a Mountain Rescue Team before you can have a dog. 'We qualify for lowland searches and then mountain searches in my team,' I explained, 'because of the different conditions and terrain.'

She listened intently, putting in a question here and there, and said that even after trekking in the Himalayas she preferred the mountains of North Wales of all the mountains she'd seen. I described Teg and how I'd had her from a pup, how she'd passed grade one, and how we taught the search and find sequence first with people going off with the dog's toys, then with people only. I described how 'bodies' lie on the hills in bivvy bags on training weekends so the dogs can find them – often for hours in all sorts of weather. I was in my element. I forgot I was talking to Megan's aunt, a lawyer from London, even forgot Meg's dad had died. It was great to share my love of dogs and mountains with someone who'd never heard of SARDA and its work.

'My friend keeps gun dogs on his farm,' she said when I had finished. And we discussed the relative merits of labradors, collies, spaniels and retrievers as working dogs and particularly in search and rescue.

'You'd love Teg,' I said, 'she's my smooth-haired collie. You could see her tomorrow afternoon if you're here when I call for Meg. We're going training on the moors.'

'I'd love to watch,' she said and before I knew it I'd invited her along.

'Thanks, I'd enjoy that. I must ask Ben if he knows about the work. He'd be interested, I'm sure.'

We went on to chat about other things, my plans to do research after my degree, the Welsh Assembly and student loans, even rugby. She was easy to talk to, letting me rattle on about my likes and dislikes and pet theories. She let me taste her Bolognese, which was nowhere near as bad as she'd led me to imagine – it was quite good in fact – and was incredibly disorganised about the kitchen. 'Look at me, I can organise training courses and oversee complicated cases but I can't even cook a simple meal.'

I thought her charming but a tad eccentric. She polished off two glasses of wine while I was there, assuring me she only usually stuck to one. We talked a bit about nationalism and the effects of foot-and-mouth. Then we swapped experiences of Aberystwyth. A friend of hers had lectured there, she said, but she admitted she'd turned her back on Wales for the bright lights of London. 'For someone brought up in a village like Llanfadog the whole atmosphere, the culture, the pubs, the folk clubs and the simmering political scene was a different world,' she explained. 'I was captivated by it, by the ferment of change and new ideas. I could never see myself coming back here after that.' She sighed then and pushed her empty wine glass away. 'But I'm wondering now if cities aren't places for young people rather than for those of us who are getting on. But could I retire to the country? I don't know. There's not a lot of buzz in the rural scene unless you make it yourself. Maybe I should jolly it up a bit, organise steeplechases for Friesians or start the second peasants' revolt.'

She could switch from flippant to thoughtful in the blink of an eye and I wasn't sure when to take her seriously. But I liked her. She was unexpected and different and her joking reminded me, painfully, of Megan's dad.

And here she was, come to view Teg's progress, looking very different in Meg's old coat and wellingtons. I was keen to show Teg off, proud of the way she was shaping. This would give Aunt Elin something to tell her gundog-owning friend, I thought.

Teg was on brilliant form. She 'found' four times with no problems, even with the distraction of a stranger watching and a group of crows flying overhead, landing and taking off again in her line of scent, and startling a couple of stray sheep in the process.

Meg's aunt was impressed as I'd hoped she would be.

She didn't chatter or get in the way, just stood at a distance and watched quietly, one hand in her pocket, one holding her cigarette. I was surprised to see she smoked. Maybe it was something hard-pressed city lawyers were driven to.

'I think she's glad to be out of doors,' Meg whispered between searches. 'She can smoke here for a start. Things aren't that easy between her and Mum, though it's better now than it was at the beginning of the week. I'm surprised she doesn't look out of place – you should see her best clothes – but I suppose she did have a rural upbringing. She used to shoot, Bryn said.'

We worked for ten minutes more then called Teg in and made a fuss of her. Aunt Elin came over then. 'She's a lovely dog,' she agreed, patting Teg. 'Thanks for the demonstration. And how does one get to be a body?' Her eyes were laughing. 'Maybe it could be my next career. Curling up undisturbed in the heather, with a good book, looks quite attractive from here. On a good day of course…'

'People volunteer,' I said.

'And is there an age limit?'

I'd never thought of that. 'Maybe lying outdoors on a cold day wouldn't appeal to the elderly. You have to be fit. No good getting pneumonia, even in a good cause.'

'I assume you don't get paid but there must be perks. Do search dogs carry flasks of brandy?' I saw she was teasing but pointed out that 'dogsbodies' did it for love.

'Like Megan,' she said with a smile.

Meg and I usually go for a walk after training. We looked at each other, wondering what to do about the aunt. But she solved our dilemma for us. 'Your Dad and I used to come up here as children,' she remarked to Megan, looking round. 'There's a place where this stream goes down to the valley where we used to hide out and make a camp. I wonder if I can find it.'

Meg was surprised. 'Do you mean Nain and Taid let you come up here on your own?'

'Not exactly.' Aunt Elin grinned. 'But we used to take ourselves off for the day when…your Nain wasn't feeling well. We never came to any harm. Children were much freer then.' She glanced at the sky. 'I'll wander off and take a look, if that's all right with you. I'll see you back at the house.'

I opened my mouth to say, 'Fine,' but Meg butted in. 'Dad never showed us. Can I come and see?' I looked at her questioningly but her eyes held mine and I saw she was determined to go. This was obviously something she needed to do because of her Dad.

She took my hand, 'You don't mind?'

'Not if it's important.' But I hoped it wouldn't take long. We weren't going to be able to meet again for a week or two because of exams.

'Come if you like.' Aunt Elin sounded non-committal and I couldn't make up my mind if she wanted us with her or not. She didn't bother to wait, anyway. She was already striding down the path while we were deciding and she didn't look back.

I took Megan's hand, called Teg, and we followed, though Teg didn't stay with us for long. Eager to follow new smells, she was soon bounding ahead of Megan's aunt, leaping from tussock to tussock, rock to rock as the downhill gradient steepened towards the stream's narrow gully.

Limestone, I noticed, looking at the rocky outcrops

below, and tried to remember from my geological map what sort it was. Carboniferous of course but was it Tournesian or Visean? The going got rougher and more slippery as we descended. This was no problem to Teg, but Meg needed help in places and I saw her aunt taking care in her rubber boots. For a city dweller she was pretty agile, slim and wiry, built like a whippet. I wondered what she did to keep fit. Smoking didn't seem to affect her speed. She'd discarded her cigarette before we started, I'd noticed, grinding the dog end under the heel of her boot at the road's edge.

'I've never been here,' muttered Meg beside me. 'Fancy Dad not showing us.'

'I expect he was busy,' I said, 'and didn't you go to the beach when he was free?'

'Mum doesn't like country walks,' she added, 'I guess I spent more time around the house or with friends in the village than walking the hills.'

Meg's aunt stopped suddenly and scanned the rocks which overhung the stream on the far side. She was below us now, standing where the fall of the stream leveled out into a succession of pools, overhung by spindly rowans. She was looking at the stream, perhaps gauging where it was best to cross.

'Is that it?' called Meg, and she let go of my hand and jumped down to join her.

'I think so.' Aunt Elin frowned. 'It's hard to tell, the trees have grown so high, but it looks like it. See that cleft in the rocks on the other bank? I believe that's where we used to go. We crossed just here I think, paddling in our bare feet or wellington boots.'

'I'll look.' Meg crossed the stream using rocks as stepping stones, her aunt waded through the water to join her and

I stayed where I was. Teg ran back and forth splashing us till I called her to heel. I didn't want her pushing the others into the stream in her eagerness to join what she thought was a game.

'This is mad,' Megan's aunt said, edging along the strip of grass between the cliff and the stream, one hand grasping the rock face. 'I ought to have better things to do than risking my neck looking for the past.' But you could see she wasn't going to give up. Slimmer than Megan she managed the traverse easily, arriving without much trouble at the cleft.

I watched from my seat on a rock, Teg panting beside me, aware that the moment belonged to Megan and her aunt. Did I mind? Not so long as Meg and I had time together before we had to go our separate ways.

'I forgot we were smaller then.' Aunt Elin's voice carried clearly across the soft burble of the stream and echoed off the limestone outcrop. She craned her neck to see into the wedge-shaped hollow. 'Yes, this is it. I remember the vein of black on the far wall.' You'd think she'd found gold the way she spoke.

'God, did I manage to sit in here once?' she exclaimed, 'I must have been much thinner then – or a lot more flexible.' She rubbed her shoulder where she had caught it on a jutting rock.

'So this is it.' Meg followed, swift and surefooted. She stood beside her aunt and bent her head to look in. 'It's awfully stony. Did you sit on the bare ground?'

Aunt Elin shook her head. 'No, we brought coats.' She laughed. 'To think I suggested sleeping here overnight. What ideas children have. But we'd stay whole days in the holidays. When it was fine, of course. The stream was impossible in very wet weather.'

Meg looked at her, eyes wide, 'Couldn't you have got swept away if it rained suddenly? And fancy being here all day. They'd send out search parties now, thinking you'd been abducted. Didn't Nain and Taid wonder where you were?'

'They'd be sending search *dogs*.' Aunt Elin turned to grin at me. 'No. As I said, children were freer then. We'd take sandwiches and a bottle of made-up squash – or drink from the stream. Mam knew we'd be back when we were hungry.' She smiled and looked around, her hands in the pockets of Meg's old coat.

'What did you do all day?' Megan's voice was eager.

'Oh...played games. We had good imaginations. We were outlaws or red Indians, Twm Sion Cati, Robin Hood, soldiers of Owain Glyndwr, explorers, children escaping wicked stepmothers. You know the sort of thing.' Aunt Elin laughed. 'Gareth liked playing schools and chapels, but I wasn't so keen on that. Sitting on a rock listening to your brother parroting what he'd heard in church wasn't my idea of fun. He could imitate a sermon beautifully though, just the right amount of *hwyl*. He used to wave his finger and berate me for my sins but I used to heckle and answer back. His congregation rebelled once and pushed him off his perch.' She laughed. 'I always told him he should have a regular pitch in Hyde Park.' She pointed to a flat rock on the opposite bank. 'That's where he used to stand.'

I could see all this was music to Meg's ears. She listened intently, head on one side, drinking in her aunt's words, then bent again and peered further into the cleft. 'You two must have been small if you could both get in here at once.'

'We couldn't. We had to take it in turns.' Aunt Elin gazed downhill to where the stream dropped steeply again, its narrow gully turning into a miniature gorge with sheer ten foot cliffs on one side. 'It's quite spectacular even now,' she remarked. 'No wonder we thought it a magical place when we were children.'

'How did you find it?' Meg asked, standing straight again and looking about her.

'Accident, I think.' Her aunt paused, reached in her pocket for cigarettes and lighter and lit up. 'We must have wandered upstream exploring in the school holidays. Of course, we claimed it as ours then. We each made a solemn promise that we wouldn't bring anyone else here without the other's permission.' She went quiet as if remembering.

'And did you?' Meg asked. 'Bring anyone else, I mean?'

'Only a school friend, later on. We scratched our names.'

'Where?' Meg bent down to scrutinise the rock face.

'Inside, I think.' Her aunt blew a smoke ring and watched it disappear.

Megan crawled into the cleft then cried out excitedly, her voice sounding muffled and echoey, 'Yes, there's something here. EP JM 19...is it 63 or 65? I can't make it out.'

'63, I expect,' her aunt said, drawing on her cigarette. 'That's us. JM is Jenny, the friend I saw on Friday. I brought her here once when we were teenagers. But she wasn't so keen on roughing it as I was. I came on my own after that, it was a good place to think.'

'You came later on?' Megan asked, surprised. 'When was that? Didn't Nain worry about you going off on your own?' She was like a search dog on a scent. And when her aunt didn't answer she went on, 'I can't imagine Mum letting me take off on my own without knowing where I was.' She sounded envious.

Aunt Elin shrugged. 'I never told her.' Her tone was throwaway, careless as if it didn't matter, as though the idea of telling her mother had never entered her head. 'Well, there you are,' she said, 'the Pritchards' secret hiding place. I'm glad I was able to find it after all these years.'

Megan crawled back out of the cleft and stood up, brushing specks from her hair and jacket.

'We vowed we'd come back here when we were older,' Aunt Elin went on, 'when I'd travelled the world and Gareth had made his millions.' She laughed. 'Gareth loved getting us to make solemn promises – I'm surprised he never became a lawyer. We promised we'd bring our children and grandchildren here to show them where we'd played as kids and each took a pebble from the stream to remind us of what we'd said. Goodness knows what I did with mine.' She shrugged and blew another smoke ring. 'Fancy remembering all this. I'd forgotten till just now.'

For a moment the two stood looking at the little half-cave, still and attentive, the way people stand at war memorials for Remembrance Day. I guessed Meg was thinking of her Dad.

'Well. I've shown *you* at least.' Aunt Elin gave Megan a brief smile, then added, her voice brisk, 'Better be going. We can't stand here all day.' With a sudden, deft movement she stubbed out her cigarette on the rock face, put the butt in her pocket and began to retrace her steps along the bank.

I could tell from the way Meg was standing that she wanted to stay longer. Knowing her, she had more questions to ask, more of Aunt Elin's memories she wanted to tease out. But her aunt was already stepping into the stream.

Meg watched her cross it, disappointment in her face.

As she reached the near bank, Aunt Elin bent down and put her hand in the water. She stopped to pat Teg before straightening up and as she did so slipped something in her pocket. I caught her eye and she looked away. I don't think she wanted me to see.

'I'm meeting Elfed at half four,' she said, looking at her watch, 'so I'll push on. Lily will be wondering where I am. We don't want her laying on a search.' She nodded at Megan, 'Now *there's* someone who likes to know where people are. You've got a good mother, Megan.'

Meg gave a weak smile in acknowledgement.

'See you later, then.' Aunt Elin lifted her hand then set off downhill at a cracking pace considering the terrain.

She didn't look back. I watched till she disappeared from view, surprised at her surefootedness. Then I remembered she'd been trekking in the Himalayas, no doubt that was good training.

Meg waited till her aunt was out of earshot then leaned against the cliff and put her head in her hands. Teg and I were with her in a flash, Teg jumping up to lick her hands, myself with a comforting arm.

'Did you see that?' Meg asked through tears. 'How she backed off? She does that whenever we get close. It's like she shares something of herself then pulls away. It's so upsetting.'

'She told you a lot,' I reasoned, 'and she did have an appointment to keep.'

'But I feel as if I'm just beginning to know her properly, learning more about her – and Dad – and then I lose her again.' Meg was unconvinced.

'She's maybe not the sort to dwell on things or look

back.'

'But she was the one who wanted to find this place. She was full of it, remember? And then she stopped remembering and clammed up. What did I do? Was it something I said?'

'I expect she's had enough.' I pulled Megan across the stream. 'She's lost a brother after all. She's probably as sad as you are in her way.'

'We're all sad, for God's sake. She is, I know. I can feel it sometimes through all the joking and stuff. It's nothing to be ashamed of. Why doesn't she have a bloody good cry like the rest of us? We might feel closer, then, get to know her better. It's as if she doesn't admit to any feelings. Not most of the time anyway.'

I said nothing. I thought Meg was being over-sensitive and a tad unreasonable. Understandable in the circumstances for her to feel dumped but I didn't think her aunt meant it personally. Meg and her Mum are touchy-feely people, warm and open-hearted. They would have hugged each other and cried back there. From what I'd seen Aunt Elin wasn't from the same mould.

I remembered my first find in mountain rescue. We'd spent hours on a raw, autumn morning searching for a missing person in Clocaenog forest. Then when we located him he was angry at being found. He'd gone off to commit suicide and we'd stopped him. His reaction was unexpected. I'd been disappointed, had thought him ungrateful, but the other team members took it in good part. They taught me to accept things as they come, to accept people as they are, no judgements, no expectations.

Was Megan feeling as I had done then? She had found her long-lost aunt but her aunt wasn't behaving as she wanted. Maybe she had to learn the same lesson.

'You can't alter how she is, but you can cry if you like,' I teased. 'Then I can have the pleasure of cheering you up.'

Megan laughed and buried her face in my chest. 'Good old Huw. Where would I be without you?'

We started back. Then I remembered something. 'Did you see what your Aunt Elin did back there?' I asked.

Megan shook her head. 'No, what?'

'She took away a pebble from the stream.'

'Really?' Meg raised her eyebrows. 'Like she and Dad did years ago to remind them of their promises.'

'I think she was embarrassed when she knew I'd seen her.'

Meg broke into a smile. 'But that's the sort of thing I'd do.'

'Didn't I say there's more to her than you think?' And, linking arms, we walked up the hill to the Land Rover, Teg racing ahead as usual.

Lynne, the Vicar

'*The Parochial Church Council will be hell on Thursday evening,*' a cutting from a parish magazine pinned on the vestry notice board, a legacy of Gareth's, along with an extract from the litany:

From all envy, wickedness and alice
and all evil intent, Good Lord deliver us

and a misprint from my own Family Service leaflet,

Our God resigns.

Bittersweet reminders of my late Treasurer's eye for a joke… How I would miss him, his talent for laughter and making light of things. I was afraid Tuesday's PCC with its discussion of urgent repairs to the church roof really would be 'hell' without him.

I thumbed through the Treasurer's folder, delivered the day before by his sister, Elin. She wasn't the easiest of guests, I gathered from Lily when I met her in the village shop. 'Elin's so restless, Lynne. She's helping with the will so I mustn't grumble but we don't find it easy to get along. We hardly know one another.'

Elin had appeared cold and distant at the funeral but yesterday she arrived at the vicarage running up the garden path to deliver the things I'd sent for, looking altogether more approachable in casual jacket and cords.

'You phoned for these.' She handed me the folder with a quick smile while Moses, my large, black, neutered tom wound his body round her legs in an effort to ingratiate himself.

'Thanks. You needn't have driven down 'specially.' I had seen her car parked at the gate.

'No trouble. I was going out anyway.' She bent to stroke Moses who flirted with her, arching his back, a sucker for attention. 'A Magnificat.' Elin Pritchard grinned.

'You sound like your brother.'

She straightened up. 'Joking kept us sane.' She seemed reluctant to go so I waited to see if she had anything else to say while Moses, his mind on a meal, slipped between us, indoors.

'Might I see you briefly?' she asked. 'Not now. Before I go back sometime.'

She was due to leave on Monday, I knew. Not much choice then.

'Tomorrow evening,' I suggested, feeling virtuous. I try to keep Sunday evenings for unwinding after a four-service day. 'Come for coffee after church.'

'Thank you.' Watching her go I thought how unlike Gareth she was with her slim build and English accent, and reminded myself, in case I was tempted to feel put upon, that I had intended to have a word with her before she left. She and Gareth had been close, I gathered, both from his brotherly pride – *Elin's the clever one of the family. Done really well for herself she has* – and from Lily – *she rings him every week almost, even from abroad. I can't think what they can find to say to each other with only seven days between calls.*

I began to arrange the vestry for Tuesday. Gareth would

have done it if he'd been here – he'd always gone the extra mile. What were we going to do without him?

As I shifted chairs I recalled my first visit...

I'd arrrived at Llanfadog on a covert fact finding mission after seeing the parish advertised in *Church Times*. Taking a detour home from climbing in Snowdonia, I was perfectly dressed for the role of undercover agent, no dog collar, walking gear, birdwatching glasses. No one could have guessed I was a potential vicar. But I had reckoned without Gareth.

He was sweeping bird droppings from the porch, a stocky, middle-aged man singing softly to himself in Welsh.

'It's not locked, *cariad*.' With a beaming smile, he swung open the heavy oak door for me to enter, then followed at a respectful distance as I sauntered into the church, spiritual antennae alert. 'Been here before?' he asked as I stood to breathe in the scent of wood polish, the smell of old books and the special atmosphere loved churches possess.

I shook my head. 'I'm on holiday. I come to Wales a lot but I've never been here.' I ran my finger across the service books on their shelves. I'd forgotten the Church in Wales had its own prayer book. I picked up a copy to look inside.

'Thinking of coming?' he asked.

I nearly dropped the book and he burst out laughing. 'Don't worry, I won't let on, but I can usually tell. It's the way people try to look as if they're not looking.'

He was the local joiner and undertaker, he said, as well as churchwarden. We had a conversation about the village and its people. His love of both showed in every word.

'Will you come, then?' he asked, as I made to leave.

'Depends what God wants,' I smiled. 'And the bishop.'

'I understand.' He winked. 'I'll take it up with the Boss.' He nodded heavenwards, then picked up his brush once more. 'We're not particular about women priests,' he called, as I walked down the path. What a nice man; I fell in love with him and the place. I couldn't think of a better first parish.

Before my induction, I met him officially.

'I knew you'd come,' he smiled. 'I've prayed for you every day since we met.'

That was six years ago. Since then we'd become firm friends. There was little Gareth didn't know about Llanfadog and its people. Though he might sigh when individuals refused to speak after a falling-out, or groan with impatience if the PCC tried to backtrack on decisions, he never had an unkind word for anyone. I could always count on his support – and his honest opinion. He wasn't above telling me if he thought I'd done something wrong, but I knew I could trust him, that everything he said and did sprang from a desire for everyone's good, including my own. I couldn't have wished for a better teacher as I struggled to learn Welsh and negotiated my way round the pitfalls of running a rural parish.

'A grave business, being an undertaker,' he said once, his blue eyes twinkling. But he was good at it, kind, courteous and sensitive. And after years as churchwarden he had become an able and reliable treasurer. He and Lily had looked after Gareth's ageing parents, I gathered, moving in with them for his father's last clouded years, a byword in the village for devotion and caring. Unlike Elin… *She never visited them. Never even came to their funerals*, local gossip went. A serious crime in Welsh eyes.

'She was abroad,' Gareth defended.

'Even so, you'd have though she'd have got leave.' Lily sounded hurt as well as critical.

I wondered how brother and sister had come to be so different.

Leaving the chairs neatly arranged, I thought of Tuesday's meeting with misgivings. Gareth's death had not only left me to bear the brunt of the financial questions that were bound to be asked, but cast doubt over my own plans. A month earlier a friend in a hospital chaplaincy team in the Midlands had approached me about applying for a vacancy there. 'You've done long enough in a parish, Lynne. Your experience and pastoral gifts would be useful to us and I can vouch for you as a colleague. Why not apply?' So after much thought, and a confidential consultation with Gareth, who could be trusted not to say a word to anyone, even Lily, I had gone ahead. The interview had been the Wednesday after Gareth died. I'd considered not going. But John, my friend, had persuaded me and I had just received a letter offering me the position. Now I had to make up my mind whether to accept.

At first I reacted by trying to forget the whole thing; it seemed unreal. Still in shock after Gareth's death I felt I'd interviewed badly and had given up all idea of getting the post. I wasn't sure I wanted it anyway. Now I was thrown into confusion. Did I wish to leave Llanfadog with the church roof in serious need of repair and the village and congregation mourning one of its favourite sons? Would it be right to abandon Lily and the family in their grief?

And where was God in this, especially when Gareth

had said I ought to apply since I had gifts that weren't being used in Llanfadog? 'I'll be sad for you to leave. But you've got a lot more to give than you're using here. Don't let us hold you back. Six years is long enough in a first parish.' God must have known what was going to happen to Gareth, so why hadn't he made me feel uneasy about attending the interview if I wasn't meant to move?

'Don't be silly,' I told myself that morning before church, as I re-read the letter with its offer. 'This is what free will is all about. You can't expect voices from heaven all the time.' I'd have liked some guidance, though. A fat cheque for the roof repair for a start, like those I read about in those Christian paperbacks with a miracle on every page. But when I prayed heaven seemed silent. Which wasn't surprising. I suspected I was angry at Gareth's death, at his removal from parish and family at such a strategic time.

I picked up the treasurer's folder and glanced at my watch. I ought to be home for Elin's arrival. As I locked the church I wondered what she wanted to see me about. Not spiritual guidance, surely? She wasn't a regular churchgoer, I assumed. Sitting with Lily, Bryn and Megan in the front pew reserved for the bereaved family that morning, she'd seemed unfamiliar with the service and hadn't taken communion, though she came to the rail for a blessing. Praying along the row I'd been aware of tension in her clasped hands, of Megan's tears, Lily's self-control and Bryn's numbness. I'd felt a love for the family and congregation and thought, 'I can't leave them now with all this going on. Surely, God, this isn't what you want?' But I received no answer, only a sense that if I put one foot in front of the other I would find the right path.

Maybe Elin wanted to talk about her brother. I would

enjoy that; it would be good to find out more about my friend from one who'd known him well. And meeting her didn't seem such an intimidating prospect as I'd imagined from her appearance at the funeral. She seemed quite human on the doorstep the day before. 'You two would get on,' Gareth said once, 'two professional women in a man's world.' I'd reserved judgement, thinking of Lily's reticence and village gossip. Now I could see for myself if Gareth was right.

Walking across the churchyard I felt in my cassock pocket and found the card given me by the young man I'd talked with after Gareth's funeral. He'd called Gareth 'Uncle' but was diffident about being seen or approached. Had Elin Pritchard noticed him, I wondered. I had my own idea who Stephen Loxley was. He looked so like Gareth I was sure he was related and after I'd spoken to him I was almost certain he must be Elin's son. Gareth hadn't wanted him to meet the family, he said. Yet in giving me his address he seemed to be hinting that he would like to be contacted if things changed. At that moment I couldn't see how he might make himself known to them without causing upset. But his grief and isolation had affected me. *God sets the solitary in families* ... I found myself quoting from Psalm 68. I wasn't sure Stephen Loxley was solitary. He might have a wife and children for all I knew. But he had lost his adoptive parents and Gareth who, in some measure, had taken their place, and I felt he needed roots and a sense of belonging. I prayed for him and the family as I closed the churchyard gate.

The phone was ringing as I reached the vicarage. I ran to answer it but failed to get there in time. Dialling 1471, I found it was John's number and decided to ring him back later. He would be bound to ask if I'd written my letter of acceptance and I didn't feel like being hustled. I went to close the front door and saw Elin Pritchard walking up the path.

'Am I too early? I wasn't sure exactly when "after church" was.'

'No. We finished Evensong twenty minutes ago. Come in.' I took off my cassock and hung it in the study. 'Would you like tea or coffee?'

'Coffee. Black, no sugar, thanks.' She waited in the hall, looking at my pictures and I felt suddenly flustered beside her obvious poise and grooming. Grow up, I told myself, she's only a human being. Remember she's the sister of a friend. And you're just as much a professional as she is, even if *vicars* can't afford Jaeger trouser suits.

'Is that Anglesey?' She paused before an original oil, my favourite.

'Yes. Red Wharf Bay.'

'It gets the atmosphere perfectly. I had a friend in Bangor once and he and I used to walk that beach often. I remember crunching over hundreds of washed-up sea potatoes after a winter storm.' She moved closer to read the signature. 'I ought to have something to remind me of Wales. A painting might be just the thing.'

'Not thinking of coming back to live?'

She shook her head. 'I don't think so. I'd die of boredom. Too used to city life.' She paused. 'Though what I'll do in retirement's another matter. Or before, come to that. Lots of imponderables. Decisions to make.'

She sounded as uncertain as I was. That was encouraging. People who had everything taped could be infuriating when you yourself were in a fog. 'Come through,' I said.

Jaeger trouser suit or not, I decided I could let her see my kitchen.

'Did you enjoy being brought up in Llanfadog?' I asked as I put my best china mugs on a tray. 'A country childhood and all that?'

She leant against one of the kitchen units, her back to the window. 'Oh yes. Outside was fun. We ran wild and had a wonderful time. Climbing trees, damming streams, making dens. But those things lose their attraction as you get older, don't you think?' She was smiling at me, amusement in her light hazel eyes – they were unusual, the colour of amber or topaz, not like Gareth's at all. 'Indoors wasn't exactly a barrel of laughs, though,' she added. A throwaway line but the edge to her voice was unmistakable. She twisted to look out of the window. 'Don't you get a lovely view of the church from here? I've never seen it from this angle before.'

'Yes. It's best in the morning.' I eyed her curiously, aware of communication on two levels and hidden shoals. She wasn't like Gareth with his gentle simplicity. I could see why Lily found her difficult.

She saw the look. 'Sorry. I'm trying not to be negative. No one warns you that grief can turn bitter if you're not careful. I suppose I'm cross with myself for not coming back and seeing Gareth and the family earlier.' She smiled sadly. 'My own fault. You think you have all the time in the world and suddenly it's gone. I've been too immersed in my own career.'

'Don't let it eat into you,' I warned, 'it doesn't lead anywhere. Gareth never criticised you for not coming. He was proud of you, always singing your praises.'

'I know.' She sighed and I saw the suspicion of a tear

in her eye. 'He could never get over my success. As if that mattered. He was a much better person than I'll ever be.' She fiddled with the silk scarf at her neck.

'Shall we go into the sitting room?' I poured her black coffee and my white one and picked up the tray.

'Yes, fine. Thanks for seeing me at such short notice by the way. I won't insult you by saying it's your busy day. But I see from the notice board that you've taken four services.'

Someone who reads notice boards, I thought, leading the way. But she was a lawyer. 'I wanted to see you before you go back anyway. We didn't get a chance to talk on Monday.'

I sat in my favourite leather-covered chair and Elin Pritchard sat on the settee opposite the big picture window. Outside on the lawn blackbirds were listening for worms and I could hear the swifts screaming round the church tower in their usual frenzy of feeding before nightfall. We sipped our coffee in silence while I wondered what she had come for and searched her face, discreetly I hoped, for any resemblance to Gareth. Apart from the red hair and freckles they were not alike in appearance. Even Elin's red hair was a different shade of red, enhanced, I assumed. She was thin-faced and not unattractive, with those startling hazel eyes. Gareth had been broad-featured with wide-set eyes and a ready smile. Yet there was an echo of Gareth in the way his sister carried her head, in her profile, laugh and sense of humour.

She was watching the birds on the lawn and seemed in no hurry to get to the point. Suddenly she turned to me. 'So, what's it like for a woman in your line of work? I've always wanted to know.'

For a moment I felt like an exam candidate, asked a

difficult question in a *viva*. 'Oh, not bad.' I gathered my thoughts. 'People are getting used to us. There's the occasional person who won't receive communion from a woman, but we're becoming accepted. In fact I think there are more women candidates coming forward in some places than men.'

'That's progress.' She leaned forward. 'But what do you do? When someone won't take communion from you?'

'Move on. Pray for them. Try not to take it personally.'

She made a face. 'I'd be tempted to bless them with a heavy hand.'

'Not very Christ-like.' I grinned, picturing it.

'Ah, but then I'm not a Christian.'

'So you wouldn't be in my position, I hope.'

'No.' We laughed. 'But what about women bishops?' she asked. 'Is there a *stained glass* ceiling?'

'Yes. It has to be passed by Synod before I can be Archbishop of Canterbury.'

'I *mitre* known.'

'I'll *cope*.'

'So long as you're not *surplice* to requirements.' She covered her face with her hands. 'Sorry. A bad *habit*.' She looked serious then. 'I supported you, you know. I was a member of MOW, but I missed hearing the big debate. I was abroad.'

'The Church in Wales waited even longer to ordain women priests,' I pointed out, 'but that earlier debate was quite an occasion. I was in theological college at the time and the atmosphere was electric.'

'I can imagine.' She paused for a moment. 'Does that mean you haven't always been a vicar?'

'No. I was a social worker before that, working with

families.'

'I suppose that comes in useful now?'

I nodded and set down my cup. 'How about your job? You'll have started earlier than me?'

She looked thoughtful. 'It was awful for women in the firm when I began there. Too many public school men who didn't think a woman could have brains. I nearly gave up in my first year, but I'd already made one false start and couldn't afford another.' She stared into her coffee. 'It's better now, but there's still a glass ceiling. Particularly for women who take time out to have children. It's easier for those of us with no family commitments.'

Was that why she had had Stephen adopted, I found myself thinking. If he was her son…

'When I became a partner I was the first woman in the firm at that level,' she went on, 'but it can be hard even now. The culture's very male dominated. I used to joke about "club clients" – contacts made at Rotary or golf or the Masonic lodge.'

'I remember being on Diocesan committees as an ordinand and never being listened to. If you're assertive, you're strident, if you're quietly spoken you confirm the expectation that you've nothing worth saying.' I smiled. 'Things are improving, though. And did you know women deacons were running parishes in Wales long before they could in England?'

'No I didn't. One up to the old country then.' She smiled back. 'Better than when I was young. I gave up on Welsh academia because I couldn't see myself making a career here. I was far too radical, the way I was then.'

'So you weren't a solicitor to start with?'

'No. I wanted to be an academic first of all, lecture, do

research. Teach.' She finished her coffee and put her cup on the table. 'The interesting thing is that the part of my work I enjoy most is mentoring trainees and setting up courses. So I seem to have done what I wanted in the end. When I was in Singapore I introduced courses in conflict resolution – giving people the skills to resolve disputes before they come to court. Saves a lot of expense if it works.'

'My PCC could do with that. Or rather, I could.'

She grinned. 'Most people who knew me when I was younger would have said my gift was for starting disputes not resolving them. I could have done with all this theory then, though I'm sure I wouldn't have taken any notice.'

She changed the subject abruptly. 'But I haven't come just for a chat, pleasant though it's been…I meant to ask whether there's anything the church needs. I want to give something in memory of Gareth, if that's acceptable to you. I know his faith meant a lot to him and he was very fond of Llanfadog church. It'd be my way of saying "thank you" for all he did for me.'

At first my mind went blank. Then I thought of the roof. 'If you don't mind contributing towards repairs rather than donating a particular item, we've got a problem with the roof. Slate sickness. We're going to have to replace all the slates.'

'Slate sickness?' She stared at me in disbelief.

'It's when the slates have worn so much the nails can't hold them. The holes have become too big.'

'If you say so.' An amused smile. 'It sounds nasty anyway.'

'But if you'd prefer to give a specific item. I shall have to think. A new service book for the altar would be useful.'

'I'll opt for the roof,' she said decisively. 'Gareth was

a practical man. No point having new books if water's dripping on them.'

I could have cheered.

At once she took a chequebook and pen from her shoulder bag and began filling in a cheque. 'Do I make it out to St. Madoc's?'

I nodded.

'You should be able to claim back the tax,' she said, 'if I fill in a Gift Aid form. Who's your treasurer?'

She had obviously forgotten. 'It was Gareth,' I said after a small silence. 'The forms'll be in the folder you brought yesterday.'

I saw her fingers tighten on the pen. She stopped writing and sat still for a moment, staring at the chequebook on her lap. 'Damn. I should have remembered.' She passed a hand across her eyes.

I found her a box of tissues and went to fetch the folder from the study.

When I came back she'd recovered. 'Sorry. It was the surprise. I should have known. Stupid of me.' She blew her nose discreetly. 'It's the little things that get you.'

'I know,' I said, 'like at Communion this morning. I expected Gareth to be sidesman as usual.'

'He thought the world of you, you know. Said you'd done a lot for the parish.'

I could feel myself blushing. 'The feeling was mutual. He was a good friend, my greatest ally on the church council. He could defuse tension better than anyone else I know.'

'He'd had plenty of practice.' A wry smile from his sister. She was silent for a moment, then asked brightly, 'Did he tell you about our nationalist phase?'

'He hinted you were into language protests.'

She launched into an account of their exploits… Their part in the demonstration against the drowning of Tryweryn. 'I was still at school then. I was only allowed to go if Gareth and I went together.' Her court appearance with her boyfriend of the time, and their involvement in the language campaign… Gareth's ancient Morris: 'The Ffestiniog moors in a snowstorm are no place to push-start a car with a flat battery.' Their night hike up Moel Fammau: 'We lugged a primus stove all the way up to the top so we could cook sausages for breakfast.' Their joint love of shooting: 'I liked targets, Gareth preferred to bag something for supper.' Their childhood games in the countryside around Llanfadog…

Elin Pritchard was a gifted raconteur and made Gareth come alive again. I countered with his Harvest Supper entertainments, his achievement in reconciling two warring families at a funeral, and the stuffed mouse he left on my prayer desk one morning to amuse me. Time flew as we enjoyed memories of her brother.

'Was your father an undertaker too?' I asked, when we'd run out of anecdotes.

'No. He was a carpenter and cabinetmaker. His workshop was where the chapel of rest is now. Gareth took over the business when Tad retired. He developed a sideline in coffins,' an amused smile, 'and it grew from there. He did one funeral, almost by accident, and he was so much better than the other local undertakers that people started asking for him. He wanted to be a teacher originally. In fact he completed a year's training in Bangor.'

This was news. 'Why did he give up?'

'My father damaged his hand and Gareth came back to help with the business.'

She frowned. 'A pity. But I suppose it turned out all right in the end. Typical of Gareth, always putting others first. It made our lives easier when he was back home but I'm sorry he had to leave college.'

She looked out at the garden. The swifts had stopped flying round. The blackbirds had gone to roost. 'My father was a difficult man, a brilliant craftsman, but a perfectionist and impossible to live with. He was a bully. He made our lives hell at times.' The harshness in her voice contrasted so starkly with the lightness of our earlier conversation that I stared at her in amazement. She gave an apologetic smile. 'Sorry to spoil the rural idyll, but not all country childhoods are perfect. The stories I told just now are true, thank God. We had a lot of fun and friends outside, good people who looked out for us. If we hadn't we would have been much more damaged. But our home life could be awful, like living under a thundercloud. You didn't know when lightning would strike next.'

She paused and looked at her hands. When she went on her voice was softer. 'It was only Gareth and Aunt Tibby next door who made it bearable for me. Gareth was my protector and friend. I don't know what I'd have done without him.' She took a tissue from the box and crumpled it. 'Don't worry. I don't intend to dissolve on you. I'm more likely to throw things.'

'I had no idea,' I said. 'Gareth seemed such a laid-back, relaxed sort of person.'

'He was. How he managed it I'll never know. Except that he was closer to Mam than I was. She was a gentle soul who had all the life crushed out of her. She hardly spoke at home except in whispers.'

'Gareth never hinted there was anything like this.'

'He wouldn't. Unhappy families keep their unhappiness to themselves. Mam would have died rather than let anyone know how much she was terrorised. We learnt to pretend for her sake. It was important no one should find out what went on, especially in a community like Llanfadog.'

'Denial's very common in that situation,' I agreed, 'but Lily knew, surely?'

Elin shook her head. 'Things were easier when Lily met the parents. Tad's energy was declining and he was getting confused. I suspect the pills he was on for depression calmed him down. And Gareth wouldn't have wanted to tell tales, 'specially as Mam and Tad needed caring for. He wouldn't have liked Lily to think badly of them.'

'Don't let this go any further, please,' she added quickly, 'I didn't plan to say any of it, but it's been hard this week, being in that house. I thought I'd managed to bury it all,' her voice trembled slightly, 'but I haven't, obviously. I can't tell Lily and the children. I've had to be on my guard sometimes when Megan or Bryn have asked questions. No one in the village knows and Gareth wouldn't have wanted them to. They live with the illusion that everything was fine even if our father *could* be awkward and unpredictable.' She stared at the screwed-up tissue in her hand. 'Anyway, what's past is past. No point going over it.'

'There is if we can undo some of its effects,' I said. 'Have you ever talked this over with anyone?'

She turned on me a look of sceptical amusement. 'Counselling, you mean? And, yes, I did talk about it once. Had to. A hospital doctor dragged it out of me like pulling teeth. Not again. I thought then that if I make a mess of my life it'll be my own mess, thank you, not something I can blame on someone else. I didn't want everyone muttering, "*Poor thing. She had such a dreadful childhood, an abusive and tyrannical father, no sense of self-worth. We must tiptoe round her in case she explodes.*"' She frowned. 'Besides I don't trust those who meddle with the insides of other people's minds.'

'A good counsellor wouldn't do that,' I persisted.

'So you say.' Her hazel eyes challenged me and I was aware of the stubborn will that kept her going.

'How did you survive? You and Gareth, as children?'

'We made our own world. We were past masters at make-believe – or I was – and we played outside as much as we could. We'd slip away for whole days when Tad was in his black moods. Aunt Tibby, my godmother, lived next door till I was twelve and her house was a safe place. At home we kept out of the way as far as possible, hid upstairs, told each other jokes and stories. It was much harder when Tibby moved. There was no escape then. And when Gareth was away at college it was my mother and myself coping on our own... Not a good year.' She paused and I could see tension in her hands, fingers clasping and unclasping, twisting round one another, unable to keep still.

'Was your father violent toward you as well?'

'Not...*violent.*' She stopped suddenly and put her head in her hands. 'Sorry.' Her voice was muffled.

I put my arm round her while she sobbed but tried not to. 'I don't do this. What on earth's the matter with me? I've survived it all ...I've got over it... and anyway, I don't cry.'

'Maybe you need to.' I supplied tissues till she'd gone through half the box. 'You can't have people dying and not feel it. Nor have bad things happen and expect them to have no effect.'

'I thought I could manage. I've always coped before.'

'There are times when it's right to let go. You can't carry all this pain inside forever.'

'Perhaps.' She sounded grudging.

Eventually she detached herself. 'Sorry.' She pushed the hair from her eyes. 'It's a bit of a shock, giving way like this. Not like me at all. I've always had everything under control.'

'Bereavement can stir up grief from the past as well sadness for immediate losses,' I explained.

She digested this in silence, looking at her hands. Then she shook her head. 'I can't talk about all this. Not yet anyway.'

'You don't have to. And *I'm* sorry. I didn't mean to push you. But you've helped me understand a lot about Gareth and the family, about where you're coming from. And crying's not a sign of weakness, you know.'

'But once you start you don't think you'll be able to stop.'

'It's usually manageable. Grief comes in waves, I find. With spaces for recovery in between. And you stopped just now.'

She laughed through the remains of her tears. 'Well argued. You'd make a good lawyer.' She sat up straight. 'What a self-pitying sod you must think I am.'

'Not at all, just human, like the rest of us.'

She smiled weakly. 'Heavens, but I must tidy myself up. What on earth will the family think?'

'There's a cloakroom across the hall if you want.'

She didn't move but sat still, looking at her hands. 'Maybe it *has* been helpful to get this out. I've been trying to push the memories away all week, after years of forgetting they were even there.' She took another tissue and blew her nose. 'The thing that's hit me hardest,' she said, 'is that I'm afraid part of the reason Gareth gave up his teaching course was because of me. I think he suspected that, as well as Mam, I needed protecting. He used to sit with me while I did my homework downstairs so I wouldn't be alone with Tad – Mam was on tranquillisers by then, knocked out and in bed most evenings.' She looked at me. 'Gareth was a very special person. To think he cared for Tad after all that happened – I could hardly bear to be in the same room – he deserves to be canonised.'

'A very special person,' I agreed.

She took another tissue and dabbed her eyes. 'You couldn't have included any of this in your funeral tribute,' she said with a sudden wicked grin that reminded me of Gareth at his most mischievous, 'but I'd love to have seen people's faces if you had.' She was recovering.

'Would you like another drink?' I decided we both needed it.

'I could murder a whisky. But I'll have coffee, thanks. I don't suppose you allow smoking in the house, do you?'

'I don't generally, though I could make an exception. But I do have whisky. I keep it for after difficult meetings and visits from church architects and other bearers of bad news.'

'You ought to qualify on both counts then. This hasn't been easy and I'm bad news. I've wasted most of your evening.'

'You're the sister of a good friend,' I said decisively. 'We both need cheering up and we can drink to his memory.'

What a surprising evening this had become, I reflected as I fetched the bottle of Bell's and the whisky glasses my brother had given me for Christmas. Nothing like I'd anticipated. I wished I could have met Gareth and Elin together. No wonder Lily had found it hard to break into that relationship. Bonds forged in adversity were as strong as climbing ropes.

I pondered about Gareth. I'd never dreamt his joking had its roots in an unhappy home nor that he and Elin were the products of a dysfunctional family. But people always said clowning hides tears. It was their way of coping, as Elin said.

She had tidied herself up when I returned with the drinks. We sipped our whisky as the sky outside darkened.

Then she broke the silence. 'When Gareth and I were talking on the phone a month ago, he sounded me out, to see if the memories of home that were coming back to him were true or not, some were so bizarre. He needed me to reassure him that he wasn't going mad or making things up, that the events he recalled really happened.' Her eyes softened as she spoke about her brother. 'We were the only people who knew, you see. I think that's what bound us together so closely, even though we tried to break free in our different ways.' She finished her whisky. 'Gareth married and I'm ashamed to say I resented it. I went abroad to work and refused to come back to Wales, and he found that hard.'

She was thinking aloud. I needn't respond, I decided. I listened, intrigued, to her musings while a dark shape – Moses – landed on the window ledge outside and demanded attention with his hard, imperious eyes. I would let him in, but not yet. I didn't want to disturb Elin's train of thought.

'I was always Gareth's kid sister,' she was saying, 'the

one he looked after. Even though I could lead him by the nose at times. Perhaps we were too close. We grew up depending on each other because there was no one else in the house rooting for us, or capable of rooting for us. Mam was too crushed to manage more than survival. Tad was…as he was. Gareth was there for me like the fairy godmother who always turns up when trouble strikes. There aren't many brothers who'd drive down to London through the night after their sisters nearly chucked themselves in the Thames.'

She noticed my shocked look. 'It's all right.' She waved a dismissive hand. 'Not as bad as it sounds. I wasn't suicidal, just flipped – had delusions – the result of a breakdown.' She spoke quickly. It was obviously something she didn't want to dwell on.

'The silly thing is,' she continued in her ordinary voice, 'that I've been trying for years to persuade Gareth that I needn't phone him every week. He always said he'd worry if he didn't hear, that he needed proof that I was all right. Habit I suppose. But these last few years I was the one worrying about him. It's as if we couldn't stop feeling responsible for each other. Our childhood tied us up and we couldn't let go.'

Death causes so much realignment, I had reflected at the funeral. How was Elin going to manage without her brother? How were Lily and Elin going to get on, if at all? I hoped they would come to appreciate each other in the end.

I looked at the clock, saw it was half ten, and opened the window to let Moses in. He claimed my visitor's lap with one swift bound.

She made a face. 'He's a weight. Definitely a

Magnificat.'

'He won't trouble you for long. You watch him move once he hears his plate.'

The cat fed, we chatted about other things. We discovered we both liked Russian opera and folk groups like Stone Angel, that we were compulsive readers of dictionaries and shared a dream of crossing the Gobi desert by camel one day. I found myself appreciating Elin's sharp mind, her sardonic humour, her experience as a fellow professional. With more time and more opportunity to meet we might be friends.

We learnt without disclosing details that we both faced significant decisions in the weeks and months to come. 'I'll pray for you if you'll pray for me,' I suggested, downing the last of my drink.

'Gareth would have. I can't promise.'

'Anyone can pray.'

'Is that a challenge?'

'If you like.'

'You won't convert me.'

'That's not my job. It's God that does the converting.'

'You sound like my brother.' And we laughed.

At last Elin glanced at her watch. 'Lily'll think I've deserted.' She stood up to go.

'Will you be coming to Llanfadog again?'

'I'm not sure. I'd like to keep in touch for Gareth's sake. And I'm working on the will so I'll have to keep Lily informed about its progress. She might be glad of my advice if she's going to continue the business herself.'

'Might she keep it on?'

She grinned. 'I'm trying not to influence her, but I think she's coming round to the idea. We'll have to see.'

On the doorstep she turned suddenly and asked, 'as an ex-social worker, what do you think of the new provision for adopted children to make contact with birth parents? Is it a good idea, or does it just cause unhappiness?'

I paused. Stephen Loxley, I thought, perhaps my guess was the right one, and considered what to say. I was aware of Elin's attention as she waited for my reply.

'Depends on the circumstances – and the individuals,' I replied, 'I think it's a good idea generally. So long as all the parties involved have proper support.'

'I see. It came up when I was talking with a friend earlier in the week. Hearing that you'd once worked with families, I wondered what your view was.' She was studiedly casual.

I was tempted to tell her the whole story, to give her Stephen Loxley's card; organise a Hollywood-style reunion of mother and son. But it didn't feel right, not yet anyway. 'If you need a considered opinion you can always ring me and have a longer chat.'

'I might. Thank you for a pleasant evening. And for listening.'

'I've enjoyed it. Come again if you're visiting. And thank you for your donation. That was kind.'

'You're welcome.' Her smile reminded me, suddenly, of Gareth's.

I watched her go. Perhaps Stephen Loxley's hopes of meeting the family would be fulfilled one day. I prayed for Elin, that she would know peace and the right path.

Later I picked up her cheque from the coffee table where she had left it. I had to pause, stunned, to count the noughts.

Tuesday's PCC wasn't going to be hell after all.

Elin

I am being unpicked. Like the knitting I used to do at school.

It's no good, Elin fach, your Mam wouldn't want a scarf with a hole in it, would she now? I'd watch miserably as the grubby piece of work I'd sweated over for half a term unravelled in crinkly coils on the teacher's desk. Poor Miss Rees. She was on to a loser teaching domestic skills to someone like me. I'd rather have been herding sheep than knitting up their wool. *Now go back and start again. And don't rush on when you make a mistake. Put it right straight away.* Back, sulkily, to my desk to spend the rest of the afternoon doing as little as possible, waiting to go home so I could catch sticklebacks in the stream.

Dropped stitches. Nothing to an eight-year-old. But if you ignored them they ran into holes that spoilt everything, apparently.

I've never bothered about knitting, but I do care about my life. Till two years ago it was like a neat scarf: rows of professional success and personal achievement laced with financial rewards and foreign travel. I could handle its challenges and order its routine. I even enjoyed the risks. Now it feels as if everything is suddenly coming undone. Familiar patterns are falling apart. And I, too, am unravelling.

'It's a natural response to bereavement,' I tell myself, as I pack the car to leave Llanfadog. 'You're still coming to terms with the shock of Gareth's death.'

But if I am honest – and I'm trying to be – this awareness of something not right began two years ago after Ben and I got together. I tried to go on in my usual way – push ahead, don't think too deeply, get on with life – always my motto. But loving someone unsettles you and lifts the lid on stuff you'd prefer to forget. Then Tibby died, and now Gareth, and I can't ignore this 'dropped stitch' feeling any longer.

Coming to Wales for the first time in years I had my guard up and my protective armour on. I was stunned by Gareth's death and determined nothing else would affect me. But I have got to know his family and met with old friends. I have rediscovered old loves and re-visited old haunts, I have remembered my childhood and I can't pretend I'm untouched.

So what to do? I ponder this as I try the windscreen washer, check the oil, clean the car windows and measure the tyre pressure. I've already done the latter at the local garage where I filled up with petrol yesterday. But I have to do it again. I record the mileage in my notebook and make sure I have bottled water, maps and cigarettes to hand. No doubt I'll tidy my hair, re-touch my make-up and find a snagged fingernail to file before I start. Ben teases me about my preparations for a journey. *It's a sign of insecurity, all this fiddling about. Rituals to placate the road gods.*

I'm making sure everything's all right, that's all.

Maybe I *am* a bit obsessive. But a woman needs to know what's what so upstart garage mechanics can't fob her off with poor service. As to my appearance, I've found the smarter you look, the better you are treated. It's a practical issue.

At the thought of Ben I pick up my mobile to see if he has answered the text message I sent in the wakeful early hours. No. But there's a voicemail. 'Darling, if you change your mind about tonight, there's a pheasant casserole in the freezer. Ring by six if you're coming. I'll phone tonight. Love you. Ben'

I grin at this. He knows how much I like pheasant, how tempted I will be. But I've promised myself I'll be in London this evening. Why, I am not sure. I can sit up all Wednesday night to go over the case details for Thursday: I've done most of the work on it. I'd rather be with Ben but there's a barrier in me, a fear of commitment. Now he has asked me to marry him I shall have to face this, to be fair to us both. My easy answers – that I cling to independence, that I can't handle close relationships after so long on my own – don't feel like the whole truth. I sense there's something more, something deeper. And I shrink from learning what it is. There's enough pain around with Gareth's death.

I still can't believe Gareth is gone. The knowledge of his absence is with me all the time, like a deep and painful hole where a tooth has been pulled. He was everything to me, especially when we were younger. There were some things only he and I could talk about, experiences only we knew and could never share with others. How will I live without him?

'Stop that,' I warn myself. 'No point getting gloomy.' I shut the boot, put my bag on the front seat and I am ready to go as the family comes out to see me off.

Bryn offers me a CD of a Welsh folk group. 'Would you like this? I don't play it now.' A half smile from under the mop of red hair so like his father's.

'Thanks. It can play me out of Wales.' I smile at him and touch his arm.

A hug for Megan, then Lily hugs me, gracious woman that she is. 'You *will* come back, won't you? I'm going to need your advice.'

'Thanks. I will. Sorry I haven't been the most restful of guests.' Maybe one day I can make it up to her for the past. 'And you're welcome to stay with me any time. Remember that.'

We pause awkwardly, then I get in the car. They wave as I move off. Do I hear a collective sigh of relief? They need time together now without me intruding. I feel regret that I never got to know them before Gareth died, that I was a stranger in their midst not one of the family. I hope things were improving towards the end of my stay. I will come and see them again, though I do wish they didn't live in *that* house.

I stop at the churchyard to take a last look at Gareth's grave. I am alone. The morning sun picks out the church tower's limestone pinnacles and gold weathervane. The polished black marble of recent memorials looks alien amongst the older gravestones of granite and slate. We used to come here as children and read the epitaphs, work out how old people were when they died.

Gareth, here's one that was only a baby. Isn't it a shame?

Here's another, Ellie. The same family too. 'Mis oed,' it says.

We would stop and be sad for a moment, then dart off quick as wild goats to catch butterflies in the buddleia by the churchyard wall.

'I want a slate headstone,' Gareth said once. I wonder what Lily will put on it. He would have liked a suitable pun but I expect the powers that be frown on such things in these over-regulated days. 'Undertaker under here,' he suggested, joking.

I approach his fresh mound as the vicar's cat slinks away, a vole in its mouth. I am pleased my brother has company in his last resting place. He always loved the natural world, even if it *is* red in tooth and claw. Flycatchers will dart back and forth over him, blackbirds will sing and swifts and swallows will circle above in summer.

'Don't be silly, you know Gareth isn't here.' I mock my imaginings. Where is he then? I like to think I'm a no-nonsense materialist, but I can almost sense Gareth's spirit, waiting to see what I will do now he isn't around to support me. I console myself that he is free at last from the flashbacks that blighted the last years of his life. Was his heart attack the result of his childhood? Those years of strain must have affected him just as they did me.

'Goodbye, then, *fy mrawd annwyl,* dear brother, *ffrind da. Diolch am bopeth.*' Thanks for everything, Gareth, best friend of my childhood and after – I lapse into the language we both fought for, and that I abandoned. I am sorry I refused to speak it with him after I went abroad. He was upset by that and it makes me sad. Did I intend to hurt? I hope not but I can't or won't remember. Here be dragons, my instincts tell me.

I shed a few tears then dry my eyes. There are things unfinished between us, questions I wish I had asked, facts I would have wanted to corroborate, but the time for that has gone. Now I have to make sense of things on my own. I promise to do my best for the family, say I'm sorry about Lily, and turn away.

If Ben were here he would say a prayer. I'm sorry he and Gareth never met. After the initial surprise they might have got on, shared a joke and talked about shooting. Maybe they'll meet in heaven since both believed in it.

I wave at Lynne's window in case she is about. I am grateful for our conversation last night. It was good to get things off my chest even if it accelerated the unpicking. I may ring her about the adoption issue. Not yet, though. I need time to think.

I look up at the church roof that is causing so much anxiety – slate sickness indeed. Whatever next? Pew plague? Vestry virus? Then I pick my way between monuments looking for my parents' grave. I didn't attend their funerals. I could have gone but I chose not to. I wonder what the wagging tongues of Llanfadog would say if they knew how deliberate that decision was. But now I want to see where Mam and Tad are buried.

I remember the last time we met, when Gareth and Lily got engaged. I didn't enjoy that weekend. I resented Lily. I know it was unreasonable of me, but I hated the thought of sharing Gareth. How dared she stake first claim on the affections of my closest friend? I was uneasy with Tad as always, afraid of being alone with him even then. A mere ghost of his former self, he had lost the power to terrify, but I could never trust him. Mam was the same frightened shadow. The experience was painful and unsettling. I left thinking I never wanted to come back to Llanfadog again.

I find my parents' grave in the newer part of the churchyard, beside a gravel path, three rows from where Gareth lies. It has the look of being tended, red and purple anemones in the plain stone vase, neatly clipped grass and a slate headstone. Gareth's work surely – though he can't have been responsible for the fresh flowers. Lily must have left those. Do I feel ashamed that it was my sister-in-law who cared for them and now leaves flowers on their grave? Not really. The village may think me hard but when did I ever care what people think? It was a matter of survival then.

Though I had expected it, it's a shock to see them sharing the same grave. What irony, considering how unhappy their marriage was, how miserable it made us.

'Er serchus cof am Thomas Owen Pritchard a'i briod Annie Elin…' I could weep at the futility of it. Was there ever a time when they were happy together? Perhaps – before Gareth or I were born.

My hands are clenched. 'Mam, why didn't you stop it? Why weren't you there when I was hurting? Surely you must have known?' I imagine her sliding away from my questions, ignoring my cries for help. Turning deaf ears to my pain, elusive as a shadow. Even when I was little I had to be naughty for her to notice me. I feel a surge of anger at her passivity, her refusal to stand up to Tad's tyranny and lies. 'Couldn't you have fought for us, taken us out of that hell? And why did you leave me unprotected? You knew what he was like.'

Silence. Once the silence of a drug-induced sleep, now the silence of death. I wish I had known my mother. She was beyond my reach even when I was small. If I let myself, I could cry. For the *lacrimae rerum* as well as my own lost innocence – tears of grief and anger. But I don't. I set my jaw and shake my head. I am not falling into that trap. The vicar may say grief is manageable. I am still not sure. If I let go of all this it will have to be somewhere safe, secure enough to contain my conflicting emotions and stop me falling apart.

As for my father, I feel nothing for him, no grief, no

pity, no regret. Nothing. My heart is like stone. But the fear isn't gone entirely, nor the anger. '*Er serchus cof am Thomas Owen Pritchard*' – a sick joke. My memories of him aren't loving.

'What's this, then?' My father to my fourteen-year-old self. 'Homework? Waste of time. They ought to be teaching you to keep house. You'll only marry and have kids like that Meryl up the road, give it all up.' He sits opposite, glaring.

'Where's your Mam, then?'

'In bed.' My voice is quiet. My hand grips my pen. I hadn't expected him in from the garden this early. I'd hoped to be in bed before he appeared.

'Speak up, girl. Got a tongue haven't you?' He opens his Daily Post. *'And who was that boy I saw you with at the bus stop? Shouldn't have boyfriends at your age.'*

'He's not a boyfriend. That was Sian's brother.'

'Can't imagine what boys'd see in you anyway. The scarecrow in Jones' field looks better. Why don't you cut your hair for God's sake? It's a mess. And sit up. You're like a sack of potatoes slouching there.'

I focus on the map I am trying to draw, face aflame.

'Ink all over your hands, I see. Can't even write tidily. Look at that blot you've just made.'

I won't cry. That's what he wants. I won't let him get the better of me.

'Bitten nails. Disgusting.' He pauses to look closer. 'Is that nail varnish you're wearing?'

I glance down at my shell pink lacquer.

'Slut. Dirty little tart. No decent woman wears muck like that. Get it cleaned off.'

I want to escape but Tad is between me and the door, close enough to grab me if I walk past, put his hand between my legs or down my blouse. I shudder. He won't try anything else, though. Not unless I break down. Should I make a dash for it?

But he has moved his chair nearer the door. 'Of course, you know you're not my daughter.'

I shut my ears to his lies. So where did I get this nose from? – and my eye colour?

'Your mother's a two-timing bitch, know that?'

Please, Tad.

'You'll turn out the same. All women are the same. Lying cheats. Fucking whores.' Venom in his voice.

I sit still as a stone, my face expressionless. I won't cry. I won't give in.

He looks me up and down. I can't see the look but I feel it and it fills me with dread.

'I knew you couldn't be mine as soon as I saw you. "No child of mine's as ugly as that," I said. I didn't look at you again for a month, did you know that? Paid your mother back for cheating on me. Taught her a lesson.' He leans forward and I smell the tobacco on his breath. 'You're no better looking now than you were then. Skinny as a rail. Face like a ferret. No figure to speak of. What are you – a stick insect or something?'

Tad don't. Tears prick my eyes but I bite my lip and hold them back. If he sees me weakening I've had it. He will change in an instant, come for me, assault me with his twisted sympathy. 'Poor Elin. I've made you cry. I never meant to. Let Tada make it right for you, kiss you better.'

It was a battle of wills. *In extremis* Latin verbs made a wonderful mental filter. I would chant them in my head to drown out Tad's torments. I wonder what my teacher would have thought if she'd known.

I won, that time. Bolted to my bedroom while Tad made a drink in the kitchen, wedged a chair under the door handle so he couldn't barge in, then spent the night reading to rid my mind of his taunts. Other times I wasn't so lucky. I learnt to switch off from my body, pretend it wasn't me Tad was pawing and invading. And threw up afterwards when I was on my own.

I fold my arms tightly as if to hold myself intact. You can cope with anything if you have to. But Tad's behaviour marked me. I am more aware of that now than when I was younger.

It ended when Gareth came home from college. He guessed something was up though I never told him till years after. We made sure I was never alone with Tad after that, even if it meant me being out more than I was at home.

Was this how he treated my mother, I wonder, staring at their grave. Was verbal abuse and humiliation the preliminary to what passed for lovemaking in their marriage? Except it wasn't love, couldn't have been. What happened to make him like that? Was it something in her? In me? In all women? Gareth thought Tad's problems were caused by the war. I wouldn't know. He fought in the desert and would never speak of it, Gareth said. Maybe he *was* ill. But that doesn't excuse what he did. I still find it difficult to cry or show weakness because of it.

Can I marry with all this in my past?

I nearly married Ian, but I was younger then. Youthful optimism helped me forget Tad's abuse, bury the memory of his cruelties.

I don't want to dump this on Ben. He doesn't deserve it.

Question: do I shrink from marriage because it means I will have to confront all this stuff about Tad? Is that why I'm afraid? And what to do about it?

Lynne suggested counselling. She may be right. But it would have to be somebody good.

'I don't need to dwell on such things,' I tell myself. Talking to Lynne re-awakened the memories but I don't have to get knotted up over my parents. Besides, Tibby was my mother in everything but name…

She would turn up at our door most Saturdays. *Annie, would you like us to take the children out today?*

Would you? That's so kind. It'd get them out of Tom's way.

Every weekend it was the same. Except for those days when we'd been sent to our rooms for being naughty. Tibby and Jack would take us on the bus to distant places: Rhyl, Prestatyn, Llandudno, even Conwy. We loved it. We would have our photos taken and sometimes be given ice creams.

'Aunt Tibby, where's that steamer going?'

'The Isle of Man.'

'Aren't there any women there, then?' Gareth, wisecracking.

'Can we go on it one day?' Me, staring wistfully at the departing boat.

We never did go on that steamer, but my longing to travel was born on those trips, and my love of history. We would explore the ruins of Denbigh, Conwy and Rhuddlan castles, imagining sieges with boiling oil poured on people's heads.

On Sunday mornings Tibby and Jack would take us to church – a small price to pay for our Saturday excursions.

Tad and Mam were Chapel, but they didn't seem to mind. During sermons we would read the prayer book. Gareth would puzzle over the tables for finding the date of Easter. I would read the Table of Kindred and Affinity at the back – *A man may not marry his mother; a man may not marry his daughter; a man may not marry his mother's mother* and so on.

Tibby's house was a refuge for us. We escaped there when Tad locked us out or was angry. One year she gave us Christmas dinner after Tad threw the chicken at the wall and Mam went to bed crying. Tibby must have known what went on, but Mam never admitted it, covering Tad's behaviour with excuses – 'the meat turned out bad,' or 'I've run out of shillings for the electric,' or 'aren't I silly? I walked into the pantry door.'

Tibby was there for me when Steve was born and gave us a home for his first few weeks. She was there for me when everything fell apart and helped put me together again.

The church clock strikes eight. I have stayed too long. I hurry back to the car.

Today is a day for catching up. Time to think and meet myself. I don't do introspection as a rule but I'm being driven to it. Gareth's death and all that's followed has stirred up more than grief. It's brought me face to face with the past – and with myself.

I study the map briefly. I have picked a route that will take me to the scene of some of my memories – a kind of pilgrimage. I need to look at the past and I want to keep faith with Tibby. I can't see Gareth buried and not acknowledge the other person who made my early life bearable. I plan to go over the moors to Bala, across the Berwyns, then south to Sallowdean where Tibby is buried.

After last night I am wary of coming undone. Talking with Lynne uncovered much I never meant to look at. And now it is uncovered I can't easily push it away. Coward, I tell myself, you can't run away forever. Maybe you have to go back to go on, like the knitting, see where you've come from. It may help decide where you're going.

The weather is fine. I have the whole day ahead and I love driving. I enjoy the challenge of pitting myself against the road and using my skills – if I had the chance I'd love to try rally driving. This new model is a pleasure to drive. I am still discovering what it can do, so the mountain road will be a good test. I feel a small thrill of excitement as I settle myself and adjust the mirror. I slip Bryn's gift into the CD player, start the engine and my beautiful new car purrs into life.

I can't avoid the past even now. The bus shelter in the village stirs a vivid memory.

'What are you doing here, Elin? It's far too early for school.' Jen's mother on her way back from nursing shift.

Me, thinking fast. 'Homework. I couldn't do it back home. I came here to get some peace and quiet.' True but not the whole truth. I couldn't tell her I was running away, could I?

'You look frozen. Oughtn't you to be indoors?'

'I'm all right here, thanks.'

'If you won't go home you'd better come back with me. Have you had breakfast?'

I hadn't. I'd crept out as soon as I'd woken up. I wasn't going to stay under the same roof as Tad. Not after I'd thrown a book at him the previous night and bolted myself in my room – bolts courtesy of Gareth, blessings upon him.

She asked awkward questions, Jen's mother. I am sure she had an idea what Tad was like but I didn't let on. Their house became a refuge. If it hadn't I might never have remained in Llanfadog or stayed on at school. And if I had run away God knows where I would have finished up.

The first track on Bryn's CD is full of *hiraeth* and nearly has me in tears. Not the thing to play if you're sad. Folk music – English, not Welsh – was the background to my life with Ian. He was a charmer and no mistake. Glyn didn't stand a chance once I'd met him. Here was this tall, bronzed Australian singing protest songs to his twelve string guitar at the college folk club. For me it was love at first sight. He bought me a cider and I found out he was a sociology lecturer on a three-year exchange. We shared the same views on politics and Vietnam. We had the same sense of humour. The scene was set for my great romance.

I should have known that his attractiveness to women meant he would find the idea of monogamy difficult. But I was an innocent abroad. Tad was no guide to male character; anyone who showed me straightforward affection was a saint by comparison. Glyn and I had been passionate but chaste. Our commitment to the cause matched our love for each other. But Ian swept me into a new dimension. I liked to think it was a more mature love I had for him. In retrospect, though, I am not so sure.

Glyn was the better person. But as I got older I wasn't sure if he was in love with me or an ideal – one of the heroic queens of Welsh history or myth, perhaps. Ian was different. Here was someone who loved me for myself. Or so I thought.

Fool.

Do I mind about it now? Not really. It's too long ago. One gets over these things. It would have been just another failed romance if it hadn't been for Steve.

The week has been full of reminders. I can't stop thinking of him, especially after seeing Gareth's youngsters and hearing about Jen and Hywel's Rhodri. Is this what all women do who have had children adopted? I've tried to push away the thought of him so long, stayed busy to stop myself remembering. But listening to Jen's experience brought it all back. I wonder what happened to him, whether he is still alive, how his life turned out.

I stop and have a cigarette at Brenig then look at the lake. Man-made though it is I can't hate it as I hate the reservoir that drowned Tryweryn. A cool wind is blowing off the water so I put on my jacket then walk along the earth dam amid grazing sheep.

I couldn't live here but I need places like this to visit, to breathe fresh air and blow the cobwebs away. I love the buzz of big cities but I like wild places too. I could never live in Llanfadog, but could I cope with Cheshire? More to the point, could Ben cope with me coping with Cheshire?

On through Cerrig to Frongoch. Drawn by the past, I turn right for Llyn Celyn and park in a lay-by opposite the slopes of Arenig. I get out of the car to take a closer look.

The lake gleams silver in the morning sunshine. A faint breeze ruffles its surface. Those who don't know its beginnings may call it beautiful but to me it's a whitewashed grave. Deceptive. I could never appreciate it knowing what it cost. Under here was a valley and a community of farms and families, a village, a chapel, and a cemetery. I am still incensed at the thought of our vain protests and pleas for reprieve, at the government's contempt for Capel Celyn's people and way of life. The nationalist in me isn't dead, just sleeping – like the serpent in Llyn Tegid. I have a lot of legal knowledge I could use now in such battles. How would we handle them today?

Tryweryn was where Glyn and I got together. I smile as I remember the old days.

He was everything I admired – intellectual, idealistic, committed, handsome – but serious. Gareth and I taught him how to laugh. I encouraged him to take risks – little did the magistrate know it was I who led Glyn astray not the other way round. But Glyn gave me a passion for study and showed you could make a career of it – and I would have done if things had been otherwise. We were carefree as seagulls, wild as mountain deer. We had hours of fun together, he and I and Gareth, then we two alone.

One summer when I was staying at Glyn's we spent the day on the sand dunes at Llanddwyn checking his doctorate thesis before he submitted it. Then we deliberately got ourselves cut off by the tide on Llanddwyn Island so we could spend the night there and watch the sun set over the Irish Sea from the comfort of our sleeping bags.

We were fellow conspirators, hooked on the idea of freeing the nation. Glyn had his poetry, I had my dreams, both focussed on Wales and the language. Meeting him at the funeral last week reminded me of lost youth and unfulfilled hopes. I'd fallen in love with London by the time we parted – and with Ian if I'm honest, though Ian and I weren't actually going out together then. With Glyn I felt I could take on the whole world and win. I'm not sure

I didn't try to at school.

I can't repress a grin as I remember the rebellious teenager I once was. I could do with a dose of that spirit now: the outrageous optimism, the conviction that I was right and everyone else was wrong. I hated all authority. I'm surprised school didn't throw me out. But Finn kept hold of me when I went too far. I owe her a lot. God knows what I would have got into if she hadn't pushed me towards London as a base for study.

I sort through my selection of CDs and pick the folk compilation Bryn chose the other day: Shirley Collins and the Albion Band, Steeleye Span, Chilli Willi and the Red Hot Peppers. Takes me back to student days, working for the PhD in London.

'Ian, I thought we were engaged to be married.' After a week at Oxford working in the Bodleian I'd heard he had been seen with someone else.

He gave me his usual charming smile. 'So we are, sweetheart, but that doesn't mean I can't see other women. You can sleep with other men if you like. I won't mind.'

'I bloody well do. I'm not that kind of woman. And I don't want to marry that kind of man.'

I paused to digest his tacit admission. 'Does that mean you slept with her?'

My voice rose in pitch.

'What if I did? Come on, Elin, don't be such a puritan. I was missing you. I love you best, you know I do.'

'Not if you go with other women I don't. We're supposed to promise to be faithful. What will you do when we're married?' I was shaking with anger and the pain of betrayal.

'Depends what you mean by faithful. You're my bread and

butter. But a man needs a bit of cake now and then. Cheer up, Elin. You used to be such fun. Why get so serious?'

I threw his ring at him. Very satisfying. And stalked out taking my records and anglepoise lamp. But during the week my fury ebbed. Memories of Tad's criticisms infiltrated my mind like a fifth column. Long-forgotten taunts worked like curses. I was a mess, he said, nothing to look at, a bag of bones, rubbish. It must be my fault if my fiancé sought others to satisfy him.

I went back to Ian. But I made sure he paid. I could be awkward too.

A turbulent six months followed. We fought more than we feasted. I walked out twice more and was always on the verge of giving up. Why did I hang on so long? I loved Ian. I loved his mind, his voice, his carefree approach to life. He was the first man I'd chosen to sleep with. A real step of trust after all I had put up with from Tad. I meant to be faithful and felt cheapened when he took the gift of myself so lightly, putting me on a par with any passing attraction. But I was unable to let go. I believed him when he promised undying love and a fresh start. I wanted to. Ever the optimist, I hoped it would all come right in the end.

At last I came to my senses. Fed up with Ian's philandering, I cut up his precious bushranger hat with the kitchen scissors, left the bits on the table with a suitable note, and moved all my stuff out while he was giving a lecture. It broke the scissors and left me with a sore hand but it was worth it to think of his face when he got home. He never came back at me about it. Guilty conscience, I presume.

The thrill of revenge was short-lived. A month after Ian went back to Sydney I found I was pregnant. Of all the stupid things… I'd been on the pill and missed a couple of days because of having a wisdom tooth out in hospital. And that's how Steve happened.

I drive into Bala, park in the high street and flex my stiff neck and arms. It isn't the car making me tense, it's me. Too much remembering.

I buy flowers, taking time to choose them because they're for Tibby's grave and I want the best. As I queue to pay for my irises and white roses, I think of Ben and wish he were here. He gave me irises when he heard Gareth had died. I'm not one for flowers usually but these cheered me. Ben is so different from Ian – kind, thoughtful and solid as a rock. Ours is a relationship of equals. We can argue vehemently but respect each other's views. And we are older, more sensible. I was too besotted with Ian to stand up for myself till the end. I worry that I will lose Ben because I'm wary of taking the step of commitment he would like. He knows my struggles. He says he'll stick with me while I work things out. I never imagined myself finding this kind of love at my age. Not something I've bargained for after all these years on my own. Which is why I am so unsettled. It isn't fair of me to treat him as I do. This is one thing I must sort out. Soon, if not this week.

I smile, remembering our first meeting. I was on the verge of giving up, frustrated by the attitude of colleagues to women and to Wales. Then I came across this man who spoke a little Welsh – was half-Welsh even – and had a sense of humour I could appreciate, even if I disliked his political views. There was hope after all. If I let myself I could have fallen in love with him there and then, but he was married, thank God, and I was resolutely single.

Before setting off again I check my mobile. A text from Ben. 'U snds gd.'

My smile turns into a grin. Our old word game from foot-and-mouth days. He must think I need cheering up. I text in 'euphony' then add 'U tree.' Too easy but never mind. Without a dictionary I'll run out of 'eu' words before he does. The rule used to be that whoever gave up first bought the other a drink next time we met. We had a lot of drinks saved by the end of foot-and-mouth but Ben was more into drowning sorrows than celebrating. I took him away to Paris, I recall. It rained, but the long weekend cheered him up. We 'did' galleries and churches till we saw pictures and Gothic arches in our sleep. I smile, remembering.

Where will he be when he gets my reply? I imagine him in his study or walking the fields and drive off still smiling.

The pass over Milltir Gerrig is one of the finest in Wales. Not a route for the faint-hearted, especially in ice or fog. Glyn and I drove over here in snow one year, enjoying the challenge as you do when you're young. So what if we got stuck. We had each other and a car rug. Crazy. The thrill of fighting that icy road was exhilarating, each bend a breathtaking test of tyres and skill and luck. There was nothing we wouldn't have dared together.

The road is empty so I push the car on the curves and gradients to see how it rides. I have an idea about a case I'm handling and stop at the summit to note it down, admiring the whaleback sweep of the Berwyns as I do so. This for me is the last of real Wales. It's border country from now on.

Foreign. For years I have played down my Welshness but it's still there. I feel a pang at leaving, though it's not my home any more. The language would come back if I let it.

I will try and restore family relations and keep up my links here even though it's not my home any more. But I will have to be careful what I say about Mam and Tad. I could tell Lily about Steve, though. I never wanted him to be a secret in the first place.

'We mustn't tell Mam and Tad. There would be hell to pay.'

'I don't see why we shouldn't. It's not as if I'm planning to sponge off them or anything.'

'You know what Tad's like. If he can't go on at you, he'll take it out on Mam. He always does.'

'That's his problem. I was hoping to come back one day and show Steve off. Maybe when I've got my doctorate and everything.'

'Elin, be reasonable. Mam couldn't cope. You're not dealing with a normal situation. You've forgotten how things are.'

For Gareth's sake I agreed. He had to live with them. Even if the physical violence had ceased, the verbal abuse and poisonous atmosphere hadn't. If I went home with Steve I'd cause trouble. But the rebel in me felt cheated. I wanted to show Llanfadog that I didn't need a husband to cope with a child and a career. I was going to blaze a trail. I wanted to thumb my nose at Tad, show him his views on women and education were outdated. Pride comes before a fall, they say. At least Gareth had the grace not to rub it in.

I never told Ian about Steve. My excuse was that I'd lost his address, but in reality I didn't want him to have a hold over me, any reason for keeping in touch. I would manage on my own.

'Elin, stop! That tree's far too high for you to climb.'

'I'm all right. I can do it.'

'Well, don't go any higher then. Turn round at the second branch and come down. Remember what happened before.'

'Leave me alone. I can manage.'

It was Tibby's husband, Jack, who helped me down from that tree. It was Gareth and Tibby who rescued me from the hole I got into with Steve.

The roads between Llanfyllin and Church Stoke are twisty and demanding. I keep my mind on them and stop playing music because it awakens the sadness about Gareth. When a flock of sheep blocks the road I tap my fingers on the steering wheel, impatient, then remind myself I have all day to get home. *'Slow down,'* Ben says. *'You'll wear yourself out. Relax for a change.'* But I've always pushed myself, always needed to prove I'm as good as, if not better than, others, especially men. I wonder how far Tad's contempt for women is responsible for that. Not something I wish to dwell on.

And all the time I'm tempted by thoughts of a stopover with Ben to recharge my batteries. Was it only Saturday that we had lunch together? I can cope on my own, I think. But who am I trying to fool? Without others, 'specially Tibby, my life would have been impossible.

A winter's day in Llanfadog. Aged four, I am hunched on Tibby's doorstep shivering. Gareth is at school so there's no one else about. Tad has stormed back to work after losing his temper over dinner. Mam has shut herself in the bedroom, crying. I've crept out of the house to seek comfort next door but Tibby isn't there.

I sit for a long time, getting colder and colder, but I don't want to go back. Home isn't a safe place.

It dawns on me then, that I must learn to cope alone, build a wall round myself if I want to survive, because even Gareth can't be with me always.

At last Tibby returns with her shopping. 'Elin, what are you doing? Come inside. You shouldn't be on that cold step.'

Into the warmth of a friendly kitchen, a lap and loving arms.

'What's the matter, pet? What's up?'

I can't tell her. My throat hurts from crying. But it's good being there – Tibby makes the fear and the cold go away. I wish I could stay with her forever.

I feel like crying. Tibby was my salvation. Her love kept me attached to life and relationships, stopped me giving up altogether. She brought me in out of the cold again, years later, when I was in deeper trouble. My mind reels forward two decades to that other time and not such a happy ending.

'What would you do, Tibby? Gareth thinks I should have Stevie adopted. I don't want to let him go. But he says it'd be better for him, kinder.'

'That's your decision, pet. I can't tell you what to do. But I know I'd find it hard.'

I stare out of the window at the hospital grounds. A squirrel is playing under an oak tree with one of last year's dead leaves.

It sticks in my mind, that squirrel. It is alive, enjoying being alive. I am not.

'You're sure you don't mind having him? I believe Gareth thinks I'm putting too much on you.'

'Don't worry what Gareth thinks, love. It's what you and I think that matters.'

If we'd had our way, Tibby would have continued looking after Steve till I was over the depression – that hospital had no provision for mothers and babies then. But Gareth had argued for adoption from the beginning.

'How are you going to manage after it's born?'

'I'll cope. People do.'

'What about Mam and Tad?'

'It's nothing to do with them. They needn't know if you don't tell them.'

'Adoption'd be much better. Leave you free to get on with your degree and everything.'

'Gareth, look. It's my baby, understand? I'm choosing to bring it into the world. I want the responsibility of it. It's not an unwanted kitten you can drown.'

'I'm not suggesting that. I just think you'd be better handing it over to someone else to bring up.'

'I'll think about it. Okay?'

Why was he so certain I wouldn't manage? He'd always been my ally before. It was awful having to fight him. One of the worst things about the whole business.

'Look, Elin, you're not well. You could take months to get better. And all the time the poor kid doesn't even know who you

are. Even when you come out you don't know if you'll be able to manage or not. Wouldn't it be sensible to have him adopted now? Give him a new beginning, a proper start in life?'

'You think I'm mad, don't you? Like Tad. That's the problem. Only you're not daring to say.'

'No I don't. Only you do seem…I mean you're still in pieces. Having a baby to look after won't help you get better.'

'I'll think about it.'

He wore me down, wore down the combined efforts of Tibby and me. His was the voice of reason. All I knew was that I loved Stevie. He was mine and I wanted to keep him. I'd never dreamed I could love anyone as much as this. It seemed a betrayal of the worst kind to give him away. But Gareth said it wasn't. I would be doing the best for him, giving him a proper home. In my right mind I would have argued him out of court. In that fragile state I was a pushover. Can you be held to that sort of decision when the balance of your mind is disturbed?

'You say you meant to jump into the river to escape from your father?' The consultant looked at me over his glasses. He sounded like the counsel for the prosecution.

'Yes. That's what I said. I thought I saw him in the crowd. I just panicked. I…'

I wondered how to explain the odd feeling I'd had that if Stevie and I hid under water we could swim to the bank after an hour or two. Maybe I'd better not try. Even talking felt like trying to run through porridge. All I could think was that it seemed a reasonable idea at the time.

'Those pills can have side effects but…' His conclusion hung in the air.

That was it. I was loopy. Just like Tad.

'Why should you have been frightened of your father?'

A black hole yawned. I didn't just stare into it. I fell in and disappeared.

I was helpless as the past swallowed me up.

In the end after they'd dragged the facts out of me, they blamed it on my childhood. 'No psychosis,' was the verdict. 'Hormone imbalance leading to reactive depression' – PPD on my notes. *Not surprising considering what happened to you in the past,* they said. It was just Steve's bad luck that his birth was the trigger. But it was fear of Tad that pushed me over the edge.

The whole business left me wary of telling people about the depression and its cause. So much that is talked of now was never discussed then, wasn't even admitted. I was left feeling I couldn't trust myself any more. With Steve. With anyone. I lost confidence completely.

The diagnosis came too late for me to keep Steve. I had decided to give in to Gareth. I couldn't withstand the pressure. And what child wants a mother who can't cope? Though discharged from hospital I wasn't eating properly, couldn't concentrate to read, couldn't follow the simplest thought through and was so drugged I lived in slow motion. Part of me wondered if I'd ever be well.

The adoption was done properly. A social worker interviewed me at Tibby's to see whether I really wanted Steve adopted. Gareth had some people he knew in mind and private adoptions were more common then. I held Steve to say goodbye before they took him away, though, goodness knows, Tibby had more to do with him then than I did. I had only been out of hospital a fortnight and he knew her better than he knew me.

I'm not just a failure but a failed mother, I thought, rocking him – he'd been taken suddenly from his cot and was beginning to protest. I looked into his eyes, blue like Ian's – and like Gareth's oddly. What was he thinking? What did he know? Would he remember me?

I didn't cry, though I wanted to. The drugs I was on, or the grey fog of depression – I don't know which – dulled my responses. I touched Stevie's pink cheek, trying to print his features on my mind but it was as if a blanket separated me from him, from everything. I sensed the others looking at me, Gareth in particular. Did they expect me to explode or something?

I wished I could have taken Steve away on my own, away from prying eyes, to say goodbye. I would have kissed him, whispered that I didn't want to let him go but it was best, hugged him for the last time. But I felt wooden and inhibited in front of an audience. It was one of the worst moments of my life.

I was tempted to go back on the whole arrangement, escape with Steve, live on our own away from interference and other people's opinions. But I knew I wasn't well enough. Afterwards when Gareth and the social worker had gone, Tibby made us a pot of tea and I sat staring out of the window at the forest, feeling there was no point to anything any more. Gareth was right. Adoption was best.

But I never forgave myself.

Or Gareth.

Which is a revelation as stunning as if I had just seen the sun fall from the sky.

I pull into the nearest lay-by, my heart thudding in my chest. I can't drive in this state. I take deep breaths, light a cigarette and walk round the car. I had never realised this was how I felt. I am angry, full of blind, helpless rage – at my dead brother, who was my greatest friend.

My first instinct is to ring Ben. To have a normal chat and hear a friendly voice. A silly idea. He would guess at once that something was up; we don't phone during the day without good reason.

Then I argue with myself. I can handle this. Okay, so I'm angry with Gareth and I've denied it. Common sense tells me he was probably right. So what if my feelings say the opposite. I have to get on with life, learn to live with it.

That's a cop out, part of me reacts.

So what do I do with all this fury swirling inside me? I stub out my cigarette because it tastes revolting. I chew a fingernail, wishing I could use my teeth on something more substantial. I pick up a brittle stick from the roadside and start shredding it between my fingers.

'Calm down,' I tell myself, 'think. There must be a way of dealing with this.'

If Gareth were alive, I would have it out with him, ask why he was so insistent I let Steve go, ask why he thought I couldn't cope as a mother, why he pressured Tibby and me till we gave in.

But Gareth is dead and I am still grieving for him. How do you reconcile anger and grief? How do you cope with the knowledge that your best friend, who has just died, is the one who betrayed you?

I press my knuckles against my forehead and try to make sense of things.

I am troubled by another question. Did Gareth see anything in me that made him doubt my ability to bring up a child? True, I had become depressed. I was incapable then. But he was against me keeping Steve from the beginning. Why? Gareth, I thought you were on my side? You always used to be.

This lifts the lid off my own doubts. Was I – am I – capable of love and caring? I had thought so, had hoped so. I daresay every new mother has doubts but once I saw Stevie I fell in love with him, absolutely and unconditionally. Tibby was supportive. Gareth seemed amenable at the time. It was only when I was back in London that I began to be anxious, dogged by fears for Steve's safety, worried I wasn't feeding him properly, afraid something would happen to him. Isn't that normal to some extent? I wasn't a bad mother, just inexperienced and feeling my way.

I thought I had got my father and his bullying out of my system. But my own fears and Gareth's concern to keep Steve secret brought him to the fore. Tad became the proverbial bogeyman, haunting my dreams, stalking my daytime imaginings. He defeated me in the end. My own mind defeated me. I can't blame Gareth for that. Nor myself, though I do.

This is going nowhere. Mind whirling, I get back in the car and prepare to move off. But, pulling out of the lay-by, I am startled by a sudden hooting and squealing of tyres. I brake sharply as a red Polo veers past and speeds on. I hadn't seen it – hadn't even looked. I, who pride myself on my driving. I take a few minutes to recover, breathing deeply and cursing my stupidity – at least no one was hurt – then, chastened, drive on to Churchstoke, taking care to allow for other road users and my own state of mind.

I could argue the rightness of Steve's adoption on an intellectual level, weigh up the arguments, come to a fair conclusion. But this is not where I am. Emotion is what overwhelms me, sadness for the child I barely knew. And fury at those who took him from me, even though I agreed to it under pressure.

I wish we could have talked about this, Gareth and I. But it was a no-go area between us once Stevie had gone.

Okay, Gareth. You got what you wanted. But I never want to hear Steve mentioned again. Do you understand? Never.

No wonder he looked upset. Poor Gareth. He would have been wrong whatever he did or advised. Angry and hurt beyond bearing, I wasn't reasonable. For all our closeness we never talked of Steve after that. I pushed away all thought of him. I don't know what Gareth did, though he said he would keep the photographs he took of us after Steve was born in case I ever wanted to see them. He left them in his desk at the office and I picked them up when Lily and I cleared it out last week. I haven't had the courage to look at them yet. They're in my case somewhere.

I feel a twinge of guilt about Lily and push it away. I can't look at that now – *un peth ar y tro* – God, I'm thinking in Welsh. Unravelling. I need a drink after that near miss.

I stop at Harry Tuffins, buy a *Financial Times,* and go to the café. There, still shaken, I sit with a black coffee and try to gather my thoughts.

Am I justified in blaming Gareth for something that was essentially my fault?

I chose to live with Ian. I chose to keep Steve. I chose to go back to London too soon after Steve was born when I should have stayed longer with Tibby – my stupid independence again. I said I didn't want to be a burden to her and look at the trouble she got in the end.

And I broke down. Which wasn't my choice.

Then I punished Gareth for trying to help as best he could. After all he had done. But he didn't have to badger me into letting Steve go. Gareth, why did you do it?

I put my head in my hands and try to see the situation from my brother's point of view. How would he have approached it, I ask myself. Practically, knowing him. Steve was a threat to peace at home. I imagine Gareth saw him as a threat to my career prospects too. He was very old-fashioned. Look how protective he was of Lily, not letting her learn to drive. He probably thought he was saving me from a life of poverty as a single mother. Get Steve out of the way and all will be well – the logical solution. The trouble is, love isn't logical.

He seemed doubtful when I told him how I planned to manage while Stevie was small. He wanted me in a proper job. But I had thought it all out, I wasn't stupid. I had coaching lined up, and secretarial work, teaching in an adult day class. I would have coped if I hadn't been ill.

I decide to talk to Ben about this. He knows about Steve though not the detail. He could give me an idea of the traditional male view – he thought like Gareth till I and his daughters subverted him and he can still be fairly conventional. He might help me understand. To understand all is to forgive all, isn't it? I can't forgive yet, though I want to.

I open my paper and flick through it but without taking anything in. I can't blame Gareth any more than I can blame myself, I reason. I didn't know I was going to flip. At the time each of us thought we were doing the right thing. I can't change what happened. Gareth probably thought he was acting for the best. But he could never have understood what I felt for Steve. No man could.

I sip my coffee and try to relax. I have clamped the lid on all this for years, denied the breakdown and, along with it, tried to forget the baby whose arrival helped tip me over the edge. It isn't surprising I'm thrown.

I never cried for Steve then. I've only cried for him once, briefly, when Ben came to supper in my Dulwich flat. His adoption is a loss unmourned. I am reminded once again of school knitting. My son is a very big dropped stitch, I can't say if it will ever be right for us to meet, but it's right to remember him, to acknowledge the short time we had together, not try and pretend he never happened.

It's also right to admit I had a breakdown, post-natal depression or whatever, that I spent two months in hospital and seven months at Tibby's being put back together again. Brought up when mental illness was something to be ashamed of, I've buried that too. It is failure and I find failure hard. It is weakness and I've always tried to be strong. A second dropped stitch.

'You're human like the rest of us,' Lynne said last night. Time I took that on board. Perhaps I'd be less trouble to others if I did.

Calmer but exhausted, I finish my coffee. I have spent most of my life blotting out painful memories – that's how you survived in our family. I did that after Steve was adopted. Had to, to go on. Which is where Tibby comes in. She kept me going when I could have given up. Thank God for her – and for Gareth.

I remember what happened after, how I stayed with Tibby till I felt able to live on my own, working in the village shop when I was well enough, how I went back to London to pick up the threads of my old life but gave up the PhD because I'd lost interest, how I worked in a bookshop before enrolling in Law School to train as a solicitor. The rest, as they say, is history.

I fold up my paper. I have a lot to be thankful for. More than I deserve. I've done well in my career, I love and am loved by a wonderful man and I'm not badly off. So why shed tears over this?

'Because you need to,' part of me replies. 'Because it comes with the package of mourning Gareth.'

I won't do it here though.

In the cloakroom I comb my hair and look at myself in the mirror.

What sort of mother would I have made, I wonder. I didn't have much of an example at home. But I learnt a lot from Tibby. Between us we could have raised Steve, I'm sure.

And what sort of woman am I? I touch up my lipstick and scrutinise my face. Successful? Intelligent? Independent? Ambitious? All of those.

But motherly? Feminine? Caring? Not words I would choose immediately to describe myself. My figure is slim, more boyish than maternal – I'd make a good Viola playing Cesario, I think. My face is too thin, my features too sharp to be pretty. And I have the Pritchard nose – long and narrow, with a slight bump on the bridge. A nose for sniffing out legal loopholes, Ben teases. I smile ruefully at it and look away.

Tad rubbished my looks so often, I grew up believing I was the ugliest female on the planet. I was saved from total self-loathing by the knowledge that there was something amiss with him and the way he saw things. Deep down I knew he was wrong about me as a person. But I swallowed his assessment of me as a woman. I put a brave face on things, a devil-may-care, take-me-as-you-find-me face that fooled everybody, even myself. Till I had the breakdown. It's taken me years since to feel comfortable with how I look but I think I've succeeded. I like good clothes, I enjoy dressing well. But it's my mind that defines me. That's where I live. That's who I am. Which is why its disintegration was so catastrophic.

I close up my lipstick and put it in my bag. I brush a hand over the shoulders of my jacket, then take another look at myself before pushing on.

I'd planned to be an unconventional mother. I wanted to travel the world with my son, lecture and write books – be an academic gypsy, an intellectual hippy. In that other life I would have gone on demos, camped on Greenham Common, been a political activist. I remember the tomboy eight-year-old with grubby knees and unruly plaits, the nationalist teenager with long hair and unisex clothes too large for her, the socialist student with her idealism and passion for study. Yet here I am a City lawyer. What happened?

Did I opt for a legal career after my *annus horribilis* because it was safe? Law relies on definitions and detail, requires a diligent mind, reasoned argument, good sense and a clear head. Not much room for a free-spirited rebel there. For passion, yes, but under control. For idealism, but it has to be disciplined. Did I choose it because I believed it could hold me together after all the upheaval, provide a solid structure as I picked up the threads of life and won back my confidence? Maybe. But I have never regretted the choice.

I am not bad at handling people. I am good with clients, and excellent with trainees, so I'm told – particularly the women, which is odd because I get on better with men as a rule. Isn't that mothering of a sort? I have always thought I lack sensitivity but they come to me with their problems, personal as well as work-related. Despite my reputation as a stickler for detail who can't stand poor work, they seem to find me approachable, even sympathetic.

I got on with Megan and Bryn last week and I'd like to see more of them. Jenny's granddaughter seemed to take to me. And Ben's grandsons always want me to join their games at the farm. Maybe I wouldn't have been such a bad mother after all.

But it's all academic now.

I close my bag firmly and return to the car.

On via Bishop's Castle, Leintwardine and Leominster towards the Forest of Dean where Tibby used to live. I fancy some music so pick a CD of Monteverdi Psalms, one of Ben's. Restful.

These borderlands are alien to me, with their orchards, rolling fields and red soil. A No Man's Land. I am in No Man's Land, suspended between England and Wales, Llanfadog and London, town and country, past and present. I am at the centre of three threads but attached to none. The thread that joins me to Llanfadog, thinner now Gareth is dead, has stretched and sprung back. The thread that binds me to London is slack - I haven't picked it up yet. The thread that links me to Cheshire where Ben lives is waiting for me to take it up if I choose. Who am I and where do I belong?

'That's bereavement,' I tell myself, 'you've lost your bearings. You'll find them again.' But part of me fears the past will swallow me, as before.

*

At half eleven I stop for another cigarette. I hadn't thought meeting the past would be so harrowing. To distract myself I play mind games. Ben hasn't replied to my puzzle so I invent cryptic crossword clues, compose funny epitaphs and limericks – things Gareth and I used to do to amuse ourselves.

There was a smart lawyer from Wales,
Who spent the time painting her nails.
Paid off by a client
She went all defiant
And now she's gone right off the rails.

Gareth sent me this on a postcard when I started working at the firm. I replied with one about coffins but I can't remember it now.

Gareth…I wish you were here…We would laugh at this together…But you aren't…And it's your death I'm mourning…I'm stuck with the knowledge that I've been angry with you for years without realising it, blaming you for the loss of Steve…refusing to acknowledge your family…I want to say sorry but you aren't around to hear me.

We were always such friends. We never quarrelled even as children – or does my memory deceive me?

Gareth and I are running across a field, muddy and breathless. We have been playing in the stream and lost track of time. I am four. He is eight.

'Ellie, hurry or we"ll be late.' He is ahead of me. I can't keep up.

Suddenly I see a caterpillar on a ragwort leaf. 'Wait, let me just look at this.'

The caterpillar is beautiful. Striped browny black and yellow like a wasp with tiny tufts of hair that sprout the length of his body. I gaze fascinated as he chews the leaf. Can I pick him off and take him home? I move in closer, break off the leaf and stem that holds him and he is in my hands. Mine.

'Leave that!' Gareth's voice in my ear makes me jump. He has run back for me, cross. He knocks leaf and caterpillar from my hand and grabs my arm.

'We've got to get home, Tad'll shout at Mam if we're not there.'

I begin to cry, roars of grief and frustration.

'Come on!' Gareth drags me roughly after him. 'And stop crying. Don't you understand? We've got to hurry. Tad'll be mad if we're late.'

We aren't late as it happens. Tad hasn't even come in from work.

Gareth hugs me then, his normal kind self. 'Cheer up, the caterpillar will be there when we go back.'

But it isn't. I sulk briefly but by mid-afternoon we are friends again.

Gareth always needed to keep the peace. At all costs. Was it fear of Tad's anger, fear that Mam might suffer that made him pressure me to give Steve up? Or did he fear for me? For my capacity to cope, for my sanity even? It hurts to think he may have considered me incapable. It didn't do much for my confidence as a woman.

I consult the map at Mitcheldean. Not far now. Gareth and I came a year ago for Tibby's funeral. I remember the last time I saw her in a Gloucester nursing home. I used to visit regularly from London once I was back in England.

'Hallo, Tibby, how are you?'

'All the better for hearing you, pet.'

She was bedridden and blind. I kissed her and arranged the scented lilies I had brought. Then I read her the paper and combed her hair and we talked of my work and our Saturday outings in the old days.

Suddenly she asked, 'Do you go back to Llanfadog, love?'

'No. I haven't been for years. Not since I went abroad.'

'You should, you know. To make it up with Gareth.'

'Gareth and I are all right. We talk on the phone most weeks.'

She pursed her lips and went on as if I hadn't spoken. 'You need to forgive him, love. I've had to. He was only doing what he thought was right.'

I said I would think about it but forgot her words in the pressure of work. She knew more than I did. She could see what I couldn't. I understand what she meant now. How much was my refusal to go home or speak Welsh a payback to Gareth for Steve? And what else am I hiding?

Gareth and I organised Tibby's funeral. She had no living relatives. We'd taken responsibility for her care ever since she became too frail to live at home.

Sallowdean churchyard is overgrown but there are mown paths between the drifts of wild flowers and grasses. A notice says it is being maintained for wildlife. The iron gate is stiff and rusty. I graze my hand on it and feel like scribbling on the notice to suggest that the gate be maintained too.

There is no outside tap and the church is locked, so I fill the little marble vase with my bottled water and arrange the flowers carefully.

Four graves in one day – Gareth, Mam and Tad, Tryweryn, and Jack and Tibby. A record for me. I don't go in for this sort of thing usually. The headstone is back in place with the additional inscription. It is simple 'In loving memory of Jack Alan Watkins...and Elisabeth Ann (Tibby)…a dearly-loved wife and godmother.' But you would need whole books to explain what Tibby was to me.

All the tenderness I knew as a child came from her. It was to Tibby I went, not Mam, when I hurt myself. How did Mam feel about that? Did she mind or was she glad not to have to bother? She always preferred Gareth to me. Too much to cope with, I imagine, and I was the difficult one. I wish I had taken flowers to her grave, if only to mark my recognition of all she suffered. Maybe next time.

But it is Tibby I grieve for. I wipe away a tear. 'Thanks, Tibby, thanks for all you did.'

I hate emotional excess. There was too much of it at home when I was little. Not for me sentimental 'In Memoriams' and tearful outpourings. I wander round the churchyard, hands in pockets, listening to the rustle of the breeze in the oak trees and the hum of insects in the grass. It is a quiet place. I'm glad Tibby has somewhere peaceful for her final rest.

This is where Ben and I differ. He believes in an after-life and I don't. I can't swallow all this stuff about harps and angels and clouds. He says it isn't like that; these are images to express the inexpressible. If all fathers were like Ben, I think, watching him with his daughters and grandchildren, maybe I could believe in a loving father God.

What would you do in my place, Tibby? Would you marry him? Would it be fair?

I find a seat in the sun, brush the grass seed from it, and sit down.

I must bring Ben here. If he wants to understand who I am and where I've come from, this is the place to start. And if I want to be straight with him I must admit what happened over Steve, tell him about the depression and what followed. It isn't that I've hidden it intentionally. I've blotted it out. My way of coping.

'Tibby, am I like Tad?'

'Of course you aren't. What gave you that idea?'

'It's just that I thought such odd things. My mind was out of control. Perhaps that's what he was like. I wonder if what he had can be inherited.'

'Whether it can or not, you haven't got it. You were ill because of what he was, but not in that way. Don't give it a second thought.'

'I'm scared it could happen again, that's all.'

'Forget it. You'll be all right soon, pet. I know you will.'

She was right. But I had already decided. No marriage. No romantic relationships. No more children. Too dangerous. Yet I have proved I can cope with pressure as well as any in the firm. Maybe it's safe to look at the past with all this solid achievement behind me.

I take a deep breath and give myself permission to remember Steve. It's not like in the past when I've had sudden, painful glimpses of him and been left saddened and bereft. I choose to think about our brief time together deliberately, disentangling his memory from the darkness I've always feared to face, pushing aside the blackness like a swimmer diving through weed, bent on treasure beneath.

I had him at Tibby's, or rather at her nearest hospital. I had stayed with her the two months before. Her husband had died the previous summer so she was glad of my company, and a college friend who needed somewhere quiet to write up her thesis had my rooms near the university. All very convenient. I remember congratulating myself on how well everything was fitting together, imagining – how stupid I was – that Steve's birth would be a mere blip in the plans I had for my life now marriage to Ian was no longer in prospect.

How wrong can you be? What shocked me about his birth wasn't so much the experience itself, but the overwhelming love I felt for Steve as soon as I saw him. I had never thought of myself as a maternal type. I had assumed I'd have children one day, but pictured myself having a matter-of-fact, bread-and-butter love for them, like the affection I'd had for pets in childhood. Nothing prepared me for the rush of possessive, protective love that bowled me over when I saw how tiny he was and how much he needed me. That I was capable of such feeling overturned all my ideas of myself. Where had I got it from? I never imagined my mother had felt anything like that for me when I was little – or at any other time, come to that.

And Steve was a beautiful baby. I know all mothers say that of their own but he truly was. You could see he was going to have red hair, though there wasn't much of it. I called him Steve, not Stephen, deliberately – after Stevie Wonder, whom I admired at the time – and because he *was* a wonder, conceived as he was, with my history and the tooth operation and the pills and the break-up with Ian and everything. I smile as I recall his tiny fingers and ginger eyelashes. I thought I was so clever producing him. How could someone so adorable be anything to do with me? I had been afraid I might see Ian in him but I forgot Ian completely once Steve appeared.

For his first month at Tibby's we lived cocooned in our own warm bubble. I forgot everything else – my studies, worries about my parents, concerns about money and whether my plans for supporting us would work out once we got back to London. I enjoyed him for the ten weeks I was in my right mind, amazed that this tiny person should depend on me, of all people. It was scary but affirming. I wish I'd been able to discharge that trust but I wasn't. No point punishing myself for it.

I remember the blue hat and jacket Tibby knitted for him, the room where we slept in my London flat, the hot summer nights when I would creep over to his cot and stand, not daring to move, listening for his breathing, marvelling at his smallness. I remember the crying too, the broken nights – not many, I was lucky – and how I used to sing to him in Welsh, rocking him to sleep in my arms. Then the anxiety and fear that brought an end to it all.

I am shivering, despite the sun. I fumble for a tissue in my bag. This is the first time I've allowed myself to cry properly for Steve so it isn't surprising I'm undone. The grief is raw, untapped. No matter that I'm in a public place, though it's out of the village, away from passers-by. No matter that I dislike showing emotion, even in front of myself. I sob quietly – for Steve, for Gareth, for Tibby, and for myself – for all the years I've stored up this grief and not allowed it to be expressed, for my anger against Gareth and my envy of Lily. It is painful and draining. Like lancing a wound that has been scarred over for many years. And it seems to take forever.

Even now I can see the funny side. Weeping in a graveyard is so definitely not me. Victorian. Like the books we had as Sunday school prizes, full of dying children and sentimental verse. I laugh aloud and dry up. 'You're hysterical,' I warn myself. But I am not. Laughing, too, is a release. I *am* in my right mind. I haven't slipped into a black hole, or been swallowed by the past.

Note: I must tell Lynne some time that she is right.

The sunlight hurts my swollen eyes. What a mess I must look. All that emotion. How self-indulgent can you get? Mothers across the world are losing children in dreadful circumstances and here I am wailing over a child who is probably still alive. 'Be thankful you had him at all,' I tell myself. 'And grow up.'

I fetch more tissues from the car, dry my soggy self and take stock.

It's no good pining for the past. No point wondering what might have been or what sort of mother I'd have made. I must let Steve go. I can't cling to what he was, romanticising his memory. If he is still alive, he is grown up. If we ever meet – and I would like us to one day – it will be as adults, the people we are now. I must let go of my baby before I can think of meeting the person he has become.

I feel done in, but better. Not so tense. Being unravelled is an exhausting business. But, for now, I've lost the desperate longing to find Steve that has haunted me since I went to Jenny's. I must leave the rest to fate – or as Ben would say – with God. I stand, pick up my bag and smooth the creases from my clothes.

What next? I could find a pub for lunch, tidy up, then drive on to London. I could take a walk in the forest, then push on. I could ring Ben to ask for that pheasant casserole and meander back north.

I opt for the forest. I spent my convalescence walking these woods. If re-discovering the past is my aim I may as well do it thoroughly.

A wet morning, February, 1974. I am walking the forest in my long, beige trenchcoat and Tibby's sou'wester and gum boots. I am so thin you could get two of me in that coat – Tad's stick insect taunt would fit me perfectly. Tibbys' springer spaniel, Mutt, is with me. Tibby always reckoned I'd be safe if I took the dog.

Standing under an oak to shelter from the rain I realise I don't feel empty and sad any more. I can smell the wet grass and notice the pattern of bare branches with their buds ready to open. I can hear the raindrops dripping from the trees, see them glistening on the outermost twigs, recognise the mistle thrush's song and feel the solid earth underfoot.

A month earlier, locked in my own grey world, I had seen, heard and felt nothing, just wanted to hide under the drifts of last year's leaves and sleep, never to wake. Now, everything is different. Mutt begs me to throw a stick and I respond, playing tug-of-war when he brings it back.

At first I can't believe my exile is ending. I hold back, not daring to trust what I feel in case it is an illusion and the darkness returns. Then I realise I have a choice. Even if the depression does reappear I know there is life beyond it. I can choose life and go on till life becomes a reality, till the shadows recede and the sun shines again.

Living again was like waking up to find you've been asleep for decades and have missed all that has been going on, like thawing out from being frozen with the pain of throbbing veins. I felt older than my contemporaries. I didn't fit in with them any more. I didn't fit anywhere. It took my legal work to give me back my confidence and get me on my feet.

Thirty years on I face other decisions, one more important than the rest. Should I accept Ben's offer of marriage or not? And why do I find it so hard? It isn't that I don't love him. We are right for each other. All our friends agree.

'Because you have lived too long trying to play safe,' my reason tells me, unprompted. 'You're scared of taking risks.'

Laughable when I remember the rebel I was, the eccentric I intended to be, the junior partner who leapt at the challenge of work overseas.

I frown as I consider this unpalatable thought. Then I realise it is loving that I fear. Since the disaster with Steve I've been wary of loving anyone I might lose. No commitments, no heartbreak. Logical.

I am shocked. I never dreamt I was such a coward. My image as a well-adjusted, got-it-all-together professional takes a knock. I am nothing but a tangled heap of unravelled wool. So much for my pride. The forest echoes to the sound of my laughter. God, woman. You take yourself too seriously. Lighten up.

But as I walk on it seems my earlier choice is being replayed. And it is serious. I can live or I can turn my back on living. As simple as that.

We can't expect a pain-free existence any more than we can control the universe, Ben wrote after Karin died. He is willing to risk marriage again. And to me. Not an easy prospect, I'd have thought. Why can't I match his courage?

Because I don't trust myself, I answer. Because I'm afraid of risking Ben's happiness and his sanity. Who in their right mind would want me for a wife?

You must let him be the judge of that, common sense replies. He's an adult. You can't be his keeper.

Suddenly I feel like a caged bird shown an open door. Outside is dangerous, but think of the heights you can reach. And what's the point of being a bird if you can't fly free, be what you were meant to be.

The track enters a clearing and divides in two. Appropriately I have to choose between them. I sense the forest holding its breath, awaiting my decision. I hesitate for a moment, then walk firmly down my preferred path, wishing Tibby and Gareth were here for me to tell.

Back in the car I drive through Mitcheldean and on to the A40. There, instead of heading East for Gloucester I turn for Newent and the scenic route north. In Ludlow I ring Ben to tell him I'll be staying after all, and break into a smile when I hear the delight in his voice.

I am going home.

Postscript

Ben

At supper we drank the burgundy Elin had bought in Ludlow and celebrated our new commitment. We were both a little drunk, not on wine but on the surprise of it all, and the euphoria of the moment. I think we were both relieved too, Elin to have given up her long-held resistance to attachments, and I that my – as it seemed to me – precipitate proposal had gained the hoped-for response.

Afterwards we relaxed in the sitting room and she told me about her day. Not everything, I was aware of that, but all she could manage to speak of for the moment. She was concerned that I should understand about Steve, that she hadn't wanted to let him go, and that, if possible, she would like to find him again.

I had been expecting something like this and offered no objection. 'If it'll make you happy,' I said, 'then I'll be happy too. You know what I think about families. A young man to side with me against all these women might be an asset.'

'You've got two perfectly good sons-in-law,' Elin pointed out, but I could see she was pleased. 'There are photographs of him,' she said, 'in my case. One day I'll show you. When I've plucked up the courage to look at them myself.' Her voice trembled and I knew not to push her. She would let me see them in her own time.

There was something different about her. Despite her

bereavement, she was more relaxed, less driven – the result of letting go after all these years, I assumed.

'What you haven't explained,' I said, my arm resting comfortably round her shoulder, 'is why you had to go all the way to the Forest of Dean before you decided to turn round and come back here. You're usually so direct with your navigation, anxious not to waste time.'

She smiled and stretched like a contented cat. 'It was a journey into the past, I suppose. A pilgrimage I had to make.' Abruptly she sat up straight and searched my face with those amazing eyes. 'There's a lot about me you don't know, Ben. Even now, when I've told you so much of it. A lot I didn't know or had forgotten. Do you still want to take me on with my background?'

'Haven't I been taking you on for years?' I joked, 'I think I can cope.'

'Silly.' She relaxed again and rested her head on my shoulder. 'I could fall asleep if I let myself,' she yawned. 'I've come a long way.'

Other titles from Honno

Facing into the West Wind by Lara Clough

A debut novel with an ethereal, deeply felt focus on characters and relationships. When Haz meets the rejected and lonely Jason on the streets of Bristol he decides to take him home to the family's beach house at Gower. What follows is a series of confessions and revelations which will change everything.

"A tender and perceptive tale of secrets" The Guardian
"A deeply felt and accomplished first novel" Sue Gee

ISBN: 978 1870206 792 £6.99

Girl on the Edge by R V Knox

A chilling story of love, betrayal, secrets and lies....

Just how did her mother die and what did Leila witness on the cliff top, if anything? Leila knows that there's something about her childhood she can't quite remember.. that haunts her dreams and sometimes her days. This year she's determined to find out the truth... but someone has tried very hard to keep their secrets and will go to extremes to make sure it stays that way. A compelling psychological thriller set in the moors of North Wales.

ISBN: 978 1870206 754 £6.99

Hector's Talent for Miracles
by Kitty Harri

A gripping human story set in this century and the last: heroic, tragic and compelling...

The small spanish town of Torre de Burros is known to pilgrims the world over for its miracles; there Hector Martinez, his mother and grandmother live in the shadow of dark secrets. Mair Watkins arrives in a clapped out yellow Beetle, all the way from Wales, on a mission to find her lost grandfather. Their meeting is explosive and their lives revealed as fragile constructions forged in the fire of a vicious conflict...

Praise for Kitty Harri (writing as Kitty Sewell) and her previous novel *Ice Trap*:
"an involving narrative, a sharply observed cast and an atmospherically evoked and unusual setting" The Guardian.

ISBN: 978 1870206 815
£6.99

Everything in the Garden

by Jo Verity

Jo Verity was the winner of the ***2003 Richard and Judy "Write Here Right Now"*** *short story competition.*

When Anna Wren and her husband Tom buy a rambling farmhouse in Wales with three other couples the intention is to grow old with the support of tried and trusted friends. But life turns out not to be the bed of roses she had imagined... as she teeters on the brink of an affair the relationships that have shaped her life begin to crumble and Anna is forced to confront the changing nature of her own sexual desire and the consequences of giving in.

ISBN: 978 1870206 709
£6.99

About Honno

Honno Welsh Women's Press was set up in 1986 by a group of women who felt strongly that women in Wales needed wider opportunities to see their writing in print and to become involved in the publishing process. Our aim is to develop the writing talents of women in Wales, give them new and exciting opportunities to see their work published and often to give them their first 'break' as a writer.

Honno is registered as a community co-operative. Any profit that Honno makes is invested in the publishing programme. Women from Wales and around the world have expressed their support for Honno by buying shares in the co-operative. Shareholders' liability is limited to the amount invested and each shareholder has a vote at the Annual General Meeting.

To buy shares or to receive further information about forthcoming publications, please write to Honno at the address below, or visit our website: **www.honno.co.uk**.

Honno
'Ailsa Craig'
Heol y Cawl
Dinas Powys
Bro Morgannwg
CF64 4AH